Lie of the Land

Lie of the Land

MICHAEL F. RUSSELL

First published in Great Britain in 2015 by
Polygon, an imprint of Birlinn Ltd.

West Newington House
10 Newington Road
Edinburgh
EH9 1QS

www.polygonbooks.co.uk

ISBN 978 1 84697 319 2
eBook ISBN 978 0 85790 840 7

British Library Cataloguing in Publication Data
A catalogue record for this book is available on request
from the British Library.

The publishers acknowledge investment from Creative Scotland
towards the publication of this volume.

For Helena, Danny and Joe

October

1

Carl closed the graveyard's rusty metal gate, breathing hard, lungs aching from the effort of walking. What was it – about half a mile from the hotel? Too fast, he'd gone far too fast for a body that had spent most of a month lying flat and then a week shuffling between rooms.

Crows rasped in the trees as the wind freshened from off the sea. The place reeked of wet earth and rotting leaves. He felt light-headed, dizzy, the fresh air knifing his lungs. He coughed, hawking a gobbet onto the gravel path that skirted the graveyard.

He soon found Howard's grave, a fresh mound next to those of the two German tourists. Carl stood for a while, then dropped to his haunches and scooped a handful of earth from Howard's grave.

An oystercatcher alarm-called as it flew, arrowing level with the dark-rock shoreline. He had come to know the sound of the bird. The soil was cold and sticky in his hand.

'Sorry,' he whispered, throwing the handful back onto the pile. His throat tightened. 'Why did I fucking listen to you? Why did I let you do it?' He gasped for breath. 'Where is everything? What am I doing here?'

Now that the fever had left him, realising where he was and what had happened threatened to blot out every other thought and feeling. Consciousness without purpose was now the dominant state. Never waking up at all would have been better.

Mistakes: to the nth power.

The world was dead, and he had helped kill it, in his own little way. Call it a sin of omission. Carl could add his only friend to the list of the dead while he was at it. There was guilt enough to gorge on, with extra guilt to go. It entered his bloodstream with every breath, all washed down with a cold glass of grief.

He stood for a moment, staring down at the grave. Insects crawled on the rectangular mound of earth. They had a job to do, above and below the ground. Wind stirred the trees again, making them sway and creak. Everything had an appointed function, except him.

There was an obvious destination: somewhere he had to go. As he looked around the bay, judging distances, Carl wondered if he could make it. Going back to where Howard died meant taking one of two routes: he could cross to the south headland, on the main road, before heading inland and into the hills. But that meant going through the main part of the village. Which meant people, and the gauntlet of shock and sympathy. Or he could continue the way he had come, up the back road over the north headland. That way he'd avoid people, but it also took him away from where he needed to go, behind the village, over rough ground, circling around Inverlair and to the south. Call it nine miles of trudging through heather and bogs. That would take him hours, if he managed it at all. With no real conviction, he set off for the hard way.

On the back road up and out of Inverlair Bay, past the church and the community hall and the start of the forestry track, he made it as far as the roadblock, a line of shin-high boulders splashed with red paint. Never mind being at the edge of the world, he couldn't have gone much further anyway.

He sat on the stones, gasping for breath. To his right, over a rusty barbed-wire fence, fields of rushes and thistles sloped down towards the grey sea. He scanned the horizon for a white boat, for salvation, but saw nothing except the fusing of cloud and water.

Some way off the road was a derelict old house, windowless,

with a ragged corrugated-iron roof. To his left, the hills rose to the fissured rocky summit of Ben Bronach, and beyond, to the deer forest. After a few minutes Carl got up and, standing at the roadblock with his hands in his coat pockets, considered the road ahead. He stepped over the painted boulders.

Maybe today was the day when the world would open up again. He could drive away from Inverlair. He could leave Room 14 and Simone and the baby, today, the eighty-second day of his confinement. This would be the last day he'd have to spend here, in this prison refuge. The redzone would open. Its signal would fail.

He took Howard's deltameter out of his pocket and watched the EMF waveform on the screen, spiking at 85 microtesla today, close to the active neural level. Another hundred metres or so and, he knew, the buzzing sound would start in his head. Another two hundred after that and the pain would skewer through his head, from temple to temple. Any further and sleep was death.

Today was not the day. But he'd known that anyway. There would be no escape. Even before he took his dead friend's gadget out of his pocket to check the signal he knew what it would tell him.

•

The next day, he stood in Room 14's en suite, in front of the mirror. Pits of ash where his eyes had been, thick phlegm-flecked beard and limp coils of oily hair.

With a pair of borrowed scissors he cut his beard to a point where shaving could finish the job. Without hot water it stung and he nicked the skin a few times as he went, hair filling the sink, red drops on the thin scum of soap and grease. Even though the razor was blunt he managed to shave off half his beard, stopping to touch the hairless side of his face, the fever-scooped hollows where his cheeks had been. Two months ago his face had been full and he hadn't felt like a decrepit wreck of a man.

Death had looked in on him, given his lungs a squeeze, then let him go. *I'll be back later for you, pal. Take care of yourself – until I take care of you.*

Neck next, and he was done; now to complete the transformation, from stinking caveman to heroin chic all in a few snips. Reaching above his ear he gathered a handful of greasy, matted hair, and started cutting until he was right down to the scalp. Getting rid of his hair made the scab on his forehead stand out. He tried to forget how it had happened, and continued cutting. The person he'd been must be somewhere underneath this feral disguise. He must be.

That night, Carl stood on the hotel's first-floor landing. Above the dark stairwell there was a stained-glass window, red roses and green petals on a blue background, the full moon blazing the colours alive. He heard an owl hooting. This is Tuesday, he said to himself, as he gazed, open-mouthed, at the moon-bright glass. Nearly a week since the fever had left his bleached bones washed up in a single bed.

He was hungry again. Appetite had been reborn. And that was a good thing, on balance. Resurrection. Coming back from the brink. Five days he'd been up and about, and now it was time to visit the ground floor. Maybe even rejoin what was left of the human race. He was in the grip of life now. He took a deep breath and, as planned, his lungs cracked a volley of phlegm, which he spat into a hankie. In the soundless night, it wouldn't do to cough in an inconvenient place and alert anyone to his presence.

On his seventh step down, the stairs creaked. Carl held his breath, gaping up at the stained-glass roses shining in the moonlight. What did he expect to happen? Simone's dad come stomping through from the annexe, dressing gown flying, shotgun at the ready? The only sound was the clock ticking in the lobby; moon glinting on the brass pendulum as it measured the night.

It was even darker on the ground floor as Carl made his way

along the lobby past reception, through the fire door and into the annexe, cupping the candle, which he'd stuck onto a saucer. He waited a few seconds, listening out for signs of life, letting the fire door swing gently back into place. But there was nothing except his own breathing as he crept into the kitchen. It was still warm; he could feel heat radiating from the stove. There wasn't much to eat: the remains of a mushroom omelette in the fridge along with milk and some butter, still chilled, even though the generator was off for the night. And fish, of course. At least there was no question of an Omega 3 deficiency. No danger of that in this place. Insanity maybe, but at least his heart wouldn't pack in.

He set the candle and saucer down on the worktop, next to a kid's storybook. Simone kept things as normal as she could for her boy. Fair play to her.

Carl ate.

Scoffing the greasy slab of omelette with his fingers, he saw an open black bin bag on the wicker kitchen chair. He reached into it.

His jaw stopped working.

The bag was full of baby clothes, sleepsuits and tiny vests. He lowered the candle to read the handwritten label taped to the bag: Under Three Months.

He laid a sleepsuit out flat on the table, adjusting the position of the candle so he could get a better look. The suit was pink with little smiling teddies on it. The bag of clothes certainly answered The Burning Question. Carl imagined the pink suit filled with a screaming, red-faced baby.

Without warning the candle fell over and went out, the air heavy with smoke.

Darkness.

Fuck. He hadn't melted enough wax on to the saucer.

He wondered if he could negotiate his way back upstairs, in darkness, without knocking anything over. As he visualised the obstacles, his eyes grew accustomed to the lack of light. Gathering candle and saucer, he crept into the hallway. There were no windows in the corridor between the annexe and the actual hotel, and it was darker there, but he could still make out all the important shapes to avoid, the edge of the reception desk. And the big brass bell, on its stand by the front door, a touch of baronial charm for the tourists. Better not knock that bugger over.

He was near the annexe fire door when he heard a sound from upstairs. It was Simone's dad, George, sobbing, groaning and calling out in his sleep. Carl froze. There came another, quieter moan. Then silence.

Bad dream, probably. Everyone had them. Dreams of death, playing on a loop. Anyway, there was now food in his belly, and he felt like he needed something to wash it down.

Making his way through to the public bar he nudged a table, low to his left, and set something rocking on top of it. The ornament, or whatever it was, shook, but stayed upright, thank Christ.

And breathe again. Take it slow through another fire door, between the chairs and tables. Past the pool table, baize under his fingertips. He mustn't rush it. There was always the unexpected obstacle.

He reached the storeroom door. There were no windows here, so the moon couldn't light his way. Easy does it now, one slow foot-sliding step at a time. He edged to the back of the storeroom, knew which forgotten cardboard box to find, felt the edge of the cold metal filing cabinet, then down and along to the box. Flipping the flaps open he took out four bottles, one at a time, careful not to let them clink together. Carl put a bottle into each pocket of his dressing gown, carried the other two in one hand, by their necks, candle and saucer in the other hand. He was fully laden now, and there was no room for mistakes. Watch that table in the corridor. Mind the big brass bell. Ease open the fire door, hook it with a foot. Let it sink back nice and quiet. And whatever happens, don't bloody cough.

For the second night in a row Carl sat in Room 14, on the edge of his bed, four bottles of lime-green alcofizz inside him. He watched his palmpod's on-screen clock count the seconds, considered – then rejected – the idea of watching a certain personal video file.

Tomorrow he would have to endure real-time interaction with George and Simone. He'd put that off for long enough.

The booze he had just guzzled equated to less than two pints, but he was pissed nonetheless. Weight loss and illness had reduced his tolerance for alcohol. It was 2.37 a.m. He lurched over to the windowsill, unsteady on his feet. The fat bluebottle that only this morning had bounced and buzzed against the room's dormer window, in thrall to the light, was dead, stiff legs in the air. He had watched the fly pound the glass, unable to stop what it was doing. If only the fly had known the impossibility of breaking through the glass it might have stopped. It might have accepted imprisonment and fate, making no fuss about its situation and inevitable end in Room 14 of Inverlair Hotel. That would be the sensible thing to do.

Rolling into bed, he pulled the duvet around him and closed his eyes. He dreamed of a giant baby that cried all night and would never go to sleep. Being so big, the screaming kid was dangerous. It might roll over and crush the life he'd only just regained back out of him.

2

Brittle brown leaves swirled around the garden. Staring into space George stood, rake in hand. Wind ruffled his grey hair. It was cold today. Dry. His jacket was on but wasn't zipped up against the morning chill. George tried not to look at the carved oak bench nestling beneath the ivy-covered trellis at the bottom of the garden. Maybe he should store it in the shed now. The bench could do with a coat of wood stain anyway, and that's something he could never face doing.

It had been their bench; the two of them used to sit on it. In future there would be only him. Maybe he should stick the bench in the shed after all. No luck with the leaves today, too windy to rake them up.

He stood there, clutching the rake, as the dead leaves flew where the wind took them. Part of him wanted to smash the bench into pieces.

Unless George kept tight control, it would start in his stomach, the spasm of awareness, and from there it would engulf him. Pain and sadness would sweep him away, and he would crumble again. But remembering was so sweet, even as it made ashes of his heart. That was the thing he couldn't get right in his head: the sweetness of letting memory swim in his blood, and the nausea of grief that came with remembering her. He was frightened of remembering his wife, and just as frightened of forgetting her.

He examined the rake he held in his hands, looked towards the pine trees and the hills as if someone was there, in the distance, waiting for him.

What had he been doing? No luck with the leaves. Too windy to bother with them.

'Dad!' Simone stood on the back step of the annexe, a cardboard box in her hands. George thought he heard a voice. He found himself staring at his daughter, and remembering laughter from long ago.

'Come and see what I've found in the loft.'

Let the leaves swirl and leave the rubbish in the loft, girl. Nothing up there but dust.

George straightened his back. 'What is it?' He put the rake back in the garden shed, in its proper place.

Simone came over, took a small paper sachet out of the box for her father to sniff; in the box there were many more: coffee, sugar, tiny cartons of milk and — holy of holies — about twenty cellophane mini-packs of biscuits, two in each. Shortbread, mainly, but there were a few custard creams.

George's face fell. 'We ordered too much stock. Then the bookings dried up. It was before you came back.' He sniffed the coffee again. 'We stopped putting them in the rooms after that.'

He dropped the sachet back in the box, bit hard on the memory. Can't keep that kind of pain in the fucking shed. 'This should really be handed in to the committee,' he said, wiping his hands on his trousers.

'It will,' said Simone, trying to catch her father's eye. 'But I thought we could sit down and have a cup of coffee and a biscuit first. One each, that's all.'

She smiled. George nodded, touched his daughter's arm, and they went inside.

Stale. He figured the biscuit would be, but it was still satisfyingly sweet. George sipped his coffee, fingering crumbs on the tabletop. He thought about how he could broach the subject of the father-to-be who was lurking upstairs.

The oak bench would not be moved from its place.

•

That evening, Carl crept along the annexe hallway. The kitchen door was open and he could see the table laid for dinner, pots bubbling away on the stove; George was fussing over the food as Simone sat at the table, her son on her lap.

'I can't fix the games visor, darling. I don't know why it's broken.'

But Isaac wasn't entirely convinced by his mother's lack of expertise. She had to fix it. The visor had to be fixed so he could play the game. Why couldn't she see that?

Carl coughed in the kitchen doorway, rubbing the stubble on his head self-consciously. The kid looked at him, open-mouthed, eyes wide.

Clothes too big. Shirt like a sack. Trousers belted on a skewered hole. Carl felt like shit and probably looked it too. Can't blame the kid for staring.

Standing at the kitchen door, he wasn't quite sure what to do. He shifted from foot to foot. 'Smells good.'

Startled at first, George said hello and went back to his pots, ladling stew into bowls. Carl sat down at the table.

As he ate, he became conscious of the watchers and the silence. Maybe he shouldn't have made the effort to smarten himself up. He glanced round the table, carried on eating. 'I'm still alive,' he stated. 'I'm not the ghost at the feast, I hope.'

George sniffed. 'I wouldn't call it a feast.'

Carl smiled. 'Thanks.' He caught Simone's eye. 'For everything.'
She nodded.

The boy had lost interest in his food. Isaac was silent, eyeing the skeletal stranger from upstairs who had appeared like magic, like the first time. Only back then lots of bad things had happened. Maybe he was going to make more bad things happen this time.

Carl slurped his stew, though he had no appreciation of what he was eating, only a studied lifting of the spoon. He began to sweat, food and silent awkwardness going to work on him.

'The *Aurora* was out the other day and came across a yacht, a big one,' said George, trying to ease the tension.

'Yeah,' said Carl, the food dry in his mouth. 'Simone said.' He took a sip of water.

George offered another forkful of food to Isaac, but the boy squirmed in his seat, lips clamped shut and eyes on Carl. George shook his head, exasperated. 'You're far too old for this nonsense. Do we have any of those biscuits left?'

'I don't know,' she said. 'But I do know there is something sweet for boys who eat their dinner.'

George pressed the fork up to the boy's mouth. It could have been a shit-covered slug Isaac was being asked to eat, but, after a prolonged show of disgust, he accepted the piece of boiled carrot.

'It's a pity about the yacht,' said Carl.

Isaac chewed another mouthful. Every time Carl spoke he felt pinned back by the boy's stare. Maybe the kid knows the truth.

'A lot of gear on a boat that size,' agreed George. 'She wasn't in sail, probably broke her moorings down the coast in the storm last week. But the tide took her into the redzone.'

The only two questions that mattered to Carl had been answered: the redzone was still there and Simone was still pregnant. Nothing else really mattered.

'Too bad,' he said.

His mind blank, Carl ate quickly, desperate to leave the table. Isaac's unyielding scrutiny hastened his exit.

Stop staring at me, you little fucker, or I'll stick that fork in your fucking eye.

After dinner he made for the hotel's residents' lounge, where a fire burned beneath a grand hardwood mantelpiece. There was a massive portrait above the fireplace, of some bewigged gentleman of yore gleaming with brocade and buckles, a sword hanging by

11

his side. The guy had more or less founded Inverlair, back when war meant Napoleon. Captain Theodore Melkins looked very satisfied with himself, his military colours and stern smugness glowing above the mantelpiece. It's amazing how something as simple as processing potash from seaweed could make a man important enough to be preserved in oils.

Carl went over to the bookshelves. He pulled out a book on geology, and sat down by the fire.

He read: 'The Moine Thrust is a linear geological feature in the Scottish Highlands which runs . . . extensive landscape of rolling hills over a metamorphic . . . Ben More Assynt (pictured) in the centre of the belt, is a typical example that rises from a glen of limestone caves . . .'

He recognised the picture in the book straight away. There was no mistaking it. Now he had a name to go with the unmistakable image of the mountain. Suddenly, as if a switch had been thrown, a hail shower machine-gunned against the high casement windows. Carl jumped at the sound of ice clattering on glass.

Fetching a dog-eared road atlas, he traced a path all the way up from Glasgow, along the edge of the Moine Thrust, until he found Ben More Assynt on the map. He recognised it from the drive up, a million years before, looming like something out of legend. Now he knew the mountain's name; maybe he'd climb it one day. Everything has an identity: a name and a purpose. Even hills. That was the rule. Surely there were still rules to obey.

Tectonics and the Moine Thrust were the reason for Ben More Assynt's existence. Shifts and faults and time: a combination that could produce innumerable consequences.

He pulled another book from the shelf: *Highland Animals*. Flicking though the pages he learned that adders are Britain's only poisonous snakes and are found throughout the Highlands. *Vipera berus* was sure to sink its fangs into him at some point. Perhaps its bite would prove fatal.

3

Thick cord rattled against the metal flagpole. Maybe another electrical storm was on its way.

Carl looked up at the gathering clouds, and wondered what would happen if lightning struck the viewpoint flagpole. Would an arc of current reach out and fry him?

No flag flew above Inverlair. Maybe the pole had never been used. But there were wooden picnic benches, flaking apart, below on the crumbling concrete platforms, and the concrete stairway that led to the viewpoint was overgrown with a gnarled prickly plant. It had yellow flowers: dollops of sunlight on stunted branches. Honeysuckle was yellow – he knew that, so maybe that's what the plant was. Surrounding the flagpole, at the highest point of the picnic site, was a waist-high concrete wall. Carl picked his way up the steps, his jeans snagging on inch-long thorns.

He was now facing inland and had a clear view of the whole village, the steel-grey length of Inverlair Bay, and the tops of the mountains beyond, to the south and east. The hills in the distance could be five miles away, or they could be fifty. It was impossible to tell. There was an interpretative weatherproofed plaque, angled like a lectern, set into the viewpoint's wall. Each mountain peak on the inland horizon was named, and the area's geology described. The plaque told him he was exactly 190 metres above sea level.

The wind whipped the flagpole's cord again. Carl turned up his collar against the cold breeze, read the rest of what was written on the plaque, then took the steps back down to the path that eventually came out near the hotel's moss-covered car park. One old car – tyres flat, packed with junk – lay abandoned in a corner.

Almost a thousand metres of ice. That's what the plaque had said. Ten thousand years ago there would only have been the tops of the highest hills poking through, nothing but rock and scree and the grinding ice advance.

The path down to the hotel branched off and took him onto the north road, beyond the last house, where he could relax, the pressure of curious others falling away. He turned up the forestry track and headed inland, between blocks of tightly packed pine trees, up the boulder-strewn slopes of Ben Bronach. Two hundred metres up from the road, beyond the greying swarf of felled timber, an excavator-type digger stood, hydraulic arm poised. Yesterday he had seen it working, roaring, buzz-sawing, stripping and sectioning trunks into manageable lengths, each one processed in less than a minute. He walked the wide access track into the scented forest, climbing, then along a narrow trail, teasing out the contours of Ben Bronach, on a walk he knew too well.

On the hill's shoulder he looked down on the village. Inverlair was definitely a rosier prospect from here than seeing it up close. He felt his mind wander, growing less focused. Up here on the hillside there was nothing but wind and open sky to bother him. Even in the middle of Glasgow he hadn't felt so suffocated, even with CivCon snoopers breathing down his neck 24/7. It was good to get out, to get better, good to walk out of the hotel and away from the village. He was stronger now; a week of generous portions had fattened him.

He walked.

There was only one destination that mattered. No point in pretending otherwise. Now that he was well enough he could get there easy enough, following the sheep track through Ben Bronach's gullies, along the hill's northern ridge.

He made the edge of the inland moors in less than an hour,

through heather and rushes and bracken, past wind-shivering pools; a bird, some kind of raptor, vigilant, gliding away over the village and the arms of the bay. He walked on, heading downhill off the ridge this time, to where the River Lair rose, oozing from the blanket bog through numberless pores and streams and capillaries.

Dr Morgan had told him not to overdo things for at least two weeks. A stroll around the village was okay, she said, until he got his strength back. Perhaps she would take a dim view of a nine-mile hike up into the squelching hills on a chilly October day. But he was stronger now, and anyway, he had to go to a certain place. There was unfinished business to finish. And he had to walk. If he stopped he would go crazy.

Skirting an outlying house at the head of the bay, he started climbing the southern hills, moving away from the sea all the time, but still able to make out the river, sunk deep into the fathoms of peat, before it plunged through Inverlair at the head of the bay. Further on and he crested the hill's swelling moorland summit, where he could no longer see the sea or the bay.

Here he was.

Below him, in a deep glen, was the same farmhouse, the door still wide open, the Range Rover still with one wheel in a stream, and the driver, or what was left of him, scattered between the vehicle and his idyllic downsized cottage-industry-cum-bolthole. The recording in Carl's head raced to its screaming climax.

This is the edge of the Inverlair notspot. This is the end. This is where it happened.

Heart pounding, Carl spun from what he saw and remembered, and half-ran back towards the village. After a while he stopped, turned around.

No point in running away. Better to let it in, to face it. That was the way it had to be done.

A while later he was sitting on the ground, looking down at the farmhouse and Range Rover, waterproof trousers keeping out the wet but not the cold on his arse. He took Howard's deltameter out of his pocket; there were spikes right across the waveform. This was almost as far as he could go before the redzone started to bite. He coughed, pain in his chest. Perhaps he'd pushed himself too hard.

This pilgrimage, this penance, hadn't turned out the way he thought it would. Here was the place where the knife had been twisted, where Howard had died. There should be a reckoning, or at least a revelation of some sort. But, after the shock of remembering that day had subsided, there was nothing, just the impassive context of land and sky.

From his pocket he took out a bottle of water and a plastic bag containing four slices of venison and two waxy cubes of polycarb. Without taking his eyes from the farmhouse, he ate and drank. It might rain; in borrowed clothing he'd be safe and dry.

He just wouldn't mention it. That was the way to handle things with Simone. Keep ignoring it and it'll go away. It: growing inside her, not yet a bump. A lump? Embryo or foetus? There was no accelerated hormonal flood to swell her like a balloon, give her all sorts of cravings and mood swings. She would be an invalid in a few months' time. Isn't that what happened? He would end up doing everything for her. She would expect that, and so would everyone else.

He shook his head. It was hard to believe. The more he thought about it, the more unjust and unfair it seemed. It was almost funny. By next spring, it would come along, and the non-stop crying and shitting would start. Isn't that what happens? And what would Isaac think — the kid who already thought the Grim Reaper stayed upstairs?

Man appears. Granny vanishes. Everyone gets sad and starts crying. Now man reappears, and Mum's talking about a baby. Man is the baby's daddy, but he is not my daddy. The man from upstairs was the angel of life and death. But maybe kids didn't think like that, didn't mull over all the ins and outs of a situation. He didn't know how they thought.

It couldn't be ignored, though. Not a hope in hell. Younger guys might carry on as before until reality kicked them in their dog-blind bollocks. But he couldn't push it away, could he? There was no bump yet. Nothing obvious. But it was coming. He could wriggle and struggle and ignore it all he liked. She could miscarry. There was still time.

From the north a gunshot cracked, breaking Carl's febrile cascade of thoughts. The sound bounced around the bay, fading into a scatter of echoes. He cocked an ear, looked towards Ben Bronach and the ridge, but the gun was not fired again.

Must be the stalker.

Should really go and say thanks to the guy. But Carl didn't even know what he looked like. He'd get round to it. Soon.

It was no small thing what the man had done.

A crescent moon came out from behind the clouds. Birds flew towards the forest for the night, and the wind picked up.

Better get used to it. Better forget about what once had been out there, including himself. Everything is here. There's no point trying to deny the truth of that. But it wasn't easy, and just thinking about it made him want to tear his hair out, hurt himself, do something crazy. How could the world just cease to exist? How could it all be unreachable, a shadowy realm of the past? What kind of arrangement was that to come smacking out of clear blue nothing? The whole thing was deranged. Rotten. But the world had been pretty deranged and rotten before the redzone threw a curtain of delta wave sleep around Inverlair. It was no change of state, really, just an end to all the familiar derangement he had known.

Carl pulled his hat down over his ears and shivered. It was getting dark, and the first nameless stars had come out. At the far end of the glen, pools of still water, like spilt mercury, reflected the half-light in the soundless, windless evening.

People were watching him, judging him.

From somewhere below – in the farmhouse glen, but from precisely where he couldn't say – an animal noise boomed, a deep bellowing that rolled around the slopes. He stood still, listened.

A cow? It certainly wasn't a sheep or a dog; hell of a racket whatever it was, as if someone was retching into a toilet bowl. A deer?

He strained to hear.

Not a sound came from the glen, its electricity pylons carrying their dead wires to the silent south.

Wind gusted from the east.

In an instant it started blowing, with force, picking up bits of dry grass. A few seconds later and the first crackle of electricity fizzed across the upper atmosphere, then another flash, and another, until the ionosphere blazed with a tracery of angry voltage.

It was just like Howard had said.

The electrical storm crackled across the eastern sky, lighting up the dark hills. He felt small and exposed under the storm.

Carl hurried down the rocky slope to the main road, the Atlantic horizon still aglow, sky flashing and sparking behind him in the east. For a split second, he was relieved to be going back to the hotel. He almost formed the word home. There were four walls, a bed and a regular supply of calories given to him by other people. But there was nothing and no one he had known from the life before. Now there was just hunger and the redzone and the consequences of action and inaction.

As the wind dropped a little, the animal noise came again from the glen below, a roar that rang around the regimented forest. From deep in its throat the cow-dog-bear called, a moaning bass note that swelled and echoed.

Carl quickened his pace down the gloomy track, between the gorse, and into the dark trees that loomed along the back of isolated houses, stumbling in the fading light. The old fear was behind him, on the hunt. After every few strides he cast a wild glance back through the wind-tossed trees, as if he were being followed, as if he were being watched and there was no escape, and nowhere to find rest.

July

4

The 11 p.m. surveillance drone, tail-light blinking red, banked at 600 metres over the city centre, heading north towards Bishopbriggs. There was something comforting in the regularity of the machine's routine, beyond his window, as it flew past, on the hour every hour, by day and by night. No matter what was going on in the rest of the world, the CivCon drone turned at the scheduled time, banking left over Glasgow, scanning for ID defaulters and clocking up their zonal debits for the council. Everything was as it had become.

Carl sat at the window of his third-floor flat. He wasn't really paying much attention to the drone's tail-light as he thought about the following day. Pollokshaws Road was dry and quiet.

Reports and photos and witness testimony covered his desk. It all added up to a great story, and one his boss would undoubtedly spike. It wasn't really Eric's fault though; he didn't make the rules; he just knew what would happen if they weren't followed. The newspaper had run out of last-chance saloons. It had called the Emergency Authority's bluff once too often.

Carl got up from his desk and made himself a fruit tea. As he flopped onto the sofa, the wall screen bleeped again, for the third time that day.

He let it ring until his ansa clicked on, watched Sarah's moon-face in the inset as she left her message. She was still playful, sarcastic, even though it was her fourth unreturned call of the day. Her blonde hair was more ruffled than earlier, her lipstick smudged.

'Hello, my darling,' she crooned. He reckoned she was stoned; her voice was hoarse. 'Are you there?' She waited. 'Are you trying to tell me you've really and truly had enough?' She smiled, seemed to look right into him. Even though she couldn't see him, Carl turned away towards the window as she left her message. 'Sorry I'm making a show of myself,' Sarah continued. 'Sorry I over-stepped the mark the other day. I mean, this is as good as it gets, right? Me here and you there, but that's okay because ...'

Carl sighed. 'Mute ansa,' he ordered, and Sarah was left to plead with her mascara-lined blue eyes alone. After a minute or so she hung up. Call and message logged.

He couldn't figure her out. First of all she seemed not to care about anything expect having fun and sharing her new lenses with him. It was a turn-on; the lenses she'd sent him were amazing. An imitation of life, every pore and hair, reproduced in high-res perfection and beamed right onto his retinas. Like she was actually in the room with him. But it was still just self-stimulation, for all the cleverness embedded in the biogel lenses. With spraysuits they could have crossed over into the promised land of personalised virtual togetherness. Without them, it was literally wanking 500 miles apart. The company promised a secure connection, but Carl had his doubts about that. There was always a chance that CivCon were listening in, although they had more to worry about than a largely neutered journalist at a failing newspaper.

It had been Sarah's plan, her idea, to try out the lenses. Now she was getting heavy, and the fun was over. When he'd suggested spraysuits, he thought she'd jump at the chance, but she had resisted the idea, before suggesting a meeting, somehow, of the meatspace sort. Transit endorsements and endless biosecurity bureaucracy would make the 500 miles to Bristol unbridgeable; CivCon could make the separation permanent, and probably would, given Carl's probable status on one of their watch lists. Surely Sarah knew all that, but still she banged on about meeting up.

If only she'd shown some sign of this honest yearning before he'd become too involved.

No. All things considered it would have been better to keep their relationship a netspace one. Women always want more from you, thought Carl; they're never content with being content. And when you become the kind of person they want you to be, they crap on you from a great height, from out of the blue. Well, he wasn't going there again. No chance. He hoped Sarah would leave him alone and not become one of those saddos who couldn't let go, who keep trying to wheedle their way back in. No point in doing that. Once it's finished it's finished: pleading and emotional blackmail just pushes the other person further away, makes them more convinced that they were right to chuck you. It was like some kind of Newtonian law: for every action there is an equal and opposite repulsion. Life would be less complicated without Sarah. It was already complicated enough.

Carl sipped his fruit tea, studying his reflection in the dark window, flicking through the papers and photos that littered his desk. There wasn't much he could do about any of it. All the ingredients were there, but he couldn't do any cooking.

Back at the bay window he caught sight of lights ascending from the helipad on top of the Hilton. The spires of the uni were black shards against the western sky.

The wall screen resumed its scan of his crowdmap, drip-feeding the chatter from 457 individuals and organisations, picking out key words and logging the information. Some of it mattered, but Carl wasn't sure if he could be bothered processing what his wall had to tell him any more. It was like some mythic jug he could never empty, no matter how deeply he drank from it.

•

The following morning, sunlight and birdsong awakened the notion of actually going in to the office. He could sit in the flat tweaking press releases and fluffing official announcements. He could lose himself in lensed-up exploration masquerading as research. Or he could leave the flat, walk through the hot dusty streets, and join the bedside vigil for a dying newspaper.

Today, he wanted to get his hands dirty, see those happy few helping speak truth to power. And it would be better if he spoke to Eric face to face about his latest article, give him the righteous spiel, for old time's sake. The online contributors were invisible, compliant, but Carl knew Eric was better persuaded in person if there was a hard sell to be sold. He would pick his moment to pounce for a result.

As if.

Walking to the bus stop he saw a mini-drone hovering over Queen's Park, the morning sun glinting from its rotors. There was loud popping and seconds later a large group of ragged men, women and children emerged from the trees, panicked and angry. The mini-drone barked a command, in several languages including English, about no unauthorised settlements and warned that a mobile unit had been despatched and was en route. Carl doubted the mobile unit would turn up within the hour, but if they did there would be more than loud bangs to worry about.

The bus came and he rode it into town.

Besides Eric, Caroline was the only other person in the office when Carl arrived, just after nine. She was yawning over supplier invoices. She took her glasses off and rubbed her eyes.

'Too many late nights, my girl.'

'More like far too many jobs,' Caroline replied. 'For one person. And this heat's making me sleepy.'

'It's only another week till the volunteer accountant starts,' said Carl. 'Then you'll have more time to spend on important stuff, like making me coffee.'

'You'd better be careful, or I might get round to installing that new payroll software,' said Caroline, smiling. 'A mistake with someone's salary could easily happen.' She returned to her printouts. 'Don't you have some pretend work to be getting on with?'

Carl gave a little bow. 'But of course, Liebling.' He straightened. 'Ajay and Val out and about?'

Caroline nodded. 'Yeah. Eric's in.'

Of course Eric's in, Carl felt like saying. Eric hardly ever left his cave.

An hour later, and Carl had pounced with his story and, amazingly, managed to persuade Eric to phone the Press Liaison Committee. The subject matter made approval unlikely.

The active denial shield was a crowd control weapon – a tightly focused microwave pain stick wielded from 400 metres that caused intense pain by exciting the water molecules in the epidermis, but did not actually damage the skin. At least, that was the manufacturer's pledge, picked up and parroted by the Emergency Authority. But it wasn't true. Carl sat at his desk, trying not to listen to his news editor in convo with the Press Liaison Committee.

There was a photo of a young Asian girl on Carl's desk screen. If he put his hand over one side of the twelve-year-old girl's image, she was pretty, but the look in her eye said something was very wrong. That something was the other side of her face, the bubble-blistered, angry red and black-crusted vitrified side, where the active denial shield had been a touch heavy on the dermal excitation. He had another dozen or so photos from the food riot at the Kelvingrove centre, of young and old, male and female. None of the images would see the light of day if the Press Liaison Committee slapped on a Section 4 interdict. Sentinel protocols would have locked down every mobile device in the neighbourhood while the riot was in progress, so that nothing would leak out. But there was always a leak, somewhere in the pipework, and this kind of damage was hard to hide.

He had the evidence and the testimony and, a fact he knew full well, zero chance of a publishable article.

The door of Eric's office opened and Carl knew straight away there was no deal. Eric would have been dancing if Nigel Fuckface at the PLC had agreed to a page two down-pager, voicing concern but nothing too strong. Hints of errant behaviour by the crowd at Kelvingrove. The manufacturer's spotless safety record. Immediate inquiry. A caring Emergency Authority in action.

At least the story would have been a start, something to build on. Carl looked at the photo of the disfigured girl on his computer. Tough luck, love.

'Mr Nigel Flitch-Pace,' said Eric, as he had a weary habit of doing, 'has the manufacturer's assurances that the aforementioned product's "calibration issues" have been resolved and that, as an added safeguard, efforts will be made to explore the inclusion of governors, fitted as standard, on the next generation of active denial devices. Mr Nigel Fuckface regrets resorting to Emergency Order Section 4 but ABC, XYZ, goodnight and fuck off.'

He studied the crease in his trousers.

A few workspaces away, Caroline looked up from her invoices.

'Guy's a prick,' she called.

Carl smiled, chewing his lip.

'Efforts to explore,' he muttered, drumming his fingers on the desk. He looked up at Eric, 'And what did the board say when you told them?'

Eric stiffened. 'I haven't told the trustees yet.'

'Hang on,' said Carl. 'How will the Emergency Authority know if the calibration issues on CivCon's new toy have been sorted?'

Eric shrugged, lowered his voice. 'Nigel . . . um, we didn't go into that kind of detail.'

'Nice one,' said Carl. He could see Eric trying not to look at the screen, at the image of a twelve-year-old girl with cheese on toast where the right side of her face should be.

'I'll tell the family,' Carl said, looking at the photo. 'They didn't really want the exposure anyway.'

'Piss off,' Eric grumbled, with no real venom. He glanced over at Caroline, lowering his voice. 'Do you fancy dinner tonight? Lesley's cooking, she got hold of a real roast.'

Carl raised his eyebrows. 'Should I be worried? The last time you invited me round for dinner we sacked everyone and moved into this leaky shithole.'

'Nothing to worry about this time.' Eric looked away. 'Just thought you might fancy some decent food, that's all.'

'What time?'

'Lesley said seven. That okay?'

'Fine by me. I'll try and get hold of something drinkable.'

Eric nodded and closed his office door. The need for privacy always meant a heated discussion with the board or the Press Liaison Committee was in the offing. Eric was up to something.

Carl studied the week's food briefing from the Emergency Authority. He'd introduce some coded ambiguity to leaven the official bullshit. There would be a place within the text where a mote of truth in heavy disguise could be inserted.

His screen flashed. Carl opened the mail.

It was Jeff from ScotNet, a low-level mole.

The email read: 'Hows trix? That gizmo you sent ovr ystrdy the custmr is a real screamr. Meet?'

Time-check. The word 'screamer' meant a same-day meeting, 4 p.m. at the usual place. It also meant something big. He had two hours before he saw Jeff – the stupid prick. 'That gizmo you sent over yesterday.' Carl shook his head. Why even write that? Why give Sentinel anything to work with? Keep the exchange to a minimum, the bare bones, and don't use any key words or phrases that might alert the system.

Gizmo. For fuck's sake. It was time to tell Eric.

Carl opened a drawer and took out a postcard of a smiling cartoon Loch Ness Monster wearing a tartan hat. He rapped on Eric's door and went in.

'I got this,' Carl said, and handed the postcard to Eric.

SCOPE

Inverlair Hotel

IV54

Thursday

There was no name or address.

Eric handed back the postcard. 'This a joke?'

Carl shook his head. 'The card came in an envelope with some kind of chipset. I'm meeting someone from ScotNet at four – an IT guy. He's gonna give me the lowdown on it, thinks it's something big, something that might be part of an upgraded version of SCOPE. He couldn't tell me much more on the phone, but we have this code word. Anyway, there's a new hydroelectricity scheme being opened in the area – it's in the Highlands – so I could kill two birds – an on-the-spot colour piece, lots of crunchy figures and a good news story for the Emergency Authority.' Carl smiled. 'They'll like that. Then I'll swing by Inverlair Hotel and have a word with Deep Throat, or whoever the contact is. And on the way back down to Glasgow I'll swing by and have a look at the Ardmonie Yard – KBS are the new tenants there ...'

Eric folded his arms and sat back. 'That's a lot of swinging by you've got planned.' He pursed his lips. 'What kind of "big" did this IT guy say the chipset was?'

Carl shrugged. 'No idea. He'll tell me at four.'

Eric sighed. 'No story is going to come out of this, got that? You'll end up under a control order, at this rate. I'm not having another run-in with Nigel, or his prick of a boss, about SCOPE. Not again.'

Carl nodded. 'A simple reconnaissance mission.' He put his hand over his heart. 'Word of honour.'

Eric shook his head. 'Where is IV54? Inverness?'

'Yes,' lied Carl. 'Just outside.'

'Hmm,' Eric frowned. 'Transit clearance will be difficult.'

'No, it won't,' said Carl. 'The car hasn't been on the road for six months, and I'm heading north within Area 1 on work-related business, not on a jolly. The nearest white rust infection is in North Yorkshire wheat crops. It ticks all the biosec boxes. If you ask Nigel Fuckface nicely I'm sure he could expedite my transit application, just for the new hydro plant.'

Eric tried not to laugh. 'You've got it all figured out, eh?' His face fell and he leant forward. 'If you cause any trouble at all – if you chase the story – I will let you go, this time. I will. Got that? The board will be delighted if I find some more fat to trim, and you'll be queuing for polycarb rations at Kelvingrove with the rest of them. *Capisce?*'

As one of only three staffers, Carl felt he could push his luck with Eric, not that it had done him much good story-wise, of late. This time, though, he figured the guy was in no mood for further aggravation. The Emergency Authority could intervene at any time and put its own press people in charge. They could turn the paper into a mouthpiece, if it wasn't that already.

'If this chipset proves to be significant, I'll meet the contact, see what he or she has to say, then leave and do a nice piece up north,' said Carl, meaning every word. 'No more than two nights. Straight up and back.'

There was no sign on his face that Carl was being disingenuous. With a bit of blagging – once up there – he could make it three or even four nights away.

Eric nodded. 'Good,' he said. Grinning, he added, 'By the way, our friend Nigel says we can refer to injuries sustained by rioters at Kelvingrove, but we can't go into any details. The phrase "microwave pain stick" is definitely off-limits. Think you can do something with that?'

'Yeah,' said Carl. 'I'll work up some carefully nuanced truth. Between the lines is where the action is.'

5

The cellar bar was quiet, lights on low, all comfy booths and jazz-funk fusion. Carl let Jeff buy the drinks. They sat in one of the booths at the back.

'How's the dynamic world of cochlear implants?'

Jeff giggled into his half lager and lime. 'Barely enough. How's the grubby world of journalism?'

Carl girned at his orange juice. 'A lot grubbier than you could possibly imagine, young man.'

Jeff asked about the new polycarb factory at Hamilton and the latest on the white rust fungus. The guy was looking for fresh insight, for solid news. Instead, scraps of reliable information were sewn together with educated guesswork, and Carl passed it off, adroitly, as incontrovertible truth. Jeff was impressed. The Emergency Authority would tell Carl the real story, and expect it to be published as they had given it, just as soon as they had decided what the real story was to be. One thing he did know about for certain was the arrival of an aerostat that was to hover over the Central Belt, bristling with all sorts of total awareness kit. It would be the seventh such blimp deployed in the UK. Jeff was suitably impressed, but unconcerned.

Carl sipped his drink and cut to the chase. 'So what's the score with the chipset?'

'Well,' began Jeff, pushing his glasses up his nose. 'This is a plasmoid board, the smallest I've ever seen. Something special all right – a high-temperature superconducting microwave filter. Or at least part of an HTS filter.' He drooled over the tiny rectangle in his hand. 'Superb architecture. Doing a bit of reverse engineering, I would say that the whole thing can provide enhanced tunability right into the terahertz wavebands . . .'

'Interesting,' said Carl, glancing at the few punters sharing the gloomy bar. 'What does all that mean?'

'Well, HTS filters are used in base stations and repeaters to filter out noise and give high front-end sensitivity . . .'

Attention wandering, Carl's eye was caught by the barmaid, in jeans and a cut-off T-shirt, a spiral tattoo around her belly button, a stud in her eyebrow. She was bending over to pick a cloth up off the floor. She moved to another table and wiped down the dark wood surface, her breasts swaying as she cleaned. He turned back to Jeff's noise.

'. . . the RF channel time delay on this is configured to some extremely low frequencies.' Jeff nodded, held the thin sheet of plasmoid in his hands, like it was alive. 'Yeah,' he murmured, smiling in awe. 'It's a beauty.'

The barmaid moved away.

'So it's comms?' said Carl.

Jeff looked up, open-mouthed. 'Yeah, a small part of it, but the HTS filter has an unusual crystalline component that . . .'

'Is it part of something really new and advanced that's designed to cover a large area, like Wimax?'

Jeff nodded. 'Yeah, but . . .'

Carl held out his hand. 'Thanks.'

With obvious reluctance, Jeff handed the chipset back to Carl like a kid being forced to hand over sweets to the teacher.

'Thanks for that, Jeff. Much appreciated.'

Jeff fiddled with his glass. 'Am I going to get paid this time?' He watched Carl sink the last of his orange juice.

'You know, Jeff, that's what I like about you. You're very direct. It's a rare quality these days.' Carl put the chipset in his inside pocket and stood up.

'Thanks for the drink.' He tossed two unopened packets of tobacco onto the table, four ounces in total. 'Don't say I'm not good to you.'

Jeff stared at the packets. 'You're having a fucking laugh – I don't even smoke.'

'Then it's money in the pocket for you,' said Carl. 'It's just a question of finding a buyer.'

Groaning, Jeff pocketed the tobacco.

They climbed the narrow staircase back to street level. It was pissing down, but Jeff didn't seem to mind; he just turned his collar up and strode off through the downpour along Sauchiehall Street, hands jammed in his trouser pockets. Carl wasn't so sure about getting soaked, so he stood in the doorway, under the tiny awning, looking up at the grey sky. Summer in fucking Glasgow. There were jobs he could have taken, years ago when travel was easy. Jobs in hot places like Cyprus or the Costa Brava; plenty of expats there, enough to warrant a newspaper or two; local drama clubs and breast cancer fundraisers. That would do him now. Away from CivCon and the pissing rain, to settle down near the beach with some hot young Spanish nymph, or Greek, or Navajo, who'd ride him all day and then make him dinner. It really didn't matter what race she was. The only girl he didn't really want to do it with was Sarah. Why did they always make things difficult? What do women want? The answer is a million things, every day. And it's a man's job to guess the right one at the right time. That's all any man had to do.

So, he said to himself, SCOPE is a communications system, and an extremely sophisticated one at that. There was no telling what it might be capable of.

A police van splashed past the pub. The coppers were still okay, not like CivCon. In fact, the coppers he knew hated CivCon. Maybe they were jealous of the perks as well as the power. They got decent booze, for starters, not the Government pish.

Carl looked at his watch. He had twenty minutes before the Central Business District checkpoints timed out and he'd have to chase up some digs for the night, another zonal default disappearing from his account. His account couldn't take another hit. Plunging into the rain, he ran to Central Station for the last shuttle train to Queen's Cross.

•

Standing in front of his wardrobe Carl wondered how much of an effort he should make for Eric and Lesley. News preferences were updating over his bedroom speakers: two guys shot while trying to break through the white rust biosec cordon around wheatfields in Wiltshire; the latest Citizen Vote results were narrowly in favour of neutrality on the Middle East; another big blackout in Eastern Europe.

A bandwidth capacity warning flashed on his crowdmap. All his categories were nearly full and he would need to go through the feeds and delete the unwanted. Let them fill. Let the warnings flash.

Carl picked up a shirt and sniffed it. He decided against wearing a tie or anything too formal. When in doubt, clean and neat was the best bet, and he always felt better after a shave. He swigged a cold beer and pulled another shirt from the pile on the chair. One night off the wagon wouldn't do him any harm. Now where had he left the iron?

'Music,' he said out loud. 'Favourites 17 to 21. Shuffle.'

Carl shaved, showered, and put on the cleanest clothes he could find. Was he dressing to impress? Eric, for want of anyone else to fit the bill, was his best friend, as well as, technically, his employer. But Carl couldn't shake the idea that Lesley was bored and looking for something, someone. Maybe she had a yearning for disorder, because disorder belongs to the young, and to be young is to be vigorous and passionate. Isn't that right? Maybe she wanted to break out of the life that was fossilising around her. Having an affair would mean risk and freshness and discovery and stolen sex. Having an affair would also mean exploding the people you love into thousands of dagger-sharp fragments. And that meant Eric.

But she was up for it, Carl could tell; the last time they'd met it had been obvious. He saw that this could go one of two ways: either he'd shag his boss's wife or he wouldn't. That is, essentially, what the situation boiled down to. As he showered, he felt himself harden. Best not to think of Lesley in that way. Much too complicated. Messy. And there had been too much of that.

Eric was obsessed with his job. He was stressed and in his fifties, and stress could have that effect on a man of his age. It had consequences in all sorts of departments.

6

Sitting across from Carl, Lesley smoked a post-prandial fag. She had her bare feet up on the chair, curled under her, black skirt tight over her thighs, smoking and listening to the music, smiling to herself, three glasses of Cab Sauv down and sipping at a fourth. Carl sat on the L-shaped leather sofa, legs stretched out in front on the hard oak floor.

Eric came back into the living room waving a single sheet of paper.

'Here comes salvation,' he breezed. He moved empties and an ashtray on to the floor and laid the sheet of paper out on the glass coffee table. It was a front-page mock-up: the splash was an exposé of CivCon brutality and the main photo was of a gesticulating Adolf Hitler. The headline read: 'Brownshirts Batter Britain!'

In the bottom corners of the page were two arrows, one pointing left and the other pointing right.

'We're saved, lad, I tell thee,' smiled Eric, reaching out to touch the right-hand button. The text and photos on the front page immediately shimmered and turned to a perfect page two, even making a rustling sound as it did so. Hitler and his Brownshirts disappeared, and were replaced by some half-pissed celebrity getting out of a limo.

'Wow,' breathed Carl, sitting up, his head clearing of wine and whisky. Eric riffled forward a few pages using the right-hand arrow, then turned back to the front page.

'Wow,' said Carl again. He laid his hand on the page, felt it. 'It's not like newsprint. So this is what all the secrecy is about?'

Eric glanced at Lesley, then tapped the sheet. 'People keep this page and the next edition is downloaded the minute we send it. And look . . .' He handed the page to Carl. 'Try tearing it.' After a fair effort, Carl made an inch-long rip along one edge. It wasn't indestructible, but it was tough, durable, and it handled like ordinary paper.

Eric smiled: the proud father. 'Nanotube construction. Microtransducers – actually embedded in the paper itself. The upshot: we can practically give it away. A one-page 42-page newspaper, downloaded fresh every morning.' He let Carl handle the page. 'So, what do you think?'

'Well,' began Carl, 'so far as distribution and raw material are concerned, we'd save a packet. The content's another matter.'

'That depends on what you want to write about. Do you want to tell the truth for a change?'

Before Carl could answer, Eric said, 'Oil hit 300 euros a barrel today, and it barely registered a blip. Why? Because the media have been told to play it down. Sentinel can block everything negative online, except DeepNet where the geeks and criminals live. It's the usual spin – pipeline shutdown or attack on a refinery. Supply chain pinchpoint. Whatever. But we can't make a big deal of it any more. That's the level of control the PLC is trying to squeeze us with.'

He smoothed out the paper on the table. 'With the new palmpods Eddie can get his hands on, you guys could file straight into the paper.' He prodded the paper. 'This paper – from anywhere. And the paper puts itself together, using preset protocols.' He glanced at Lesley and then back at Carl. 'No editing required. You see, if we carry on like this, there won't be a paper any more. We both know that. Either that or you won't have a job and it'll be press officers from the Emergency Authority who take over.' Eric laughed. 'Some of the guys we had to sack the last time now work for them. Imagine them coming back as the ones in charge.'

Carl snorted. 'Maybe I'll apply there myself.'

Eric shook his head. 'Come on, man. This is all you've known, this is what you are. What else are you going to do? Keep shelving real news?'

Carl considered his empty glass. Eric poured a couple of fingers of whisky into it.

'Countermeasures is big business, Carl, if you have the money or the contacts,' he said. 'We don't have a huge amount of one, but we do have a very well-positioned other – Eddie.'

Now the purpose of the evening became clear. It was a proposition, made all the more palpable after real meat and some lubrication.

'The main man,' said Eric. 'Always one step ahead. This time it's uncrackable quantum encryption, so he tells me.'

'Except that nothing's uncrackable.'

'Correct. But he said it was good for six months.'

'Then what?'

Eric smiled. 'Then Eddie and his . . . partners produce another set of encryption algorithms for the paying customers, for those who like their anonymity.'

Carl considered the paper on the table. He realised Lesley was looking at him, and her skirt was now riding a little higher up her nyloned leg. Eric was watching him too.

'So,' said Carl, 'what exactly are you asking me?'

Sipping his whisky, Eric squinted across the coffee table. 'I think you have a good idea about that.' He took a deep breath. 'Call it guerrilla journalism. Filing on the hoof.' He rapped his knuckles on the mock-up. 'Eddie says that half the cameras on the South Side aren't even working. The contractor hasn't been paid for over a year to fix them. There's a map of the broken ones, apparently, networked safehouses, new zombie uploading of . . .'

'Whoa,' said Carl, getting to his feet. 'Safehouses? Cameras?' He shook his head, pacing the room. 'What the fuck are you talking about? They'll close us down as soon as we publish. And what about you? Where will you be when all this is going on – directing operations from a CivCon black site?'

Eric sighed and put down his empty glass. 'One more negative story and the helpful Mr Flitch-Pace hinted, pretty much said it really, that the Emergency Authority will step in and put their own people in charge.' He looked up at Carl. 'We'll be finished as a newspaper, and so will all the noble stuff about speaking truth to power.' He glanced at Lesley. 'But the paper isn't the only reason why I asked you to dinner.'

For the first time in several minutes Lesley spoke. 'We're getting out.'

Carl frowned. 'Out?' He tried the word one more time. 'What do you mean *out*? Where?'

'My sister,' said Eric. 'She works for the Ministry of Agriculture, in Brazil. There's no white rust down there – not yet anyway.' He tried a smile. 'Travel is a bit easier for the diplomatic class. There's this house by the sea and a job for me, one that doesn't really exist. My sister's arranged it all.' He toyed with his glass, got up for a refill, taking Carl's empty from his limp, compliant hand. A weight had been lifted from Eric's shoulders. It was out in the open, and he felt better for saying it.

Lesley held her glass up behind her head. 'Thanks, darling, you're so very kind.'

'Oh,' said Eric, taking her empty. 'Sorry, love.'

Carl got up and sat down across the room, on an uncomfortable cane chair that Lesley had insisted on bringing back from a holiday in Egypt, before the biosec shutdown. Apart from a single 'fuck' he was speechless. They left him to sit, digesting the shock news.

After a minute or so he said, 'When?'

Lesley answered. 'We applied four months ago. Transit clearance should come through in another six weeks or so, and our new passports. We were more or less given the green light this week by the Security Ministry. Just procedure to go through, that's all. I think they're glad to get rid of us.'

Half an hour later, Carl was more or less over the initial surprise. He could see the sense in their leaving, and he wondered about Lesley, skirt riding high, and the looks, the suggestions, over the last couple of weeks. Was it a final fling she was after? He watched Eric dancing in his socks. Grown-up kids and a second marriage, and he can't perform when and where it counts. Do animals suffer from impotence? Of course they don't; there's nothing to interfere with their programming so long as the stimuli are right. Psychopathology doesn't come into it.

'. . . the Emergency Authority know fine well what's going on,' bellowed Eric above the music, 'no point pretending otherwise. CivCon aren't gonna let go when all this is over, if it ever is over. Like fucking Pit Bulls they are. They've got their teeth into this thing and they're not going to let go of us, not while there's money to be made, and even when there isn't they'll probably do it for pleasure and just because they can. Isn't that the way of it?'

Lesley got up and went through to the kitchen. 'Time for bed, tiger. Grab the bottle will you, Carl, before he sees the bottom of it.'

She could be a cold bitch. But it must be hard for her, Carl thought, watching Eric trying to keep the paper afloat single-handed, encased in his own space, his own struggle. A caveman trapped in ice. Anyone who still believed in the power of the press was a primitive, clinging on to some outmoded animist belief.

Lesley stacked the dinner dishes in the washer. 'Use the spare room if you want,' she said. 'It's pretty late.'

There was no denying that. At this time of night there was always the chance that if a CivCon patrol saw who they were dealing with they would put him through a full biometric, just to piss him off. That would take the best part of the night. But it was nothing too serious: not like in some places. People seldom disappeared never to be heard from again. Of all people, Carl had to stay ID- and zone-legal or they could pull him in and keep him. He watched Lesley wash the good wine glasses in the sink. He grabbed a dishtowel to help. A little potbelly at forty-seven didn't constitute horrible deformity. Her perfume mingled with lemon fresh washing-up liquid.

'Thanks for the offer,' he said to her, drying a plate, 'but I'll take my chances on the street with the Brownshirts tonight.'

Lesley was just about to speak when, from the sitting room, came the sound of Johnny Marr's chiming guitar. Grinning and swaying on the spot, Eric was sloshing whisky onto the floor. He raised his glass, not quite in time to the music. One side of his shirt had come out of his trousers. Carl watched him for a spell while Lesley clattered dishes in the kitchen. She was pissed off. That's what women do when they're pissed off, they take it out on the dishes, or the bathroom floor, or . . .

'People didn't give a fuck in the old days,' shouted Eric, the daft grin fading. He rambled some more about a pristine past that never existed.

He stopped, stood still for a moment, then dropped his empty glass onto the dining table, glass on glass knocking hard together but nothing breaking, and collapsed onto the sofa.

Carl went over to the sofa and stood, watching. He picked up Eric's legs by the ankles and hoisted them onto the sofa.

'The enemy within is the outsider, and we are all suspects,' said Eric woozily. He smiled, his eyes closing. 'Stay on the outside, eh?'

'Yes, Eric,' said Carl. 'Whatever you say.'

Within a minute Eric was snoring, mouth slack and sucking for air, flat on his back, one foot on the floor.

'I'll get a blanket,' said Lesley. It probably wasn't the first time that her man had ended up sleeping on the couch, pissed. It was now almost 11.30. Carl downed the last of his whisky and picked up his jacket, as Lesley came back down the stairs with the blanket.

'You sure you won't change your mind? The spare room's there, if you want it.'

He shook his head, afraid to catch Lesley's eye. Sex gripped him by the guts, made his voice thick and uncertain. 'It's fine. My zonal credit is good until one. I'll just head home, if that's okay.'

Why say that? She was standing next to her unconscious husband, waiting for something to happen, willing it.

'Thanks for the meal,' he said, pulling on his jacket in the lobby. 'Best bit of flesh I've had in a long time.'

Light-hearted. Easygoing. Saying goodnight to a friend. That's all. Simple. Why the fuck use the word 'flesh'?

'Goodnight then.' He stepped out into the warm summer night. The earlier rain had all but dried up; Byres Road was ten minutes away and he could grab a cab there. A quick peck on her cheek and he was gone, relief and desire churning within him. Usually, he would have given her a squeeze. But not tonight.

'Yeah,' Lesley said, watching the retreating figure. 'Take care.'

7

Most of the office space in the St Vincent Street complex had not been let since it was built. The gleaming glass had lost its shine over the last twenty years and some of the upper floors on the east side had not been fully weatherproofed. It was watertight at the other end of the building, but lately the lights had begun to flicker every time the wind rose, and there was now a drip from the ceiling near the lift.

Today, there were two large vans parked outside, half on the pavement. Eric had said Nigel at the PLC had arranged some building repairs, without any thought of a quid pro quo, of course. How nice of the man to think of the struggling newspaper without any thought of what he could get in return.

The sudden thought of driving – no, zooming – along by Loch Lomond occurred to him, then he killed the image. Best not to get carried away. There were the biosec checkpoints to get through first. Once CivCon saw who was trying to leave the city they might get antsy, focus on a minor irregularity just to frustrate him. Carl might have to spend all day waiting at their Clydebank compound for nothing, and end up back at the office without ever getting to enjoy the twists and turns of Loch Lomondside. They might just do that, the bastards, and enjoy every minute of it. He made his way down to the basement car park. The one and only company car, one tyre flat, hadn't moved for months and no one had seen fit to throw a dust sheet over it. Carl ran his finger down the windscreen and drew a clear line through the dust. He blew his finger and wiped it on his jeans. Beeped the lock, chucked his rucksack on the back seat, and got into the driver's seat. It still had that clean car smell, but the air was a little fusty.

Sitting there, his hands on the wheel, all the functions of the car still to be awoken, it was hard not to think of the long road north, music blaring and the miles blurring past. Almost a year since he'd driven a car. The smell of the interior and the smooth curves, the seat adjustable to the perfect driving position; it was all there to command and enjoy.

The stair door clanged shut and someone came walking across the car park's bare concrete, clip-clopping a scatter of echoes. A stocky man in black biker's leather, a man that wasn't Eric.

Carl got out of the car. 'Christ,' he said, smiling. 'It's Santa Claus himself.'

'How's it going, big man?'

'Fine, Eddie. Yourself?'

'Not bad. Still fighting the good fight.'

Carl smiled. 'Yeah, if the price is right.'

Eddie grinned, a gold tooth glinting. 'Eric tells me you're after a bit of anonymity.' He took a slender black case, no more than seven inches long, from his inside pocket, the leather jacket creaking over his bulk. 'Pop the bonnet, will you?'

Carl did as he was told.

Eddie put on a pair of rubber gloves, then set to work. From the open case he unwound two thin black wires that ended in crocodile clips. Under the bonnet he grunted and footled about in the guts of the engine.

'So how's life treating you, Eddie?'

'Could be worse. Countermeasures is the place to be.'

'So I gather.'

With a bit of effort, Eddie found the contacts and attached the clips. 'It puts food on the table.'

'How's the family?'

'Still giving me grief, but I wouldn't change them for the world.'

'That true?'

'I'm always open to offers.' Eddie grinned. 'But so far none have come in.' He touched the screen in the little black case, some kind of meter, and watched the results. 'Good,' he said. 'Now. I've inserted an impedance circuit into the RF tracker, to create a feedback current. Wait until you're past the emergency perimeter and out near Loch Lomond. Keep an eye on your bars and when you hit a notspot keep above forty and switch the engine off for a couple of seconds, then back on. You might smell a bit of burning, but don't worry. It's only the RF tracker circuit shorting. If you get stopped by CivCon, which is highly unlikely outside the cities, it's just a burned-out circuit and you had nothing to do with it.'

'Nice one,' said Carl. 'Thanks.'

'Thank Eric, he paid for it. He must have friends on the board.'

'Yeah, well, I suppose he must . . . if only you could give me a new ID.'

'There're guys that can do that for you, no bother. But I doubt if the paper's budget will stretch to it. CivCon are sharp, but not as sharp as they think. There're ways round most things, even who you are. So what's the scoop, scoop?'

'Not sure. A tip-off. It might be nothing.'

Eddie handed over the ignition key. 'The usual, then. This should get you up north and back. There's a full month's quota of carbon credits on there as well.'

Carl got into the car, inserted the key, and opened the window. Over the internal speakers an expressionless female voice said: 'Autodriver engaged. Smart screen display on. Fuel quota at maximum. Tyre reflation in progress. Pressure now optimal. EMS at 95.6 per cent efficiency. Have a safe journey.'

Thumbs up to Eddie. Let's burn rubber.

'Not today, honey,' said Carl, switching off the autodriver. It was easy enough to feel powerless without a car doing all the driving into the bargain.

'Autodriver disengaged. Smart screen display off,' the female voice told him in a disapproving tone. He slipped into first gear, and the car went lurching forward. The engine stalled. Carl looked rueful and started the car again.

Smoother, and for the first time in a very long time, Carl drove out of the car park and onto the streets of Glasgow. His hangover, not the worst he'd ever suffered, made him jittery.

But there was driving. Music. Control. Purpose.

They're not as clever as they think.

As he drove along Waterloo Street and onto the Kingston Bridge, he couldn't help smiling. The warm weather had brought the people out onto the streets. People, patrols, CivCon, coppers, pigeons, bouncing tits in small tops, council workers, assorted city centre misfits, and the few who still had cash to spend. Everything more or less normal, in an abnormal kind of way.

•

There weren't many other cars. Electric cabs, but not many. Lamppost scanners would already have clocked his car; maybe the drones would keep an eye on him, the city beneath laid out for their inspection. Next month they were launching the aerostat, bristling with sensors, to do the job even better than the fleet of hover-drones.

By now, the first CivCon perimeter would have been alerted; Sentinel's multivariable analysis would have produced a response. Maybe it had already allocated the appropriate resources to deal with him.

The machinery of control would swing into operation, unless it was broken, like the cameras on the South Side. In the old days he would have headed up Woodlands Road, but that now took him too close to Kelvingrove Park and the rationing centre. No chance was he going near there, not at this time of day; the road would be packed, queues out the park gate; maybe trouble, answered by microwave pain sticks with calibration issues. At least he'd written the story, albeit missing most of what he would like to have said. But there was something out there, a blip on the flatline of controlled reality.

Today he was going to leave it all behind. Today he only had one thing in mind and it was going to happen, surely it was, just like he prayed it would. As he approached the sliproad for the Kingston Bridge he saw the sign: CIVIL CONTINGENCIES ENFORCEMENT. CHECKPOINT AHEAD (INNER RING) BY ORDER OF THE EMERGENCY AUTHORITY. A few years ago CivCon had been known as the Civil Contingencies Rapid Reaction Force. Now rapid reaction had morphed into a permanent presence. This subtle descriptive shift always made him smile. By degrees was the screw tightened, turning always, by those in the background, who now took silence and compliance for granted.

Halfway over the Clyde, there were seven other cars in front of him, a few pedestrians on foot, being body-scanned in and out of the Inner Ring. He licked his lips and strained to see ahead, nervous. CivCon could put the kibosh on his drive before it even started.

The cars in front went through okay, each one sprayed in the biosec booth, and the barrier came down again. Darth Vader's Stormtroopers waved and barked, no helmets today because of the baking heat. He slid the window down and held out his ID, took off his sunglasses and waited for the iris scan. The CivCon grunt, Scottish regimental tattoo on his bare forearm, smiled when his hand-held scanner revealed the next driver to be a 'fucking journalist'.

Carl smiled right back. Without a hint of reaction, he said, 'Yes. I'm off to cover the opening of the new hydroelectric scheme in the Highlands. An on-the-spot interview with the Minister.'

His goofy smile broadened. This bull-necked prick could pull him in for no reason, find a way to block his progress. The merest suspicion would be enough. Playing it sullen never worked. They loved to pull up people who tried to ignore them. This one looked at his terminal, saw the letters SIP – Surveillance In Progress – and followed his training to the letter. He looked at Carl, checked inside the car, then stood up to look at his scanner again.

The smile was there, the sly smile around the eyes. I know about you, Mr Carl Shewan, right down to when and where you bought your last pair of socks, every preference and perversion.

'Transit clearance in order,' said the grunt, glancing up at the sky and handing Carl his ID. 'Follow the instructions in the biosecurity booth. Have a safe day.'

An awareness passed between them. Carl knew what was going on in the background, and so did the guard. He pocketed his ID and slipped the car into gear. If he'd been heading south, towards white rust instead of away, he'd have to allow himself to be disinfected as well as the car in case of white rust. Doing three miles an hour he followed the green light into biosec, stopped when the red showed, and drove off when the spray had finished, a trail of disinfectant glistening on the road behind him.

He was over the first hurdle and onto the M8; the beginning of the great arterial arc that didn't really stop; that just went on into the Highlands until there was no more road.

He knew CivCon hated a good summer because it brought people out onto the streets, and that was a very bad thing. Being outside was unsafe, as any risk management manual could tell you. Better for order and security if the unemployed stayed in their pits and played the Lottery.

At every major exit there were CivCon Humvees parked up, the new J7 models, unless Carl was mistaken, fresh from the Solihull factory. The guys inside gave him the eye as he passed. He was part way out of the shithole, though he had a nagging doubt about the Outer Ring checkpoint on the Erskine Bridge. Making it through the Inner Ring didn't mean he had escaped altogether.

Maybe this was part of their game: let him through the Inner Ring, turn him back at the Outer.

After eight years controlling the streets, CivCon knew their turf by now, knew where and how to squeeze, always tighter, like a bully not satisfied until he heard a cry of pain. They were here for the long haul and their grip would not easily be loosened. But clearance is clearance, so play the game, you fuckers. Play by your own rules.

Past the airport the buildings thinned out, more land than concrete. Almost there. Fingers and toes crossed. To feel a little freer, to breathe a little easier.

From the Inchinnan industrial estate a column of black smoke rose. Two helicopters hovered on either side of it.

None of it mattered.

Another few minutes and the road started to climb into being the Erskine Bridge. The Clyde estuary shimmered and the northern hills were massing. Right now, he was the only vehicle breaching the biosec cordon at Checkpoint 24.

There were supposed to be a minimum of twenty CivCons at each of the twenty-eight exit points in the city's Outer Ring. Most of them were arseholes: ex-army, Special Forces, the best coppers, private security from overseas; all on decent pay and food. There were meant to be twenty, but today he could only see five. Maybe there was trouble somewhere, and they were overstretched.

Same as before, he told himself. Hand the thing over. Don't get smart. Give him the spiel and the smile.

Thrash metal was blasting from the sentry booth, the singer screaming over white noise feedback. The five CivCons had their helmets off; tunics open in the warmth. An older one, South African by the sound of it, moaned about the shit music.

A black guy, English, did the honours.

Pulse quickening, Carl held out his ID card for scanning. He tried to look impassive, bored even, for his retinal scan. This time the guy didn't spit the word 'journalist'. Maybe the surveillance drone had watched him since the city centre, seen that he hadn't stopped near any known subversives. Maybe nothing had watched him at all, and he was just imagining it. He drummed his fingers lightly on the steering wheel. ID's fine, man. Transit clearance has been given. Pull a fast one or let me out.

The CivCon didn't say a word, just nodded, handed back the ID, with the same sly smile as the first. He walked away and, after what seemed like an age, the barrier floated upwards. Stop had become an invitation to go. Just the disinfectant spray-booth, and he was away. Carl followed the arrows, stopped in the booth, and waited. The nozzles started spraying, and then they stopped.

The light was red.

Red. That meant stop. No go.

Shit.

He looked up, hands trembling, at the figure striding towards him.

The CivCon bent down. 'Have you had a shower this morning, sir?'

Carl felt panic rising. 'Eh ... what? I don't unders—'

Please. Let me go. Let me get out.

The guard bent down, grinning, and looked Carl straight in the eye. 'Close your fucking window. The spray won't work if it's open.'

And he walked away.

Relief made Carl feel like laughing. He understood, did as he was told, felt tension draining from his body.

The spray-booth went to work, and the light turned green. He put the car in gear and drove away from the checkpoint, the road ahead straight and empty. For a while, he kept checking the rear-view mirror, casting anxious glances behind. There was no sign of activity at the checkpoint, nothing to indicate a change of mood, no sudden alert; only the dayshift, hot and listless.

The checkpoint disappeared behind him and he was back on the north side of the River Clyde.

Carl took a deep breath. Then he screamed at the top of his voice until it hurt, thumping the steering wheel. He cranked the music up loud. For the first time since the Glasgow Emergency Order had been imposed, he was outside the city. An exit had been engineered. Ordinary coppers and the old laws were the worst that he would encounter unless he went near Aberdeen, Edinburgh, Stirling or Inverness, and he had no reason to go to any of those places.

8

The sun was shining. For a few days he could relax. CivCon had enough trouble in the cities to contend with to go chasing after him, though Sentinel would doubtless keep a locus on him, just in case. In any event, outside the urban emergency zones CivCon were supposed to leave everything to the police, stretched and under-resourced though they were. As he sped towards Luss and Loch Lomond, Carl kept reminding himself of that. Older laws were now in operation.

Speeding past the Luss turn-off, trees drooped their lush branches over the road, and he had to swerve every so often to avoid them. Every few minutes there was a grey patch, like mould, on a far hillside where the conifers had been harvested for wood-chip fuel. He drove, loving the feel of the car, unbelieving. There were only a few other vehicles on the road, and the occasional truck from one of the few haulage firms still in existence. A bus came towards him: folk going to Glasgow to see friends and relatives, after waiting weeks for a three-day entry permit.

The car in front of Carl turned off the main road. He was on his own now, nothing in front or behind, taking the tight curves by Loch Lomond like a rally driver, dodging the potholes. On and up towards Tyndrum he went, cloud-shadows passing across hills that reared on either side; gates and fences, old cars by the side of the road; long grass and signs for closed hotels. Then the hills relaxed, settling down for a spell, stretching out, and the sky broadened. On a straight he made sure he was above forty, then followed Eddie's instructions.

After restarting the engine, he caught the whiff of burning plastic as the circuit in the engine burned out. Maybe some blip of light on a screen back in Glasgow or Edinburgh or London had gone out. Maybe someone in Command and Control had looked away as it happened, and was now scratching his or her head at the amazing vanishing car. Maybe they were alerting the rural police right now.

'Fuck them,' Carl shouted over his music. Second-guessing what the authorities had in mind for him was a pointless, stress-inducing exercise. The people who would make life unpleasant were there, watching and waiting. If they were going to pull him in for a Category 1 offence, keep him in a black site for as long as they pleased, then that's what they were going to do. No point in worrying about it.

Easier said than done.

At Tyndrum there was an automated biofuel station. The sign was missing a few letters. Most of the other buildings that looked like they might once have housed a business were boarded up and in the same condition. He sped past.

After another half an hour he pulled over into a lay-by. The last time he'd been to Glen Coe, many years before, the weather had been foul and the cloud low. But now the sky was higher and, miles ahead, the towering land was dark under cloud, spears of sun being doused as the steel sky rolled in over Rannoch Moor. The place was a gateway to somewhere else, the jaws of the earth waiting to swallow you whole. He sat for a few minutes, watching the change of light and shade, each movement of cloud casting a shifting intensity over hill and moor.

'Engage autodriver,' he said. With autodriver on, the safety parameters governing the smart screen were switched off, and the windscreen lit up with object-tags and insets, a brief history of Glen Coe, its geology, and a tag for the one hotel. Still trading, but there was no information on a menu. He switched settings and the smart screen flipped into weather mode, displaying cloud types, atmospheric pressure, humidity and the chances of the rain continuing. There was a 64 per cent likelihood that a shower would fall within the next hour.

He started the car and drove on. Within the chasm of Glen Coe itself, just twelve minutes later, the rain hit, like a hose being turned against the windscreen. It lashed down, turning the road into a river, potholes invisible, drowned. Water hammering and scorching and furious, wipers barely able to clear the windscreen. Then, as quickly as it started, the rain stopped; the tap turned tight in the off position. The smart screen was bang on the money.

'Fuck's sake,' Carl breathed, glad to be through the downpour. He could look up at scree-strewn slopes now. He stopped the car again, getting out this time. Fresh air, damp and earthy; he could hear the river now, down below, gushing and rushing through the rocks.

Where he was headed, the blue-grey hills faded by degrees into the blue-grey sky until it was hard to say where the hills ended and where the sky began. He was hungry. Sitting on a stone, he scoffed his sandwiches, gazing up at the high tops, the ragged drops. When had the massacre been? What were the causes? He couldn't quite remember. He tried to imagine women and children being stabbed to death in the snow.

He finished his lunch and drove on. The smart screen told him about rock types and a brief sanitised version of what had happened in 1692.

•

He passed scarred hillsides where conifer plantations had been levelled for biofuel and which now resembled First World War battlefields. He passed shuttered hotels, overgrown verges and, deep into the north, empty glens and the gaping ruins of old stone houses.

Wind turbines turned on a summit or two and some stretches of road were so bad with potholes that he had to slow to walking speed to weave through them. Two buses and four cars had passed him, heading south; one big Jag had overtaken him, going north. He had not seen a single police car north of Fort William.

And everywhere, he would spot a mast on some hilltop, skeletal metal and antennae against the sky. Nothing tagged with RFID moved without being monitored, and most of the under-18s had theirs implanted for 'safety' reasons. Sentinel sensed everything and everyone, except those who had the means to avoid it.

He drove through Fort William without stopping. SCOPE was just another tool in the state's outsourced security toolbox, another supply chain driver. No single journalist, he knew, could ever hope to slow that juggernaut as it moved up through the gears. The masts and the miles and the silent villages came and went. Afternoon eased into drowsy evening. He'd long passed Ullapool, still plenty of north left.

'Tourist coastal route' said a faded road-sign. Now there was a laugh.

•

An hour later Carl pulled into a lay-by. To the west the evening sun cut through the clouds. He had not seen another vehicle for eighteen miles. Rubbing his eyes and the small of his back, the thrill of being behind the wheel had soured. He stretched and took a lungful of warm air. Around him there was nothing except slopes of rock and heather, up-thrusts of naked rock. He took out his palmpod; it barely registered a signal.

The sun's rays were playing on the distant hills, shadows scooped from the hunched massifs. A bird of prey hovered, lasering its target, then dropped like a dead weight. He took it all in, the spectacle.

Satnav said thirty-four miles to Inverlair. From the glove compartment he pulled out an old frayed map, spread it out on the bonnet of the car, and traced his journey. Some ninety miles south-east was the new hydroelectric dam that he was meant to swing by. It was a bugger that he had to drive there the day after tomorrow. Anyway, here he was, wherever it was. What do people do up here? Nothing. Nothing around him as far as he could see, just the vast opening north, swallowing the line of the road.

He stretched his back again, smelling summer in the grass and on the wind, easy sun over a glimpse of sea between the hills. The surrounding summits were scraped bare of vegetation, crags fissured and scrubbed like this rhino he'd seen up close once, in Edinburgh Zoo, its skin cracked and weathered and out of the reptilian past. His sandwiches were gone, and there was no more water left in the bottle. His legs were aching. Glasgow felt a long way away.

Away from the road – he had no idea of distance – was a bare fist of mountain that burst through the thin covering of green. Somewhere in his mind, the outline of the dark shape rang a bell. He had seen this photo, he was sure of it. And now here he was, looking, open-mouthed, at the real thing. He stopped the car again and got out. After a while, he became aware of another sensation – absolute silence. Only the breeze in the grass registered in his ears, birds calling in the distance. By the side of the road, in the long grass of the verge, a bee, droning and moving from flower to flower sounded like a chainsaw. The pure air filled his lungs. There was nothing to do but look and listen, but he found himself unable to do either for very long.

He drove on.

•

At a derelict filling station he stopped again to check the map. Weeds were poking up here and there through the concrete forecourt and the station's high metal roof was missing. There were no fuel pumps on the two concrete stands. Plastic electricity cables, sheared at the root, stuck out of the ragged holes in the concrete where the pumps had stood. The booth's livery was fading under the scrub of Atlantic weathers, windows intact and covered in dust. Carl cleaned a spot with his fist and looked inside. Most of the shelves were still in place; the metal shell of a coffee machine; a chewing-gum display stand on the counter; empty plastic water bottles; a glass-fronted fridge, for sandwiches and soft drinks. He could murder a coffee. Not far now to Inverlair.

•

A few miles on, the dark scarp of a sea-cliff appeared in the distance, and the road veered abruptly down, following the curve of the bay. A road sign said 'Inverlair'. Carl pulled over to the roadside and reached into the glove compartment. Taking out a pair of binoculars he scanned the village, most of which lined the other side of an inlet – more a fjord – bordered on three sides by steep forested hills and a few dozen houses, about half of them clustered around a pier that was jutting out into the bay. Outlying houses were spread across the green and brown hillside, with fenced fields between them and the sea. A river split the rounded uplands at the head of the bay, a rocky summit rising to the north. Carl could see what he figured was some kind of boatyard, a large grey corrugated-iron building with a high doorway. Inside, he could see a shower of sparks. Probably welding gear. On the pier there were guys hauling plastic boxes, streaming seawater, up from a waiting boat. There was nothing out of place, no CivCon, and no cops that he could see. And no telecomms mast, though most houses had a satellite dish.

In the centre of the village, halfway up the opposite headland, Carl could see 'Inverlair Hotel' above the doorway of a solid two-storey stone building. Smoke was billowing from one of the chimneys. There was a church at one end, a small shop and post office in the middle, and what Carl took to be a schoolhouse at the other end.

He got back in the car and drove the last mile or so down and around the bay towards the hotel, followed the sign into the car park, parked, and made his way round to the front door. Inside, he waited in the reception lobby, all dark wood panelling and claret carpet. There was no one around. A button on the counter told him to 'Ring For Attention'. He did, heard distant bleeps within. He waited, and was just about to press again, when a man in his sixties, wearing a navy-blue fleece with the RNLI logo in red, came through a fire door.

'Yes?'

'Hi. I'd like a room, please. A single, if you have one.'

'A room?'

'If you have one, yes. I should've phoned, but I assumed . . .'

For a second the man, who spoke with the faint trace of an American accent, seemed unsure of what was taking place.

'Sure,' he said at last, narrowing his eyes at Carl. He went behind the reception desk. 'The ID machine's broken, I'm afraid. We've been trying to get a technician out for weeks.' He smiled and slid a ledger across the counter. 'You'll have to do it the old-fashioned way.'

Carl signed his name, scanning the rest of the entries as he did so. The previous signature was dated two months before.

'Did you drive here?'

'Yes.'

There was a glint in the man's eye. When Carl looked up from the ledger he saw it fade. There was a stag's head mounted over the reception desk. That's enough information for you, you nosey old bugger.

'You don't get many tourists here then?'

The man raised his bushy eyebrows, amused. 'Not by car, no.

59

We still get the odd busload and even a few by boat, but the last tourists to arrive here under their own steam was nearly a month ago, a party of Canadians in the bunkhouse, backpackers, and a German couple staying in one of the holiday homes.' His mouth drooped. 'That's been more or less our season.'

He looked at the name in the book. 'Mr Shewan,' he said. 'I'm George Cutler, the owner.' He handed Carl the key to Room 14. 'Come on and I'll show you up.'

The hallway of the hotel had a musty smell. Paintings of old soldiers – the braid-and-wig brigade – hung on the walls. A fat fish mounted in a glass case. A shiny brass handbell stood on a dark-wood side table. A stained-glass panel lit the staircase to the first-floor landing.

Cutler opened the door of Room 14. 'Coffee over there,' he said, pointing to a kettle and basket of sachets. 'It's old stuff but it should be okay.' He pointed at the TV. 'We've got satellite, broadband that works, just about. Would you like breakfast?'

Carl nodded, inspecting a tatty brochure that listed local attractions: walks, heritage centres and archaeological sites. Half-eight was the time agreed for breakfast.

'You can have something to eat now, if you want?'

'Sounds good. What is there?'

Cutler smiled, his soft colourless face cracking. 'Plenty of fish. Potatoes and veg. I think there's some venison pie left as well. It's good stuff.'

Not exactly the seaweed gruel that Carl had been expecting.

'Venison pie it is. I'll be down in ten minutes, if that's okay?'

Cutler said that was fine. As he made his way out, he stopped, reached into the pocket of his fleece.

'Oh, this was left for you at reception yesterday.' He handed over an envelope which had CARL SHEWAN printed on the front, nothing else. Carl turned it over a few times. There was something inside.

'Thanks,' he said absently.

Cutler closed the door and Carl ripped open the envelope to see what was inside. It was a memory stick, and nothing else.

He unzipped his bag and took out his palmpod, and inserted the stick. At the password prompt he thought for a second.

He typed 'SCOPE'.

Bingo. There were two video files. He played the first one.

On his palmpod screen, inside what looked like a tent, a bald man in his fifties sat cross-legged, his tightly muscled face sombre, downcast. He cleared his throat, adjusted the camera.

'Hello, Mr Shewan. If you've come this far, then I thank you for that. I hope to Christ I'm wrong, but . . . anyway, my name is Howard Brindley and I am – was – senior head of research at GeoByte Support Services. You probably haven't heard of us, we did some work on SCOPE, just the GPS telemetry.'

Howard Brindley shifted position. He clearly wasn't used to sitting cross-legged on the ground inside a tent. He rubbed his stubbled face, clearly exhausted.

'You had some financial concerns about SCOPE, Mr Shewan,' Brindley said, looking away. 'My concerns are more . . . technical. We were only the subcontractor, but I got hold of the full spec for the SCOPE transmitters, and ran some harmonic modelling on the crystalline microwave filters, the new ones . . .' He stopped, sat up, straight-backed. 'Sorry for talking shop. The second file on this memory stick will tell you the rest . . . in plainer language. It is time-locked until twelve noon on Thursday, seventeenth of July.' Brindley pursed his lips, looked intently at the camera. He then leaned over and switched it off.

The video file stopped. The seventeenth was tomorrow.

Carl tried the other file. Time-locked. Why would he put a time-lock on the rest of his story?

The guy better not be another crank. But there was the plasmoid chipset to consider – no crank would have sent him that. Carl checked the time. He was hungry and thirsty. Brindley wasn't in the hotel – he could be anywhere in the area – and there were sixteen hours until the time-lock on the second file expired. Nothing to do except relax.

9

The pool ball smacked off the baize and clacked along the bar room's tiled floor. It thumped against the counter. A scruffy collie darted over, picked the ball up in its mouth, and spat it back out onto the floor where it bounced into a metal bowl. The dog looked expectantly at the drinkers, who chuckled and clapped at the trick. Cute Collie Dog picked the cue ball up and did it again. This time, a louder cheer went up and the dog was patted and praised by its owner. All the customers were middle-aged men, the dedicated early-evening crowd, happy enough with their price-capped product and a big screen showcasing some Reformed League football. Bellies and flushed faces in the bar, a dozen or so, and the only woman in the place was pulling the pints.

Carl told her he would take his food in the dining area.

It was a big enough room, breakfast bar and French windows. He reckoned it could sit about seventy; there was only him. Peak season and here he was, the one and only cover. What did people do around here? Maybe the Canadians or the Germans would come in, give the chef a real thrill-ride of a night.

Half the dining room was a tip, with chairs and tables stacked any old how. Boxes of crockery, piles of bed linen and curtains, garden parasols standing in the corner – a bike half-buried under it all. The place was more storeroom than eating place. He supped his flat lager. It was hardly worth a second day off the wagon.

The barmaid had become a waitress. She came through with Carl's plate of food, and set it down in front of him. She was early thirties, bobbed black hair, pretty, but not exactly a customer service expert. There was no warm Highland welcome here.

'Do you want another drink?'

'Yeah, I might get lucky this time. Is it spot the bubble and win a prize?'

The waitress/barmaid eyed him, not even attempting to see the humour in the remark. 'That's what we're given up here, Mr Shewan. It's take it or leave it, I'm afraid.'

'It's the same in Glasgow. We don't get special treatment – well, most places don't.' He took a long pull on the glass to show his acceptance. She nodded curtly, cracked the faintest smile, and left him to eat.

Three hours later Carl was well on the way to being completely relaxed. In the hotel's public bar he was being harangued by a pissed old local with a scruffy white beard. A jukebox thumped out some techno and a few lads were larking around at the pool table. The pissed local persisted with tales of the good old days at the oil fabrication yard down the coast. Most of the older men had worked there, including George Cutler as a backpacking young tourist, so the barfly had slurred. The good old days, so far as Carl could tell, lasted only a few years until production was moved to the east coast, and the yard closed. But that was several drinks ago, when the man had made sense; now he was firing off in all directions. 'Glasgow's best fuggin siddy in gundree. Always fuggin welcome there.' He shook his head. 'Can't put a price on that.' He paused, succumbed once more to thoughts that made sense only to him. 'Fuggers,' he spat. 'Not a penny from them cunts after the accident, y'know?'

He was oblivious to the white pool ball smacking onto the hard floor at his feet. Some of the pool-players roared their laughter. Flying pool balls seemed to be a habit around here. One guy shouted over, 'Hey, Frankie, you've laid another fucking egg!'

While Frankie tried to look menacing, Carl downed his drink. Time for some fresh air.

A piss first. The toilet wall told Carl that LORNA GIVES GOOD

GOBLES. Where the fuck was Brindley? He didn't want to ask Cutler about him. A direct question could arouse suspicions, and other people might be informed about these suspicions, and so on. Even up here that could still happen. Sidling in at an angle was the best way, nicey nice, terrible fucking weather, winkle a wee bit out of them, pull back, talk about footie or food but keep it behind your ear, then come back for another wee slice, and so bit by bit he could get what he wanted. If only that strategy had worked in other areas of his life.

He headed outside.

Jesus.

Under the clear sky the bay was quiet and dark, and in the east were stars. But to the west was a pink and red fugue under shreds of high cloud, each shade of colour luminous, unpolluted, diffusing from the red sun's vanishing core. Carl headed down towards the pier and away from the streetlights to get a better look.

Absolutely amazing. Dark arms of the narrow bay and the quiet breath of the night, with just the waves lapping and a late bird calling. Warm salt reek at the end of the pier. He stood for a while watching the world turn and the stars come out, stuff that was invisible in the city. No midges so far, maybe the breeze kept them away. George Cutler said to watch out for midges if he went for a walk, the buggers'll eat you alive on a quiet night. The fizz in Carl's mind came off the boil. There was nothing to do except absorb the slow ending of the day. He breathed deep at the end of the pier.

After about ten minutes he headed back to the hotel, none too steadily. Sea legs not what they never were. Was the pier moving? He hiccupped. Better not start with those fuckers. Pain in the arse when you think they've stopped and they start again. This place would do him for a couple of days, maybe try stretching it to three or four. Maybe he'd move here and never go back. No way. He'd go nuts within a week.

Brindley. Brindley and his state-of-the-art chipset . . . Carl cleared a shadow from his mind. Better not go there. Stick to the facts and not the fears. As he walked back towards the hotel, the streetlights went out, their filaments glowing and dying; little suns fading.

'Ho!'

Power cut?

But no. The houselights were still on, the sign over the hotel's public bar, and even in the few houses on the other side of the bay. A minute later, his eyes had adjusted and he could see the tarmac at his feet, the fading light in the west sharper, the church a dark silhouette, and the stars overhead. Who had killed the streetlights? His watch said 11.32 p.m. Just over twelve hours until the time lock on the second video file expired. Maybe Brindley would show up at the same time. The edge of the pavement caught Carl by surprise, and he stumbled, crossed the road to the hotel path. Guys were yammering away. He heard a North American accent, a young woman, part of a group who were smoking outside a guesthouse. Six months it had taken her to get travel clearance from London, apparently. A month for each emergency zone. She said it was her birthright, this trip, part of her emigrant heritage – so she deserved it. Carl passed them by and followed the path up to the hotel.

The waitress was in the lobby. He grinned, nodded, his brain lagging behind the desire to say something. She bustled past him and locked the outside door. 'It's chucking-out time from the bar. I wasn't sure if I could lock the door on you or not.'

'No bother. What's with the streetlights going off and everything else staying on?'

'It's the council, they're saving money.'

'I suppose it causes a few accidents, not being able to see in the dark.'

The way she looked at him, straight in the eye, as if to say here's another smart-arse trying out his patter.

'Breakfast is between eight and half-nine. There are enough eggs and toast and porridge. Night.'

'I thought you didn't lock the doors up here?'

She snorted at him. 'We do when there's strange men around.' And away she went, through the fire door.

'I just wanted to talk,' he said after her. 'That's all.'

She stopped at the doors, half turned towards him.

'It's just my cack-handed way of starting a conversation.' He looked mournfully at the floor, hands in the pockets of his jeans. 'I'm not trying to be funny . . .' He grinned. 'Well, I was trying to be funny, if you know what I mean.'

A woman laughing at your jokes was a good first step. You were on your way if you could get them to laugh, not overdoing it, but just breaking the ice, then weighing in with some well-considered remark that, depending on the woman, would prove there was depth to the man as well as a reasonably inoffensive surface. Then maybe a follow-up funny, a listening ear, a question or two. Repeat and vary until she's eating out of your trousers. That was the theory, anyway. Did the evidence back it up? His field research was ongoing, but this one didn't take the bait, he could see that straight away. She had this way of looking at him, weighing him up. He started climbing the stairs to his room.

'The guy who dropped that package off for you must be camping up at the forest,' she said, softening. 'You told my dad that you were meeting up with an old friend.' Her raised eyebrows said it all: what kind of an old friend hides in the forest?

Thankfully, Carl wasn't so drunk that he'd lost control of his tongue. There was an abridged version of the truth that could be used on those who asked awkward questions. He pointed to the glass cabinet that lined one wall of the lobby.

'Are these bottles full of whisky or cold tea?'

'I don't know,' she said. 'They've been on display for years, most of them. For as long as I can remember.'

Carl considered the lines of bottles. 'And how long has that been?'

'Since I was seven.'

Uncertain, Carl peered at the waitress. 'Bit young to start working, isn't it?'

'That's when my dad bought the place.'

'Who – George . . .'

'Cutler. I'm Simone.'

Carl processed this information. He turned back to the cabinet full of whisky bottles. 'Well, Simone, if you uncork one of these to find out whether or not it's tea inside, I'll tell you my dark secret.'

'What happens if it's cold tea?'

'Then it's name, rank and serial number, and nothing else.'

•

He threw the room key on the dresser of Room 14 and sat down heavily on the edge of his bed, tugging at his laces. He kicked off his shoes.

Struggling into bed, he lay a while with the lamp on. Simone was a funny woman. Music student then single mum, her defences too ready to come up.

There was a funny feeling in his guts, and he assumed it was to do with the booze. Eventually, he fell asleep.

10

His alarm went off at 8 a.m., the tone knifing into his head. Once he was over the shock, something like consciousness seeped into him. It hurt. Off the booze was an altogether gentler place to be. As he lay there, getting used to being awake and in pain, he wondered whether Inverlair Hotel could stretch to a full fry-up. Furred arteries and high cholesterol were best avoided, but a hangover demands such damage. Only saturated fat and sugar can make the morning-after body shock better. He lay there for a while, thinking about Simone. Sensitive subject, her son's dad. As soon as he'd touched on it, Carl had seen the shutters come down. She was happy enough to talk about playing the flute and being a session musician and living in Bristol, content to hear about his journalism and life in Glasgow. But the personal stuff was off-limits. Her dad might be American, but Simone had not inherited any propensity to gush at complete strangers, be it on the subject of medical complaints or familial tensions or any other stuff that Brits deemed too private to talk about. And thank God she hadn't.

He got up to piss, groaning as he splashed into the bowl. In the bathroom, beside the wash-hand basin, there was no mini-soap and no towel, so he splashed his face with water a few times. He made a coffee, swallowed two painkillers, pulled on yesterday's clothes, and crept downstairs. He heard Cutler complaining about how the weekly minibus from Inverness was late, and there was no answer from the brewery. Carl accepted the offer of two fried eggs and tomato on toast.

'You couldn't spare a towel as well, could you, and some of those wee soaps?'

Cutler said he would bring them up.

It was just after ten. Less than two hours until the time lock on the video file expired. Carl wasn't sure if it was the fact that he was hungover, but he was beginning to feel a bit unsettled. There was no wireless signal in Inverlair; he couldn't check his texts or his feeds. Brindley's cloak-and-dagger act was a pain in the arse. He must be on the run, to camp out like that.

Fried food was the second part of the remedy for his hangover. Showering had been the first part. Now that he was out walking in the fresh air, the fuzz of seven pints and an after-hours whisky had all but lifted. Salt on the breeze. Sun on the water, oily rainbow diesel-sheen lapping against the pier's legs. He felt better for being outside. Carl leant on a railing, looked out across the bay at the open horizon, and behind to the rising land, the dark hollow of Inverlair Bay. What the fuck went on here? How could people live?

If Brindley was on the run then he wouldn't stay anywhere official, like a hotel or guesthouse. Had he come by sea? Carl walked back through the village, along the shingle shorefront, stopping at some old boat sheds, his mind wandering. He had to tell the waitress, Simone, something. Yes, he was a journalist, and, yes, he was working on a story, but it was nothing to do with Inverlair or any of the locals. Doubtless she had her own story to tell if he could be bothered to probe for it. Everyone has a key, well hidden usually, even from themselves. He turned back along the shingle beach towards the concrete slipway.

It was 12.04 p.m.

In Room 14, Carl played the second file on the memory stick for the third time. Nothing but the inside of Brindley's tent. No sign of him. He played the first file again. Brindley looked tired, kept rubbing his bald head, massaging his eyes. He hadn't shaved for a few days. But his words were definite: 'The second file is time-locked until noon on the seventeenth – tomorrow if you made it in time. It'll explain everything.'

Yet the evidence on the screen said the opposite. File two was empty.

Okay. There was no other option: he'd have to find Brindley, wherever he was hiding. Carl grabbed his jacket and shoulder bag and headed down the stairs. At the reception desk a German couple were asking for directions to a prehistoric cave in the hills. Simone nodded to Carl as he walked past and out the main door.

Standing on the steps of the hotel, Carl let the door bang behind him. What the fuck was Brindley playing at? He could be anywhere in the forest – if he was up there at all. Nothing for it, he'd have to get his trainers wet. So intently was he looking across at the conifer plantation at the head of the bay that it took him a few seconds to register who was walking towards him along the rhododendron-lined track. Unlike the video file, this Brindley was clean-shaven and didn't look quite so tired.

It was Brindley who spoke first. 'Your picture in the paper makes you look older.' He forced a smile. 'You've tried the second video file and now you're on your way to track me down.' It was a statement.

Carl nodded. 'Yes.' He looked about, at hills and water, and wondered who might be lurking close by. 'Look, do you want to talk out here, or shall we go inside?'

Brindley's faced darkened. 'Do you have a car?'

Carl nodded.

A flood of emotions crossed Brindley's face in an instant, before settling on anxiety. He could only stare at the ground. 'Let's go then. Rather than talk, I'll show you what SCOPE has done.'

•

Two hours later, Carl came into the hotel's public bar, ashen-faced. He stood for a while at the door, watching the few regulars, Simone pulling pints.

'I'll tell them,' he said to Brindley, who sat down at a corner table.

Behind the bar, George Cutler was complaining that the bus was almost four hours late and the satellite TV was still down. 'We're nearly out of draught lager,' he murmured to his daughter. 'And the bloody power is still off.' He quietened when he saw Carl in the doorway. 'Enjoy your walk, Mr Shewan?'

Without answering, Carl pointed at the optics. Simone gave him the glimmer of a smile, but it didn't register. None of this was real any more, he thought. It was finished. There was a wrecking ball on its way. Any minute now it would shatter everything.

George shook his head and took silence for an answer. 'Feeling rough, eh?'

They don't know, Carl thought. They don't know, and he would have to show them, like Brindley had shown him. That was the only way to convince them. George went into the office and Simone eyed Carl from down the bar.

'Are you all right?'

He threw back his whisky in one gulp as George stamped through from the office.

'They're still not answering the phone,' he said to his daughter. 'I can't even get online. The shop's expecting a delivery as well.'

Another whisky went smartly down Carl's throat, firing his stomach and clearing his head. But he didn't want a clear head. He wanted a head that was unable to form coherent thoughts, so he smacked the empty glass back down on the bar and demanded another shot. The only real thing left was to get pissed.

Brindley appeared by his side.

'Who are you waiting for?' he asked George.

It was a direct question, spoken loudly and without any hesitation.

'The brewery,' began George. 'Every two weeks they arrange for a deliv—'

'They're not coming.'

George looked puzzled.

'Are there any police in Inverlair?' It was another direct question from Brindley.

'Yes,' said George slowly. 'P.C. Gibbs.' He glanced at Carl. 'Is there any . . . trouble?'

But Brindley kept firing the questions. No time to waste on politeness.

'Do you have a local councillor, community leaders?'

'Look, what's this about?'

'Do you have a local councillor, Mr Cutler? Yes or no.'

Flustered, George said: 'Yes, but . . .'

'It is vital that you get a group of people together immediately.'

'Look, whoever you . . . what the hell's all this about?'

Brindley considered an answer, then gave up. He looked at Carl, who was now well into his third double. Carl knocked back what remained of his measure.

'Come with us and we'll show you.'

•

George sat in the back of Brindley's car along with the moustachioed P.C. Gibbs. As they drove away, a woman came out of the tiny shop and wondered where they were all going in the same car.

Just over two miles into the drive they all began to hear it. George touched his temple as Carl stopped the car and turned the engine off. He glanced in the rear-view mirror at Brindley.

'What's that noise?' said George. 'Something's clicking.'

'Microwave hearing,' said Brindley. 'The sound isn't actually hitting your eardrums – it's being generated in your brain's auditory centres.'

'Where's it coming from?'

Carl started the engine again, and they drove on.

The noise changed to a continuous high-pitched intensity, growing louder and louder. They drove on, south and east, away from the bay, their headaches growing worse, until the shrieking noise cut right into them. Carl stopped the car, wrenched the gear stick into reverse, his eyes streaming, and turned back the way they'd come, the passengers shouting and grabbing at him to stop. He fought them off. 'Don't get out,' he shouted, racing the car back towards Inverlair and down into the bay. The high-pitched tone vanished, and their headaches eased.

•

They all sat in the lounge bar. It reeked of stale beer and sweat. They listened, or at least appeared to listen.

'The system is named SCOPE,' said Howard. 'That stands for Secure Communications Open Emergency. It's a system of transmitters using pulsed microwaves designed to give complete asset management and communications coverage in the event of a national emergency or crisis. Most base stations have SCOPE now, site-sharing with commercial operators.' He looked at his watch. 'SCOPE was networked, across most of Europe and North America at 09.28 GMT, just over three hours ago. An imperfection in tiny diarite crystals that are used in the microwave filters has caused a standing harmonic, a signal, that has propagated throughout the entire system. This harmonic resonates at 2.14 hertz, the same frequency as deep sleep. Everyone outside a notspot – an area without signal coverage – is now asleep, and will remain that way until they die, within a few days, a week, however long it takes, unless SCOPE, somehow, shuts down. The pain and noise you felt and heard were simply interference patterns at the very edge of the electromagnetic field.'

Councillor Diane Matheson gave a nervous laugh. She turned

to George Cutler. 'What's he talking about, George? Stupid bloody nonsense . . .'

Cutler could only stare at Brindley. The councillor waited for an answer.

'We can't leave,' said Carl, helping himself to another whisky. 'And everybody who's within range of this fucking delta signal, which is a big chunk of the developed world, is as good as dead.' He looked out the window while slugging his drink. 'I think that just about covers it.'

There was silence in the room.

'Mum,' said Simone. She looked at her dad. George knew, and Brindley wouldn't meet his eye. 'My wife is in Edinburgh,' he said, pleading.

Brindley took a deep breath. He looked from the councillor, to George Cutler, to Gibbs. 'You have to start planning, because there is a chance that nothing is going to come in from the outside world for a long time.'

'For how long?' said Gibbs, tears in his eyes.

'Well,' said Brindley, 'the delta signal in rural areas is coming from hundreds of base stations, but in the cities there are thousands of smaller nodes in the grid. They all use high-temperature superconductors so they only need a tiny amount of power. The system is designed to scavenge the national grid. Solar and tidal will give it what it needs . . . for years . . . for power.'

'No,' said Simone firmly. She stormed though the fire door and into the annexe.

Gibbs stood and buttoned up his uniform jacket. 'You seem to know an awful lot about this SCOPE system, Mr Brindley.'

'Our company worked on systems integration, telemetry, for CivCon's main contractor.'

Councillor Matheson slammed her hand down on the table with such force that it made everyone jump. 'Constable Gibbs, what absolute bloody nonsense is this man talking about?'

The policeman glanced at Cutler.

'I'll take her,' said George.

'Take me? Take me where? What're you on about, George?'

Carl slid his car key down the bar.

George picked it up and walked out, the councillor on his heels.

Gibbs went behind the bar and poured himself a brandy. He put some money in a shot glass and contemplated his drink.

'For the first time in thirteen years, I'm about to drink while on duty.' He took a gulp of brandy, grimaced. 'You're a journalist, Mr Shewan,' he asked. 'Is that correct?'

'Yes.'

Gibbs nodded, paused. 'And you wrote some newspaper articles on this . . . SCOPE system?'

Carl had the feeling that that he was being probed. 'A few years ago now, yes. But the articles covered how SCOPE and its budget were being hidden from Parliament. They were political, not scientific.'

Gibbs nodded again. 'Uh-uh. And you have both managed to find your way to one of the few *notspots* left in the country, if not the whole of northern Europe.'

Carl stiffened.

'That's very convenient,' continued Gibbs. He nodded to himself. 'Quite remarkable, really.'

There was silence.

Brindley sighed. 'I managed to get hold of a partial map of where the main transmitters were. I figured Inverlair Bay would be one of the biggest notspots, judging by where the nearest masts were. As for Mr Shewan, I thought he could help me stop it. I should have gone to him earlier.'

Carl rapped his empty glass down onto the bar. 'We didn't do this, Gibbs. Surely to Christ you can see that? You heard what Brindley said. You guys had better get folk together. Set up a roadblock. Go house to house. Do something.'

Gibbs agreed, and Brindley went with him.

Carl sat at the end of the bar, staring into space.

There were distractions on which to focus the mind, blot out the impossible horror. Sun showing up the streaks of polish on the dark-veneered tabletop, or glinting on the pool table's coin slot; the movement of the clouds across the bay; stains on the carpet; swirling dust motes in the sunbeams. He sat and watched the sun and the dust and the high clouds crossing the windows.

After a few minutes, Carl got up, went behind the bar and took a bottle of single malt off the shelf and headed upstairs. Maybe it was absolute rubbish. SCOPE would stop working tomorrow and everyone would wake up. Yes, there would be deaths, but nothing exceptional, nothing that couldn't be boxed off and forgotten about. There would be an official inquiry, held in private of course, and some contracts would be reviewed. Normality would be restored.

11

He stirred after 10 a.m. the next morning, head pounding, stomach lurching. It wasn't just the hangover that hit him in the stomach. He stood up, shuffled around the room, wished he hadn't stopped smoking. There were a few sachets of coffee left, so he boiled the kettle, shut the window, made a coffee, had a shower, opened the window again, and paced the room. Birds were chirping away. Summer sun was warming the bay. The stirrings of perfection were there, all happening around him. But the view was poisoned. The prospect was desolation.

Eric. Lesley. Eddie. The girl from the Kelvingrove riot. Sarah. Jeff from ScotNet and most of the people he had ever known. His dad in a nursing home in Stirling. His sister: Brighton was bound to have it too.

No. He shook his head.

'No,' he said out loud.

There was a soft knock on the door. It was Brindley. He had to be bringing good news.

'Is it down? Can we leave?'

Brindley shook his head. 'No. We, um, we held a meeting, last night. Not many turned up. A lot of family and friends, a lot of . . . I don't think they believe it. I don't think they're up to planning anything.' He leant against the bureau, clasped his hands together, and took a deep breath. 'I was thinking we should map the delta signal, for fluctuations. Get a few readings over . . . however long it lasts. See exactly how big this notspot is. You could help me.' He shrugged. 'If you feel up to it.'

Carl sat on the edge of the bed, hangover and fear making his voice and hands shake. 'They will stop transmitting, the masts, the nodes. They might pack in tomorrow, right?'

'They might,' said Brindley. 'But SCOPE was designed with resilience in mind. It's robust. And the two-hertz harmonic is a standing wave, with a strong magnetic component. Impossible to shield against.'

Sitting on the bed, Carl considered the whisky bottle on the bedside table. Enough for a hair of the dog remained.

'I heard someone crying. Or maybe I dreamed it,' he said, taking a slug from the bottle. 'Maybe it was me. I'm not sure. But there was crying, somewhere. Everywhere. There's always someone crying somewhere.'

Brindley shifted his stance, pursed his lips. He sighed, standing awkwardly, breathing in the silence and sweat and alcohol fumes in Room 14.

'I'll leave you to it then.' He opened the door to leave. 'I'm in Room 22 now. It's down at the end of the corridor. Let me know what you think about mapping the area.'

The door closed. Carl sat there for a while, then went to splash his face in the bathroom. Another slug of whisky made him feel almost human again. He grabbed his jacket and the ignition key for the car.

It seemed like most of the villagers were out of doors, and they stared at him as he drove through the fine morning. Fair enough if they thought he was nuts. He would just drive on, drive on, drive on . . .

He went around the bay and up onto the southern headland. After turning inland for a short distance, he stopped. There were four cars up on the grass verge, and about thirty people standing at a line of traffic cones, a police roadblock sign lying flat on its back. Someone kicked one of the cones into the ditch.

Carl joined the crowd. Getting out of the car and walking

towards the cones he felt a sharp twinge of pain in his temple, and a faint clicking noise. A bit further and the faint clicking would become a sonic skewer that would make his nose bleed. Day 2 and SCOPE still hadn't packed in. How long can people live when they can't wake up, lying where they fell?

He laughed. One or two from the crowd glared at him. Just ahead of the roadblock was the road sign for the national speed limit, a fading black slash across white. 60mph had been enjoyed by the few of late, an unreachable pleasure. Now the sign may as well have been in a different universe.

Down the road. Where sleep ruled the airwaves.

A crow flew across his field of vision. The bird was already in the delta field when it veered further, deeper, where humans could no longer set foot. Animals seemed unaffected; Brindley said they had different brains. Or maybe it was just crows that had different brains. They could feast now, and the rats too.

'They'll survive,' he said to the sky and hills. 'Rats always fucking survive.'

He jumped the ditch and started walking at a right angle to the road, ignored by the crowd, up the green slopes that rose towards the heather and hilltops of bare rock. He left the crying and silence behind.

Late in the afternoon he returned, exhausted, to the hotel, his feet soaking, clothes and hands filthy, knuckle grazed from a fall. George was right about the conifer forest though: you couldn't really go through it because the trees were so densely packed. He was tired, worn out, limbs aching as he flopped onto the couch in the residents' lounge. Burned it off, he had. But the terror would be back. Even now he could feel it around his stomach, coils tightening. He lay there, dozed, imagined; tried to feel lucky. A car pulled up outside. Who was driving? He heard the hotel door open.

Footsteps. Silence.

Still lying on the couch, Carl opened his eyes, aware he was being watched. It was Brindley.

'I've been looking for you,' he said, sitting down in a leather chair.

Carl turned away, faced the back of the couch. He just wanted to go to sleep, but his curiosity got the better of him.

'How did you get here, Mr Brindley? To Inverlair, I mean.' His voice was level, expressionless.

The leather chair creaked.

'With great difficulty. Friends of mine, they tried to get me to go with them, on their boat.'

'Friends?' Carl sat up. Sleep could wait.

'Yes.'

'So where are they now?'

Brindley sighed. 'West coast of Ireland, I hope. That's where they were headed. SCOPE was being trialled in Dublin – they had their own Civil Contingencies Secretariat – and down the east coast, and in the north, but parts of the west coast should be okay, I think.'

Carl turned to face Brindley. 'So you did manage to persuade at least some people that SCOPE was a danger?'

'Yes, close friends, my sister and ...'

'That all?'

Brindley narrowed his eyes. 'Yes.'

'So why didn't you go with them, these friends of yours?' Carl sat up on the sofa. 'And why exactly did you choose to bring me up here?'

'To save you, I suppose.'

'Save me?'

'Yes. Who else would follow a lead connected to SCOPE all the way up here? It was your job.'

That was something Carl didn't want to think about. Instead of thinking he could sleep, or walk. Being hungover didn't help matters, made it harder for him to judge the truth of what he was being told. It had been his job to sniff around ugly secrets such as SCOPE. Exposing that kind of crap was supposed to be a calling, a vocation; at least that's what he'd believed. Maybe he'd failed to do his job properly. If there had been any saving to be done, he should have been the one doing it, in banner headlines over an exposé. But nothing like that had been possible.

'Why didn't you try to stop it?'

Brindley folded his arms, his eyes flashing. 'What the fuck are you talking about? You don't think I tried to stop this?' He jabbed a finger at Carl. 'You must have known that SCOPE was more than a communications system. You knew that. You must have. You said you had the full spec – you mentioned bioactive frequencies for Christ's sake in one of your pieces. You must have known, at least suspected . . . you must have talked to Cobhill or Haarland or one of these guys.'

Carl heaved himself off the couch, anger rising in him. 'I couldn't have stopped this any more than you.'

Silence.

The hint of a smile played around Brindley's thin lips. 'You think I was any less impotent than you?'

Carl didn't answer. He headed upstairs without looking back.

•

Shadow marked the deepening evening, sun sinking behind the northern headland. Carl got up to sit by the window and look out across the sun-bright bay.

In the quiet, he could hear the sea stir against the bay, a background rush of water lapping on rock. The day moved into early evening and it was warm, and the smell of the sea was strong. He leant on the sill of the open window. There was crying somewhere, though he wasn't sure where, and a steady stream of people coming back from the edge of the delta field. He reached for the cigarette he had been given by one of the locals. There was a big NO SMOKING sign on the back of the door, but he guessed that George Cutler would have other things on his mind apart from the smell of smoke in one of his rooms. The death of his wife would be fairly high on that list.

A knock at the door. He listened. It came again, louder. He heard a woman's voice, out in the corridor.

'Are you there?'

He sat up, his lips parched, wearing a T-shirt and boxer shorts.

'Come in,' he rasped, rising from the bed.

The door creaked open and Simone Cutler looked in, her face pale, eyes red. Sleepless. Just like him.

'We were wondering if you'd like anything to eat?'

She came into the room. Instead of her waitress whites, she wore a dressing gown. Her hair was loose.

'No,' Carl said. 'Thanks. I'm not hungry. How . . .' He stopped, unable to finish the question. There was no need to ask.

Simone started to shake. She was next to him now, and Carl could smell traces of perfume and, deeper, her true scent. She raised a trembling hand to her eyes. The next thing Carl knew they were holding each other, a full-on hug, in the summer stillness as the birds sang in the sun.

He stroked Simone's unbrushed hair, pressed her closer. They sat on the bed and, as her dressing gown parted Carl automatically slid his hand between her thighs. He felt himself harden, and he gave himself to an emotion that blotted out fear.

November

12

Autumn was on the move, flinging storms in a fusillade from the Atlantic. On the main road south Carl stopped in his tracks, sucking deep for air. He was pushing himself too hard, full recovery still some way off, evidently. How long would it take?

This is how it is and how it would be. Pneumonia had given him a glimpse of the future and he now existed as a weaker, older man. He'd never felt so tired and worn out. Was this to be his new peak fitness? Maybe he'd never fully recover.

Bed had suited him too well; it was as if he belonged in the hollow his dead weight had pressed into the mattress in Room 14. Try as he might, he couldn't make himself as strong as once he'd been, couldn't shake the disease. A deeper resting-place than his bed would have been no bad thing, one next to Howard and the German couple. But he wasn't going to die any time soon. There was here and now to consider; pressing concerns that demanded a response, even if it was jumping off a cliff or slitting his wrists. That was always an option.

Perhaps he'd pushed himself too hard, walking into the hills, following the invisible bars of his cage from one side of the bay to the other.

They were watching him, the villagers. Through binoculars they were scrutinising him as he plodded and puffed along the southern headland, on the road that curved up and out of the bay. He knew they were watching him because he was watching them. There were two pairs searching for him, he could see through his binoculars: the old woman in Bayview Cottage, standing at her living-room window, and one of Cutler's boatyard crew down on the pier. Well, he'd give them a good show. He put one foot in front of the other, a feat of dexterity that was bound to amaze the observers.

He walked out from behind the trees, adjusted his headphones and headed south in time to the music throbbing in his ears. Thank Christ for solar power.

•

On the main road out of Inverlair where there was an opening in a line of rowan trees, a gravel track led to a rusty metal gate that was wide enough to let a lorry through. Hidden by low branches Carl saw a washed-out sign for Levanche Aggregates, Inverlair Quarry. The metal gates were chained together and a wheelless windowless old car was taking root among the bushes. Carl climbed over the chest-high gate and continued down the rough track and into the quarry. Warning placards atop wooden posts, all flattened by the wind, urged site visitors to WEAR PERSONAL PROTECTION EQUIPMENT and DON'T TAKE UNNECESSARY RISKS. As far as the pregnancy was concerned, it was a bit late for any of that. He crunched on down the stony track, into the great gouged pit.

The main part of the quarry must have been over 300 metres wide and at least 50 deep, one side open, leading down towards a sagging ballast-filled pier where the cargo ships had loaded up with gravel sand and aggregate. Long gone now, everything rust and rot: prefab site office with broken windows; corrugated-iron works shed rattling and squeaking in the wind; corroded tank and concrete bund for waste oil; lorry trailers with flat tyres; a long conveyor-belt machine, angling into the air, a dead dinosaur like Eric. Like himself.

At the far end of the quarry another dirt track ploughed up and through banks of peat, until it opened out again into a steep-sided lagoon. Signs warned of deep water. Young pine trees had taken hold on the lagoon's stony slopes, along with gorse and tufts of heather. Wind ghosted in gusts across the dark water.

Nobody was watching him here.

On a stone track overlooking the lagoon, Carl picked up a fist-sized stone and hurled it underarm down towards the deep water. The splash echoed round the pit, setting birds to flight. Some of them sped from the quarry's floor, twittering in fright, flashing towards the safety of holes in the sand cliffs, at the far end of the lagoon. When the sun was out it was warm, but the cool breeze sped the clouds, and it was cold in the shadows, spines of winter needling into autumn.

Carl made his way down the side of the quarry towards the lagoon. The wind dropped away and, sitting next to a pile of huge boulders, he felt some heat in the sun in the rocks and on the ground. He unzipped his jacket and pulled out his water bottle.

There was sand on the quarry floor, around the lagoon. The plaque at the village viewpoint said the sea level had fluctuated since the last Ice Age. Maybe that explained why he had his own private inland beach.

Tenacious buggers, those young pine trees, half-submerged on the slopes of the lagoon, green shoots bursting through the gravel, some of them saplings barely knee-high. The earth was reclaiming this man-made scar in the landscape, creeping down the sides of the quarry, covering the pit and the tracks, the mounds of till and rusting machinery. Healing over. Carl sat with eyes closed and out of the wind until the next cloud, a big one, came and blocked the sun. Shadow lowered the temperature and sitting there became uncomfortable after a spell. He got to his feet. The book in the hotel said there was a prehistoric structure, and some caves, up in the hill. There was nothing else to do but walk and hide and think. Despite what George had said, people probably blamed him for everything that had happened; when they found out about

Simone they'd blame him for that as well. Fair enough. Rather than question their own lack of awareness, their blindness, they could pin SCOPE on him and Howard. Simone's brother seemed to have Little Man Syndrome. Carl doubted whether being an uncle again would cause him unbridled delight.

•

Two hours later he was 300 metres up on the opposite headland, at the remains of a Bronze Age broch, trying to envisage what this pile of stones had looked like, standing twelve metres high and with two-metre thick walls. There was tightness in his chest and weakness in his legs. But he'd managed the climb, all the way, whereas the week before he hadn't.

People had looked out from here once, he thought, across the same hills and bay, out to where sun and cloud danced on the same leaden Atlantic. Hungry people, perhaps, watching from this spot. How healthy had the prehistoric diet been? It seemed to consist mainly of nuts, berries and fish. How could you square a healthy diet with dying young? Simple: death had more than one trick up its sleeve. It could seep into your bones with the drizzle, or it could strangle you with your own umbilical cord. A harsh winter. The point of a sword. These were the ways before Alzheimer's and cancer and the industrialised race to extinction. Erase the main road from the picture, the forest plantation too, and you could be looking at a million years ago.

The broch was anywhere between 2,000 and 4,000 years old, according to the book in the hotel, but there wasn't much left now. The thing had collapsed in on itself, or been knocked down. A defensive structure, built to keep watch over a wide area with one face towards the sea and the other inland. Inverlair was an ideal spot: a river at the head of a sheltered bay. But something, someone, would have come along to break the peace. Did the invaders export their desperation, taking by force what Inverlair had?

SCOPE would fail – everything man-made did, sooner or later. SCOPE would retreat, mast by mast, and those who were left could take over again, could . . . what? Scavenge over relics? Worship the fucking masts like some death cult?

Looking down the hill towards the village Carl could see the spill of big stones from the collapsed broch, some of them completely grown over. He walked down the slope and knelt, touched one of the buried stones. Within this grass swelling, this bump, was a missing piece of the past, and it would stay there unless he freed it. Perhaps he should help the rock get reborn.

Stamping with the heel of his boot, he struck a solid edge under the grass, worked around in this way until he had the outline, then with his hands he pulled the sods and black soil from the broch stone. After a few minutes of effort, sweat running into his eyes and down the small of his back, lungs straining, he'd worked the boulder loose, like a molar in its socket.

Straining every sinew, he extracted, a heave at a time, a hundredweight of rectangular stone, dragging it free of the centuries and onto the grass. Many stones were buried further down the slope.

Gasping for breath, Carl sank down next to the slab, dark earth reeking from the hole. After a few minutes, he sat up. Already the soil was drying on his hands; cold sweat on his face, nails topped with a line of dirt. There were dozens more stones to dig out. Big ones on the outside, smaller ones forming the inner wall of the broch; the whole thing tapering upwards for seven metres, just like the book said. His arms were shaking with the effort and his lungs were sore. Maybe he could dig more out, maybe all of them, in time.

He lifted his binoculars and scanned the village. If he could see them clearly, then they could see him. He searched the backs of houses, upstairs bedrooms and kitchen windows. Did he see a movement in one, someone ducking behind a curtain?

Carl patted the stone he had just dug up, the first of many. He could do it. He could resurrect the dead.

That would give them something to talk about. The nutter on the hill. The guy who knew about SCOPE and who didn't try to stop it. The guy who killed his friend.

After a while he stood up, drank some water from his bottle. It was too early to go back yet; too early for the awkward silences and the hints and the looks. Simone wanted a conversation, but he doubted if anything he had to say would improve the situation, although, now that he thought about it, he wasn't sure if he could find any words of significance at all. Sometimes it felt like a dream, and at other times everything came sharply into focus; a reality he had no idea how to handle.

Best not to think about it. It was easier to push it away. He had to push it away.

13

Sitting on the roadblock on the north road out of the bay, Carl pulled Howard's deltameter out of his pocket. Howard must have had it in his own pocket, his body wet and cold from six days lying on the hill. Carl sniffed the phone, expecting the lingering scent of putrefaction, but it just smelled of plastic. One day he would be able to leave the redzone; the deltameter would tell him when it was safe. It would point the way to when he could get back into his car and drive.

Better park Howard's car somewhere. Garage it. Top it up with biodiesel every now and again. Run the engine. Keep the tyres inflated, ready for when he could take off. To where?

Somewhere. The road would open. The masts would fail and the delta field would open, and he could drive on to where he wouldn't feel like someone in a cage. But that was for the future; just now he was an inmate who would have to do his time.

There was an old stone cottage a short distance away from the road, chimney at either end, and no windows or door. It stank of animals and shit. Two rooms, the corroded hulk of a stove in one, and no floorboards or furniture in either. No internal walls as such but there were beams standing, holding up most of the ceiling. The bottom three steps of the wooden staircase were missing. Carl looked up. The roof was intact, apart from over one gable-end.

He tried the staircase and it held, so he tried a foot on the first step, let it take his full weight. The wood protested, and he thought the whole lot would come crashing down. But it didn't. He climbed and poked his head up, level with the upper floor to see what was what. A metal bed frame in one of two rooms, and nothing else. Musty smell of decay and the sheepshit stink on the ground floor.

The staircase held him. The bare floorboards in the bedroom held him. Carl edged towards the bed, testing every step, pressuring the wood, listening, waiting to plummet. The skylight in the bedroom was still unbroken. The cobwebbed stalk of a light fitting, minus bulb and shade, hung in the middle of the ceiling. He sat, gently, on the bare metal springs of the old bedstead. It squeaked. Ribbons of wallpaper had peeled and drooped; most of the paint that had once been on the ceiling lay in flakes on the bare floor.

Carl lay back and waited, his feet still on the floor, ready to rise at the first sign of trouble. But bed and floor held his weight. He lifted his legs onto the springs; they still had their bounce, and it wasn't too uncomfortable, no, not at all ...

He closed his eyes.

Eric. Lesley. Sarah. Eddie. All now populating a dream world. Were they real, or had he dreamed his previous life? This life involved Simone, and the dreaded by-product of real sex. It wasn't even that; it hadn't been sex, not really. What had it been? Comfort. A gift from terror. She hadn't been wearing underwear. Didn't say anything to him, afterwards, just left the room. Spunk on the carpet. He blanked the details, the pressure, and the urge.

At least with CivCon and food riots he knew what he was dealing with – all that stuff had origins that could be understood, oppression that could be traced and plotted. Even an ugly world moulds itself around a person, and they become the impression it makes of them.

After a while he found closing his eyes easier than keeping them open.

He was grateful for extinction.

•

It was dark when Carl came back to the hotel. As he reached the back garden he heard a stag's bellowing moan echo round the dark hills, sounding his power. George had told him they'd be shagged out in a few weeks after the rut was finished. Carl let himself in quietly and listened for activity. The clock, ticking in the lobby, was the only sound.

His eyes grew accustomed to the dark. There was always light, he just had to give himself the chance to see it, to stand and look until the black released the objects it was holding. Carl made his way to the kitchen, found the lamp on the table, and the box of matches. He opened the door of the stove to warm up. Lighting the lamp, he sat at the kitchen table.

Outside, the wind was picking up. In the silence he could hear dry leaves scraping against the back door. Fried fish and potatoes were warming in the oven, enough to take the edge off his appetite. As he chewed the food, he thought of the sleeping village, and him creeping back to it, stealing into this house, like a burglar breaking in. Was it a foetus or an embryo? He knew there was a difference. It was all a matter of time. Maybe it was awake, percolating its mother's nutrients, more thing than person, inside the sleeping Simone; maybe he and it were the only two entities awake in the village.

He heard a noise in the corridor.

The door opened. It was Simone, in her dressing gown, yawning, candle in hand

Carl collected himself. 'I thought I was being quiet when I came in.'

'People are never as quiet coming in as they think,' she said. 'I just wanted to tell you something.'

Carl stiffened.

Simone warmed her hands on the stove. 'Adam told me that they could use someone at the forestry. One of the guys hurt his arm. If you're feeling up to it – I don't know if you are – you could fill in for him.'

'Doing what?'

'I'm not sure. Helping cut more of those probably.' She pointed at the basket of logs by the stove.

Instinctively, he wanted to say no. He didn't want anything to do with Simone's twat of a brother, or anyone else for that matter. He thought for a second.

'I've never used any forestry machinery before. Maybe I'd just get in the way.'

'You don't have to use any machinery. He said he could use you.'

The wind gusted against the kitchen window, moaning in the chimney flue as the rain started.

He told her he would think about it.

•

Hard workers. All of them. Cutting wood. Catching fish. Growing food and fixing things. Everyone mucking in, unless they were too old or too young. Everyone doing their bit. Everyone except him, the parasite feeding off the hard work of others, eating their food, absorbing their heat, shagging their women. Too clever to get his hands dirty like the hard workers. He can hardly hold a hammer. Where does he go during the day? What's he doing mooching around the hills when there's work to be done? Let him get on with it. Get a grip. Get his head down and lend a hand. Do his bit. Muck in.

Well, the hard workers could all piss off. Let them watch him. Let them invent whatever stories they wanted.

It all came down to calories — energy. Young kids got the most, followed by working men and women. It was Howard's first-winter survival system. Carl wasn't young and he wasn't exactly useful. He was now on the bottom rung of the rationing ladder; he may as well have had a yellow U for useless stamped on his forehead. He lay on the bed, lime-green alcopop bubbling in his stomach, and fell asleep. In his dream, a giant adder was coiled and standing, at the foot of his bed, watching, tasting the darkness with its flickering tongue.

14

Being under surveillance, with no escape possible. He was used to that. Emails, texts and calls intercepted. His ID a permanent locus on the CivCon watchlist. Anonymity was a thing of the past for most people. At least he wasn't safety-chipped, like the kids. What he did, where he went, what he said and who he said it to, was of sufficient interest to someone, somewhere, that various procedures were enacted to ensure it was all logged and cross-indexed, put through pattern-recognition filters, and presented as a case file to some CivCon technocrat. Liberty and incarceration were entirely matters of procedure, depending on what Sentinel recommended. After a while, he had learned to live with that. If there is no immediate physical threat, people can learn to live with just about anything. There was nothing he could have done about any of it, so ignoring it as best he could seemed to make sense, otherwise it would have driven him crazy. Same applies now.

After a few days spent mulling it over, Carl finally decided to act on Simone's suggestion. Walking up the track from the north road he could hear the forestry machines before he saw them, smell the strong, sweet scent of freshly cut pine. Splintered branches, their fibrous ends wrenched apart, littered the track up to the conifer plantation; caterpillar chains had gouged a mud-trail over the rough ground. He followed the trail and the noise of the machines until he came to a clearing. There were guys there he recognised, a pick-up truck and a Portakabin. Through the trees, Carl caught glimpses of the felling machine, its claw reaching out to grip a ten-metre trunk, cutting it at the base, turning it as if it weighed no more than a broom handle. Each trunk was stripped of branches and sliced in ten seconds flat, puffs of blue smoke belching from the machine's exhaust. The roar and the wrath of a huge beast, smashing a path through the trees as it harvested low-grade carbon.

Stacks of cut trunks were waiting to be lifted by another machine onto the pick-up truck. George had said there were seven in the forestry work crew. Today, there were only two guys in the Portakabin, one older man, late fifties, wearing thick black-rimmed glasses, dozing in a plastic chair, a cap on his head and booted feet crossed on the tabletop. The other, a thick-necked younger man wore an oily orange boiler suit and was playing a hand-held gaming machine. It took him a few seconds to realise that Carl was standing in the doorway. The game-player looked up, kicked the sleeper's boots to wake him up.

'The gaffer said you might be along. You were with that other guy when he died, the bald guy.'

'Howard,' said Carl. 'Yes, I was. I'm Carl, by the way.'

'I know,' said the nameless gamer. 'And you got pneumonia on the hill.' There was nothing like the direct approach; a smirk on the guy's face, the trace of secret amusement. The CivCon smile.

'Yes, in both lungs,' said Carl, trying the bluff approach. 'That's the kind of double I could do without. Sorry, I didn't get your names.'

Gamer toggled his thumb, first at himself. 'Casper. And this is Shit for Brains.'

Shit for Brains stretched himself from his doze. 'You're a twat, Casper,' he laughed, arms crossed, boots still on the tabletop. 'It's Dennis. So you've come to join our band of merry men have you, Carl?'

Carl said yes and tried to see the funny side of it. He'd once shadowed a fire crew for the night: two call-outs, one a faulty fire alarm and the other a chimney fire. Mainly, there seemed to be a lot of eating, cleaning and playing of pool involved in being a firefighter, but Carl managed to get 1,200 words out of it. These jokers, Dennis and Casper, were different. He would have to get along with them, maybe for a long time. This was work of a different kind.

Almost two hours later he was halfway up the forest track when he stopped what he was doing. Though the day was cold, the exertion had warmed him. After dragging about twenty loads of branches up the hill, something important dawned on him. He hadn't really thought of it when Casper had shown him his job for the day, but now he was starting to wonder what the fuck he was actually doing.

He looked back down the forest track to the Portakabin, where a droning crane-lift grabbed a clawful of man-sized logs and dropped them onto the back of the pick-up. The machine in the forest had stopped felling and stripping; Casper and Dennis were standing around waiting for the driver of the crane to finish loading. A few at a time, the claw-lift picked up the trunks of spruce and placed them expertly in the vehicle, which rocked as each new load was banged down. There are supposed to be seven guys in the wood crew, thought Carl: one's doing the work, two are standing around, and four aren't even here. He looked at the head-high stack of offcuts he'd built up over the last two hours.

Why the fuck was he dragging bundles of useless branches further up the forest track? He dropped the rope and walked back to where the logs were being loaded. The more he thought about what he'd been doing, the more it didn't stack up, so to speak. And Casper giving it the old CivCon look. That bothered him. Something wasn't right, and Carl had a gut feeling that the wrongness of the situation was at his expense.

The pick-up was loaded with twenty or so logs, then it rumbled off towards the village. Someone at the boatyard would chainsaw the wood into smaller logs for the fires of Inverlair. Another guy, blond crew cut and red scar on his cheekbone, got out of the claw-lift; Casper was sitting on the Portakabin's step, playing his game as Carl walked over to him.

'I was just thinking there,' said Carl, pointing back up the track. 'Why do all the offcuts have to be moved up the track?'

In reply came the smirk, the secret smile. Casper shrugged. 'Site management,' he said gruffly, fiddling with his game.

'Eh?'

'See the gaffer if you want an explanation,' Casper said, glancing at his mate. The blond man laughed, turned back to the claw-lift. 'Adam'll fucking batter you for dropping him in it.'

Casper just giggled, glanced up at Carl. 'See the gaffer.'

As he walked back to the village, Carl was sure he heard the words 'site management', followed by more laughter.

At the boatyard, he saw Adam's pick-up, heard a rattling chainsaw make short work of the spruce trunks. It was a cold day. Though the sun was out and there were few clouds, it was breezy, from the east. That usually spelt cold and dry, George had said.

Adam Cutler had plugged an electric chainsaw into a biodiesel generator and was oblivious to Carl standing at the gate. When he finally caught sight of him, Adam eased up on the revs and lifted his goggles. He came over, leaving the chainsaw idling on a bed of fresh sawdust.

'You finished already?'

'Not quite,' said Carl. He rubbed his stubble. 'I'm sort of wondering why I have to move that stuff at all. It doesn't make sense.' His eyes narrowed. 'If you're taking the piss . . . I'm not interested.'

Adam grinned. 'Oh, lighten up for fuck's sake.' He shook his head. 'Can you not take a joke?'

Carl frowned. 'A joke?'

'Yeah, the guys are just messing with you. Of course there's no need to move the fucking branches, they just want to see how you take it, that's all, see who they're dealing with.'

'Right,' Carl said. 'I see. There's plenty to laugh about, I suppose. It's a very . . . humorous situation, this.' He gestured at nothing in particular. 'Everything's funny. Hilarious, if you look hard enough.'

Striding back to his chainsaw, Adam waved Carl away. 'Oh, come on, man. People respond to things in their own way. Crying about it won't put food on the table, and that's what's important right now, more than ever.' He picked up the chainsaw. 'The work crew get more food because they work, so thank your lucky stars you're on it.' He revved the chainsaw. 'And thank my sister as well,' he shouted.

Over the next few days, Carl turned up for work, cut kelp for the biofuel processor plant; the extra food, his work rations, slipped down nice and easy. He moved from Room 14 into Room 7, casting off some of the traces of death. Three days later, when there was no need to cut any more logs or kelp, he went down to the pier to help unload the *Aurora* of its catch of mackerel and pollock. Even that task only involved taking a few boxes to the community-centre freezers on a handcart. People were getting fed up of eating fish every day, but alternatives were thin on the ground, apart from venison and the odd rabbit or grouse shot by the old gamekeeper. He learned, as he guessed, that Casper was a nickname and that it was indeed connected with the friendly ghost. They'd never be bosom pals.

After a week, Carl arrived at the clear-felled forest. Today he was supposed to learn how to operate the log-grabber. The guys were in the Portakabin.

'Adam wants to see you,' said Casper, without looking up from his game.

'What for?'

'Dunno. He's at the house.'

Dennis was paring a piece of wood with a penknife. He didn't look up either.

Carl assessed the situation. 'I'll nip down later.'

Shifting in a plastic chair, Dennis coughed. 'I think he wants to see you now.'

'Now? I've just got here.'

'Yep,' chirped Casper, his eyes still glued to the action. 'That's what de man say.'

They wouldn't meet his eye. He turned on his heel and set off.

Adam's house, a massive harled bungalow, was one of eight ranged in a line behind the main part of the village, on the northern headland. Carl walked the main road back from the forest and along the headland until he reached the track that led to Adam's house. Built on top of a double garage and partly buried in the hillside, the house was shielded by a belt of mature willow trees that provided shelter on the seaward side.

He didn't like this; no, not one bit. Something was wrong. He knocked on the heavy varnished back door. A woman in her early twenties opened it. She was small, fair-skinned, with long hair tied in a ponytail, dark rings under her blue eyes. She told Carl that Adam was in his office.

Some people are touchy about their places of origin, especially when they're living somewhere else. The woman was definitely from either America or Canada. Carl recognised her. She'd been too hungover, the day SCOPE had gone live, to go with her friends for a drive. Her friends never came back.

What could Adam want with an office?

It wasn't really an office as such, more a storeroom, though a semi-circular desk had four screens arranged upon it. Three of them still had cellophane wrappers around them, brand new.

Another door was open. Footsteps sounded from below, coming up stairs. It was some kind of cellar, probably down to one of the garages below.

There was no greeting from Adam. 'This was going to be my nerve centre,' he said, pointing to the screens. 'Links with the boatyard and with both fishing boats. A monitoring system for the biofuel plant – we had a CivCon contract to serve their Inverness depot. We even had a contract in place with a seaplane firm; it would have cut through a shitload of biosec red tape. Just think about it: shellfish delivered fresh to European buyers in a few hours.' He pressed the tip of his index finger against one of the screens. He pushed, applied a little more pressure, and the screen fell off the desk, corner first, crashing onto the floor. 'Every litre of diesel and every rivet and every lobster. Every debit and credit with every customer and supplier, logged automatically.' He smiled. 'My accountant would've loved it.'

His face fell. 'You've made my sister pregnant, you fucking tosspot.' He looked at Carl, blank-eyed.

A response was expected. An explanation. 'Yes,' Carl said.

There was silence. Two can play at that game, he thought.

Adam snorted. 'Is that it? Is that all you've got to say? *Yes.*'

'Yeah. You asked me a specific question. I answered it.'

'Okay. Do you mind telling me how it happened?' In response to Carl's raised eyebrows, he added quickly: 'The circumstances, smart-arse. She's nearly three months gone. You arrived here three months ago. So you didn't fucking hang about there, did you?' He came out from behind the desk.

'It wasn't like that,' said Carl. 'Who told you Simone was pregnant?'

'Never mind who told me. Wasn't like what, exactly?'

'It wasn't meant to happen.'

'Is that a fact?'

'Yes. It is.'

'So, what was the scene? Let me see.' Adam clicked his fingers. 'That's it: a vulnerable woman seeking comfort . . .'

Carl jerked his thumb at the door. 'What – like yours?'

'Fuck off,' said Adam. 'It wasn't . . . like that.'

Carl put his hands in his pockets. Round 1 to him. 'So, is this where the older brother gets all protective? Are you going to make me an offer I can't refuse?'

'Look,' said Adam. 'She's my sister, for fuck's sake. I want to know what your plans are. What are you going to do about it?'

'Something,' said Carl. 'Or nothing. There's not much I can do about it, or so I've been told.'

He turned to go.

'Fine. Excellent.' Adam took a quick step forward. 'Well, don't bother coming anywhere near the pier or the boatyard until you make your fucking mind up, useless prick.'

•

Carl sat on the twenty-fifth broch stone he had managed to unearth and looked down at the bay.

The days were shorter now, and colder. A crow landed nearby, across a gully, on top of an outcrop of lichen-covered rock. He watched it, keeping quite still. This seemed to unnerve the crow.

People threw stones. People took no notice. They didn't just sit, stock-still and staring. The bird hopped from foot to foot, bobbing and blinking, confused.

'*Corvus corone*,' Carl said out loud. 'I know what you are.'

Maybe this was the bird that had pecked Howard's eyes out, the one that had tugged and nipped off bits of lip and ear. Here was another scavenger shitting out digested human. There had been plenty of those. The crow hopped and called, squawked enquiry, coal-eye glistening. Carl spied a stone at his feet. He grabbed it. As he did so the crow snapped from the rock and barked away into the grey sky. Carl threw the stone even though he knew there was no chance of hitting the bird. Just taking aim at it would do, but the crow was too quick and the stone climbed, looped to earth, well short of its target.

The bird had come to taunt him; knew the man's habits and had lain in wait for him. Your friend filled my belly. How do you like that? Why don't you just lie down and do likewise? Turn yourself into meat. Give up your corporeal tribute for the greater good of crowkind. Maybe he should do that; grab whatever pills he could get his hands on; swipe one of George's bottles of malt, swallow the lot. Find a hole to hide in, neck the lot, and fall asleep for the last time. Give the crows and the worms a good feed. Sleep and death would be reliable, this time around.

Out at sea, there was still no white boat. Howard's friends would never come for him. Even if they were able to, they'd stay where they were if they had any sense.

He'd been a journalist, once. You do a job for long enough and that's all you are. He was seeing that now.

Without a job, what are you? People don't like thinking about that, with or without full stomachs. It's easier just to work, without thinking of alternative identities or meanings. He'd been a journalist. But that label no longer meant anything. There were now other labels being written for him to wear.

15

For two days it rained, without let-up, the dry spell well and truly broken. In his room, he considered the calendar on the wall, the months in motion.

The rain didn't stop Carl going up the hill. Three days ago the river through the forest had been a delicate trickle; now it had transformed into a roaring beast, churning peaty froth as it thundered over the falls and out under the road bridge.

He could have hung around the hotel. Easy enough, he could have gone downstairs just to talk to Simone or George, or to pass the time until the rain stopped. Make the effort. Reach out. Somewhere inside him there was an awareness that that was what he had to do. It was stirring – this need to reach out – but it could yet be strangled in his inner darkness, unborn.

He climbed the stile at the back fence, near the stalker's cottage, and headed squelching through the rain up to the ridge towards the broch, spade slung over his shoulder, oilskins keeping him dry and warm. It was true: there was no such thing as bad weather, only bad clothing.

Why sulk in his room? He looked back down the hill at the hotel. It wasn't her fault. It wasn't his fault. Extenuating circumstances. End of the world, and all that. Adam Cutler was a Grade A prick though, he didn't need much clarity of thought to see that.

Not even crows out today. Sheep huddling bedraggled and quiet in any shelter they could find. Cold with it – and getting colder. The steady climb to the broch took about forty-five minutes; a few weeks before it had taken him twice as long, but now his lungs and legs were strong and he didn't need to pause on the climb. At least there was no wind today firing rain into his face.

Sitting on the low wall he had exhumed from the ground, he wondered how many other communities there were like Inverlair. There were probably some, where SCOPE and mobile coverage had been poor. Isolated rural hill villages or natural depressions. Inverlair was both. Carl watched sun and shadow fight it out on the far headlands, the *Aurora* motoring back into the bay.

Maybe Adam Cutler was just looking out for his sister. Just doing his best for everyone in the village. Like hell he was. He was playing the saviour, the man with the big plan, and he relished the part.

Carl took out his binoculars and scanned Inverlair. Walk and climb, climb and walk, pressure easing in his head, rain pattering on his hood. He was walking away from all the crap that had to do with how other people felt and what they expected from him. He could walk as far as the bars of his cage, measure them on the deltameter, and look out at the dead world that had once been alive, or at least not quite so dead. Maybe he couldn't call it living, but at least it had a point and a purpose, however basic: to stay alive.

They'd be watching him now, he reckoned, not with RF trackers or GPS or Sentinel in Glasgow, but from back windows that faced onto the hills of Inverlair. They'd see his yellow oilskins, watch him rebuild the wall of the broch, stone by stone, the nutter.

Carl took a detour, cutting south towards the road instead of north behind the village. His change of routine would be noticed, he surmised.

Down below was the road, winding into the drift-net of low cloud that smothered the southern summits. At least Howard and the German couple had been given a decent burial. They were lying next to others: people threw in their handfuls of dirt; said a few words. SCOPE had done away with all that ritual, preferring instead an open-air smörgåsbord approach. Is that not what the Indian Parsees did? Left their dead exposed on the hillside for the wind and the eagles to devour? Meat going around on the big wheel. A parade of predators to scoff the bodies: foxes, dogs, birds, rats, cats, trillions of maggots pupating in the ripening flesh. Mass human death would have caused a sudden flowering of insect life.

Good eating, all round.

•

The rain eased. Each hole that had held a broch stone was full of water; there were twenty-five holes altogether, twenty-five pieces of a Neolithic puzzle.

It was a sick fucking joke, that's what it was; a new life on the way and he'd put it there. That wasn't right. To say it was a sick joke wasn't doing it justice. What would its future be? Stuck in Inverlair, hungry and clueless about the world. Another mouth gaping for food, a burden that was his doing and his responsibility.

There had been no agenda with Simone when she'd knocked on his door, no ulterior motive. He never meant for anything to happen; he had felt something that wasn't to do with sex or lust. Maybe fear was the basic driver for so much of what people did, even when they were shagging. Even that could be a cry against extinction and terror, the obliteration of self and conscious awareness. Or was it the unmasking of the true self, the revelation of insatiable appetite in its twisted, personalised glory?

All he'd wanted to do was hold her.

The rest of it just happened. That is what he believed to be the truth.

Carl hacked round another broch stone, clearing its outline in the sticky earth. He was keeping watch, but he wasn't really sure on what.

The sea would have been scanned, when the broch was a

broch, for uninvited guests; it would have been Mission Control in the fight against invaders. Where was the threat now?

It wasn't the redzone or the sea that Carl watched. It was Inverlair. With Howard's binoculars he scanned for movement; old women finally able to hang out clothes to dry; fish unloaded at the pier; Isaac playing in his sandpit. All this was perfectly normal for a world he could not penetrate, that held him at bay; so he had to watch it. Stay vigilant.

Carl dug out another stone, heaving it up and onto the grass, purpose being regained and reconfigured. One curving section of wall – almost a half circle – was rising to join the remains of the other. Higher than knee-height would cause him problems, but he'd figure that out when the time came.

Graft? He'd show the fuckers all about that. He would rebuild this thing, stone by buried stone. Fuck it – he would live in it. He would defend the broch against all comers. He would fight.

Fight.

So there was no time to waste.

He worked faster, hacking round a stone, levering it out, muttering to himself.

What's the point in trying to make a difference? Why risk what you have when protesting – the stance you take – means nothing? You're just one man. You're being buried, bit by bit, and you're just about to go under. If only you'd stop struggling, all that weight would lift from your shoulders and you could breathe again, take it all in your stride. So why bother trying to shine a light? The darkness is all around. Let it claim you. Get used to the dark that everyone else is groping around in. He should have let CivCon take him by the hand and show him the right way to behave now that there is no light in the world. Thrashing around in the dark is dangerous. You might hurt yourself, sonny, and those around you. The dark is all around you. Accept it. Let the shit wash over you and don't try to see into it or through it because that's just a headfuck and why bother bringing that on? Just keep your head clear and down and accept what's around you, now and forever. Amen. Accept the darkness. Stop struggling. Stop resisting. Stop trying to make other people see the foul things that are whispering how blessed is the darkness. Let it alone, and keep your mouth shut.

No.

And another stone, his sixth that day, was reclaimed from the earth. Another piece of the puzzle. Another step towards wholeness. It was important. It meant something. The broch was older than SCOPE and white rust and CivCon. Only hunger and death were older.

Sweating and gasping as he spaded up chunks of turf, Carl imagined himself a savage, repelling hordes of invaders from his perch. He would club them aside. Hack them to pieces. Machine-gun the lot of them. A caveman with an M60.

He'd make a difference. He'd make them pay.

'Hello there,' a voice said.

Carl let out a cry, jumped up from his digging, sweat, mud and hair plastered across his face. Wide-eyed, he gawped at the figure standing nearby. The stalker; Carl couldn't remember his name. The man smiled, adjusting his cap.

'The view is nice, but you won't have much in the way of mod cons.'

Carl cocked his head, still brandishing the spade. 'Eh? What the fuck are you on about?'

'The broch,' said the stalker, calm and even. 'A view but no loo. Not what you'd call a des res.'

Carl looked at the guy, sixty if he was a day. He felt the blister sting on his right palm from the digging. The pain wouldn't stop him doing what he had to do. No fucking way.

'Definitely not cosy,' the stalker said quietly.

Carl clutched the spade, and took a deep breath. The wall of the broch was forming; the long dead was rising.

The stalker leant forward on his stick. He wore a dark Gore-Tex jacket and thick brown socks above his heavy boots. Wisps of greying hair stuck out from under a tweed cap.

'You're busy,' he said.

Carl sat down on the mud-plastered stone he had just spent twenty minutes exhuming. The rain had stopped. He wiped his face clear of sweat and hair, nodded, said nothing.

The stalker squinted at the sky, the fog-shrouded bastion of Ben Bronach. The day was clearing, wind swinging to the north, getting colder. A seagull soared, silent over the ridge.

'Do you mind if I ask you what you're doing up here?'

Here we go. Never mind the matey chinwag.

'Why? Are you going to tell me to get off your land?'

'No,' said the stalker, his voice steady. 'This isn't my land. I'm wondering why you're digging these stones out of the ground.' He lowered his eyes from the sky and hills to inspect the foundations of the broch wall.

Of course there was a reason why a man would climb up into the hills to dig large stones out of the ground in the pissing rain. Alec John could remember, as a boy, when stones just as big had been used to build, and rebuild, walls. But this was different. This man was not digging for a practical reason. He was digging because he was compelled to.

For a second, Carl felt like telling the stalker the truth about the stones. He was rebuilding the broch, he felt like saying, because he was sick of living in that goldfish bowl down there, and because he needed something to do with his time. He was sick of the people down there muttering about what he had or hadn't done. They were sly bullies, the lot of them. So much for Highland hospitality.

'I wanted to be an archaeologist, once,' Carl found himself saying. 'I just wanted to see the broch as it was. Not just a pile of stones, but . . .' He faltered. 'Just to preserve it, you know? Before it's too late.' He looked at the ground, eyes roving over the stones.

'That's a fair enough explanation, I suppose,' said the stalker. He cleared his throat. 'But maybe it is too late, for the stones anyway.'

Shouldering his shotgun, he gestured up at the ridge. 'I've got traps where the grouse are,' he said. 'Stoats – they're fucking pests.' He jerked his thumb towards the village. 'They're even worse than that lot down there. And that's saying something, believe you me.'

Carl stopped inspecting his blister and looked up at the stalker, his mouth open.

'I'm Alec John Stoddart,' said the stalker. 'You'll be Carl Shewan. I remember you. I found you, lying half dead with your friend.'

Carl nodded, still staring. 'I know,' he said softly. 'I meant to say thanks for that and . . .'

Before Carl could finish, Alec John set off up the slope towards Ben Bronach, his dark form soon vanishing against the dark flank of the hill.

'Don't worry about it,' he said over his shoulder. 'Sorry about your friend.'

Carl got up and continued to dig, but it took him the whole afternoon to unearth one more stone. He kept stopping to think, looking up the hill to where the stalker's dwindling form had vanished into the dark slopes of rock and heather.

A while later Carl gave up digging. Late afternoon sun appeared, spotlighting the horizon as wads of grey nimbus opened. Carl shouldered the spade and headed in the direction of the north road, down to the old house near the roadblock.

Careful in the gloom, he eased his way up the broken staircase and, almost in darkness, lay on the bare bed frame. Eventually, stars appeared above him, visible through the dusty cracked skylight.

Patterns.

16

Down to the dunes and the waves, past the quarry, behind the southern headland, among the flotsam on the shoreline, sliding in the autumn sunlight among the stink of rotting high-tide seaweed, Carl stood on the glittering shore as the water played, filling the gullies with each surge, slooping and slurping between the cracks in the rocks. The sea kept on, coming in, going out, carrying stuff in, and spiriting it away again. Label-less plastic bottles full of what looked suspiciously like piss; oil drums half buried in the sand; and wooden planks, beams and branches – tossed high up the beach to soften and rot at the foot of the dunes. The sea was patient at its business, coughing up the rubbish, the indigestible. An election placard from Ireland, washed-out blue and white, the bleached grin of some straight-up, honest candidate was lying, half covered, in a slimy mound of kelp. He wondered if a wind had ripped the placard from a lamppost, maybe at the seafront somewhere, and sent it spinning into the Irish Sea. It might have been years in the water, a drifting relic of the old pre-emergency order. All that trust: washed away and beached in a far corner of nowhere.

Carl walked further along the high-tide line; the sea fizzing on the sand as the waves dragged out, feeling the first sting of redzone in his right temple.

The sheen of oil on a stretch of sand, its rainbow iridescence spreading on the water, black gobbets in the tideline froth. The oil had no obvious source. God knows where it had come from, but here it was – the dead world, like a decomposing corpse, leaking putrescence onto the pure sand, still with the power to hurt.

Above a shingle cove, near the main road south, he could see the small cairn of red warning stones that Howard had built and painted to mark the edge of the redzone. Making his way through the soft dunes, through the spiky marram grass, he headed back to the sub-lethal tranquillity of Inverlair.

No matter what happens, the sea comes in and the deer walk their ancient paths and the wind blows, or it doesn't. Nothing else enters the equation or disturbs the equilibrium, not old oil drums or Irish election posters. And certainly not SCOPE. All that stuff wasn't even a nuisance. Arrowhead and atom were all the same to the sea and the wind. Human triumphs had come and gone in a blink, and now the tide was high and the time to move to higher ground, or drown, had arrived.

'You're an arsehole,' Carl muttered to himself as he made his way between the dunes. 'At least talk to the woman. What other choice do you have?'

The stalker: it sounded as if he didn't exactly see eye to eye with the rest of the village. The guy had made a wise choice. Up there in the hills a man could think his own thoughts, be himself. There was no one watching, judging. There was nothing except air and earth.

Carl would keep picking away at the broch, building what he was compelled to reassemble, somehow. The stones were waiting to be fitted back together, and he shouldn't let them down. They could be recast; with effort they could be returned to what they once had been. Order could be restored, a semblance of purpose and pristine machismo.

He walked back up to the main road, grass knee-high on the verges, wanting something hard and level under his feet for a change instead of soft sand and shifting shingle. The road would vanish too, just like the quarry was doing. Creeping vegetation would do for both.

He took the track that led up past the stalker's house and onto the ridge, to where in the summer he would aim for the summit of Ben Bronach, at a shade over 670 metres. In the summer . . .

As he walked the south road that swept down into Inverlair Bay he slowed, looking ahead. There was a guy putting a chain on a bicycle. Before Carl could make a detour, the guy straightened from his upside-down bike, saw him approaching, and waved. With no real conviction, Carl waved back. A bit closer and he recognised the guy from the previous month, up the ladder, cleaning the guttering along with ex-Navy Patrick or Peter.

'Hey, dude,' called the guy, wiping oily hands on his black combats. He was smoking, and Carl didn't have to get too close to realise it wasn't ordinary tobacco. Gusts of weed came to him on the breeze. Carl wished he still smoked, the craving sparked by the sight of someone doing it for real. As he approached, the guy grinned. 'Never try riding a bike when you're stoned.'

'Can't say I've had the pleasure,' said Carl. He glanced at the spliff. There seemed to be writing, tiny script, covering the paper. The guy handed it to Carl with a twinkle in his eye. 'The good book contains the path to enlightenment.'

Carl studied the joint. A page from the Bible, ultra-thin, rolled into a fat cone. He took it and had a suck, the raw weed harsh on his throat. He coughed immediately.

'I'm not a true believer.' There were tears in his eyes as he struggled to catch his breath.

'You the journalist?'

'Was. There's not much call for news-gathering any more.'

'Certainly not in this place,' said the guy. 'Everyone's a journalist in Inverlair.' He grinned. 'They make up what they don't know.'

Shaking his head, Carl declined another puff. 'I must be hot news.'

The guy mounted his bike. 'You're a household name, for sure.' He stuck out his hand. 'I'm Terry Sullivan.' He picked up a can of white paint.

'You decorating? An autumn makeover to banish the blues?'

Terry smiled. His battered leather jacket was covered in sewn-on patches: Greenpeace, Shiva, Yin and Yang. The usual New Age hodgepodge. 'I'm in the Care and Repair Detail,' he said. 'Mrs Mackay is eighty-seven and her windows need doing before the winter.'

Smoke snaked from his nostrils and was carried away on the breeze. He climbed back on his bike and set off down the road. 'Come over for a smoke any time you want,' he shouted over his shoulder. 'I'm in the caravan.'

•

Two days later, Carl considered broch stone number 34. It was the last one before the slope. The harder work was about to start: heaving the stones up the slope, a few inches at a time, would take every ounce of strength he had. And the second layer of wall, lifting one stone onto another, would need a crowbar. Making the broch higher could not be done by brute strength alone. It was stacking up to be a mountainous problem.

Binoculars poised, Carl watched Terry Sullivan's grey static caravan. A couple of hundred metres down from the main road, it sat on the opposite headland where the ground levelled off near the shore. By the look of it, Terry's neighbour was an old hippie: grey hair in a ponytail, glasses and sandals; going in and out of three big polytunnels lined up next to his house, a two-up, two-down with a flat-roof extension out the back.

Carl lowered the binoculars. He could walk round the shore or into the quarry, the forest, anywhere. All the way to 2.26 miles, if the fancy took him, as far as he could go, which was nowhere near far enough. Maybe he could pop over for a visit, and a smoke.

For today at least, stone 34 could stay buried.

•

Out in the corridor Carl heard children's voices.

'The monster will get us up here,' came a whisper. He recognised Isaac. Another kid spoke. 'Is there a monster?'

'Yes,' said Isaac. 'He makes noises, stamps on the floor. I get shaky in my bed, and the walls get shaky too, cos the monster is very strong.'

'Is it a man monster or a lady monster?' his friend asked.

'A man monster, of course.' Isaac scolded. 'You don't get lady monsters.'

There was silence, then a thud on the stairs, and something hitting the walls. Carl heard yelps of delight and the drum of footsteps going down the stairs and coming back up.

'Your go,' said Isaac. 'Why don't we make them crash in the air like planes?'

There was another thud against the wall; whoops of delight and little feet pounding the stairs followed. Carl opened the room door and crept out into the corridor, down to the corner, peered round at the two boys. They were kneeling at the top of the stairs, firing two sleek but scratched metal cars down the steps and onto the landing. They zoomed the cars along the soft carpet and off the edge, metal hitting the wall with a crash.

Carl watched. He could see the scratches from here, the white wood beneath the dark varnished skirting board. Perhaps he shouldn't be watching this. Isaac fired his car again, and it hit the wall, gouging out a big splinter.

Carl stepped round the corner. 'Guys, maybe you shouldn't be doing that. It marks the wood.' He pointed. 'See? Over there.'

At exactly the same time, both boys jumped to their feet, shouted 'The Monster' and ran downstairs, laughing, terrified. They banged through the fire door and into the annexe.

Carl went over to inspect the walls. You couldn't say they intended to cause any damage; sometimes it just happens that damage happens, especially with kids, or so he thought. Anyway, it hardly mattered if the walls were fucking scratched: it wasn't going to put the tourists off or affect the sale price. He looked at his watch. By the time he made the broch it would be getting dark, and he'd have to come down again. There was a glimmer of something that wasn't fear or despair inside him. Something had been planted.

Across the bay, wisps of white smoke curled from the thin metal chimney of Terry Sullivan's caravan.

•

Carl shivered as he washed himself in the bathroom sink. Balls and armpits. The works. Call it a reacquaintance with recent convention.

The water was barely warm; there was nothing but a stream of ice from the shower. He couldn't say he was a picture of health, but in nearly a month he'd filled out a bit. Colour in his cheeks. Other people had made that happen, fed him and looked after him. He sighed, rubbing the short hair on his head. Softer now. Not so bristly. Time for a trim, maybe.

On his way down the stairs he picked up the two metal cars. Isaac and his pal could get them later.

The fire door to the annexe opened. It was George. 'The kids said there was a monster upstairs.'

'Only me.'

George folded his arms and leant against the wall.

'Look,' said Carl. 'Don't start again, George. It's your son you should be having a go at, not me.'

'I wasn't thinking about Adam. I'm sorry I let it slip to him.' George shook his head. 'But he had to find out, sooner or later. No, it was more my daughter I was thinking of.'

'What do you want me to do, George?'

'Talk to her.'

Carl rubbed his forehead. 'I'm having trouble doing that, George – with anyone. Mass death. Being trapped here. Howard. A baby. Stuff like that, you know, bit of a shock to the old system …'

'It's a shock, yes, but . . .'

'It's extremely unfair that you guys expect me to . . .'

George started laughing, shaking his head in pity. The humour faded. 'My daughter's friend is right – you are an asshole.' He looked coldly at Carl. 'My wife going to Edinburgh and not coming back – that's not fair. Millions falling asleep and never waking up – that's not very fair. All the work *some* of us are having to put in to staying alive – that's a little bit unfair as well.'

Carl considered picking up the toy cars and hurling them against the wall. But that would only have caused more damage to the varnished woodwork.

George pushed open the fire door, chuckling to himself. 'Unfair: that's a good one. Fucking priceless.' He poked his head back through the fire door, all trace of amusement gone. 'We're here. You're here. And you're going to be a dad. Deal with it, like the rest of us have had to.'

The door swung closed.

Outside, the morning was cold in the fresh onshore breeze. An old guy on a chopper bike pedalled along the shorefront, nice and easy, going slow from A to B. Carl said hello – a proper hello, not a furtive glance and a mumble. It was returned with a wave. Acknowledgement. It wasn't so hard, this greeting lark; the old habits could soon re-establish themselves given half a chance. Anyway, he was going round to someone else's house, and that had to be a good thing. In a world of very fucking bad things smoking grass with someone who seemed reasonably entertaining had to count as progress.

He crossed the stone bridge at the head of the bay, river frothing down to the foreshore; sponge bogs, up in the hills, sluicing out two days of rain. The *Aurora* was chuntering back into the bay, trailing a raucous flurry of seagulls in its wake. The main man was bringing home the bacon. Altruistic Adam.

Carl climbed the southern road to Terry's gate, and walked

down to the caravan. A bike stood against a wall. There were fat, stunted cacti lined up inside the window of Terry's caravan. Carl knocked. Not a sound from within. He knocked again, waited. There was no one home.

Carl looked in the window: a few clothes strewn about, plasma screen propped on a bench sofa, dirty plates on the table; pencil sketches pinned everywhere, a bookmarked Arthur Koestler. Overflowing ashtray. Everyday layabout stuff. Just living: the things you have to take care of, sooner or later, no matter what has happened to a sizeable chunk of humanity.

Carl turned away from the window and started back up the track to the main road.

Down at the hippie's house, he saw Terry, waving and shouting. He walked up the path as Carl started down.

'You said to come over any time.'

'No bother,' said Terry. 'I'm down at Hendrik's. Come and have a drop of some truly foul home-brew.'

'You're kidding. What is it?'

They walked down the track.

'Elderflower wine, but it didn't turn out quite right.' Terry smiled. 'It works, but with a few unpleasant side-effects.'

People were introduced, Hendrik de Vries and his Filipino wife, Maganda. Cloudy, tasteless wine was sampled. The bible was smoked.

Up close Carl could see Hendrik's yellow toenails needed cutting, probably with a bolt cutter. The Dutchman sat, hands on belly, like the brass Buddha on his mantelpiece.

He liked the sound of his own voice, that was for sure. Carl had given the guy enough of a chance, but the conversation hadn't improved. Second hearings were all very well, but after two hours on journalism's failure of democracy, the trials of building an orphanage in Thailand, and plant nutrition, enough was enough. Carl wouldn't be popping in to see Hendrik any time soon. Shame about that. Maybe Terry was a bumptious prick as well.

Maganda was good company though. What she was doing with an old goat who must have been at least twenty years older than her, you had to fucking ask yourself. Her and Terry could share a joke and, if he wasn't much mistaken, Carl had seen a knowing smile from Hendrik at that. Prick was probably dreaming up a threesome. There was something dodgy about the guy, with his laid-back bohemian air and self-aggrandising anecdotes. Something not right about the whole thing: sitting there laughing, having a fucking party.

Through a fifth glass of cloudy elderflower rocket fuel and a few spliffs of home-grown, Carl realised that Hendrik was talking to him, directly, about something important. It was hard to focus on the words at first; the logical train of thought was always a station ahead. But then he caught up with the conversation, jumped aboard, with a little help from Terry.

'Hendrik's got issues with the emergency committee.'

Carl nodded, rubbed his face. 'Issues,' he repeated, focusing on Hendrik's face, the glasses and grey goatee. 'Issues with the committee.'

The big Dutchman nodded, sitting up straight with his hands on his knees. 'People are being greedy,' he said.

'What Hendrik and Maganda mean,' said Terry, smiling, 'is, can you have a word with George Cutler about the whole . . . situation? He's chairman of the committee, although how he got that position isn't quite clear if you come to think about it. A little bit cloudy, like this pish, Hendrik.'

Hendrik passed another joint to Terry. 'You'll drink it all the same.' He turned to Carl. 'It is not good when people think I am dishonest.'

'Absolutely,' said Carl, waving away the offer of a puff. 'That's what you said. But can you be more specific, if you can be specific about the . . .' He was getting edgy, and he felt a little nauseous. He forgot what he'd been talking about.

Hendrik cleared his throat. Maganda stopped giggling. 'I will tell you.' He smoothed his grey goatee. 'Yesterday I had a visit from the policeman, Gibbs. We grow lots of nice things in our polytunnels, you may know that.'

Carl tried to concentrate on the man's words. Policeman? Did he say policeman?

'Anyway,' continued Hendrik. 'Gibbs said he had to check that what we gave to the committee was what we produced.'

There was a shift in the air, a change of frequency. Carl didn't know what to say; his thoughts were confused, unnavigable.

Hendrik seemed agitated. 'I am an honest person, Mr Shewan.'

Terry fixed his eyes on the Escher print hanging over the fireplace. 'Come on, Hen, no one's saying you aren't.'

The Dutchman held up his hands. 'Okay.' He tugged his beard again. 'Ninety per cent goes to the committee. We have four goats, hens, tomatoes and lettuce and so on in the polytunnels – we get biofuel for the generators from Adam Cutler – and a few eggs we keep, not many.' He squinted at Carl, then leant forward. 'We have been here for over twenty years, Mr Shewan. A lot of hard work we have put into this place – our home, you know? Now we are under suspicion. This is not the way it should be. Not here. Not now.'

Carl's mouth was dry. He drank some water. 'I really don't know,' was all he could say. 'I'll have to think about it.'

What was the guy talking about? Just stringing words together. A noise coming out of his bearded hole. What did he say he'd think about? Think about thinking about . . .

'You weren't well for a long time, so maybe this is something you don't know about,' said Terry, sitting up straight on the soft, shapeless couch. 'Adam Cutler and his guys have made the food rationing system work in their favour. Food is divided by age, but also by man-hours worked, by activity levels. Your friend designed the system. See, it's Cutler and his crew who do all the work. No one else is getting a look-in. So, seven guys, plus their families and one or two others, are not exactly as hungry as the rest of the village.' He glanced at Hendrik. 'Some of us don't think that's very fair.'

Fair. There was that word again. Where had he heard it before? Was it now, or yesterday? Carl felt dizzy. 'That's right, that's fine,' he said. He stood up unsteadily, trying to breathe. 'I need some fresh air.'

Hendrik laughed, slapping his knees.

Outside, the wind had dropped. Somewhere in the hills a stag bellowed, his cry carrying round the bay. You go for it, big man, thought Carl; you let the world know you mean business because your very fucking essence is bigger and stronger than anything else is. Not even the galaxy, constellated to infinity in the clear night sky, was a match for the living illusion of perfect projected power. Give it big licks, big man, and fill your boots while you can.

He felt better in the fresh air, in the breathless night. Only the glow from the oil-lamps in Hendrik's living room stained the blackness.

Inverlair was across the bay, invisible. There were no streetlights, no warm glowing windows of welcome. Without electricity or cars on the road the place might not even exist, out there, in the darkness. It would never be home. But where else was there? Even when it became safe to leave, where would he go? Howard had said Spain was clear of SCOPE. Fair enough. Spain. Maybe things were okay there. But how would he get across Europe? He'd keep Howard's car, not let anyone cannibalise it here, pick up fuel along the way; he'd take his chances.

Really?

He felt himself grimace in the darkness, the unreality of escape making him shiver. Get a grip.

'You all right?' It was Terry.

'Yeah,' shouted Carl. 'Felt a bit woozy in there. I haven't smoked that much weed in quite a while.' He said no more, conscious that more was expected.

'Hendrik lays it on a bit thick,' said Terry. 'He can be a bit full of himself. If you can't be arsed walking back to the hotel, feel free to crash in the caravan. The couch folds out.'

That was a tough call. Creeping about the hotel like an intruder was great fun; getting hassled by George and Simone was a hoot.

Standing there looking into the night, Carl felt the stirrings of ordinary discontentment.

17

In the morning the wind picked up; Carl could feel Terry's caravan moving, even with a gable-end of brick to protect it. It had rained in the night, drumrolling on the caravan's flat metal roof.

His guts were churning. Dry mouth and pounding head. It was daylight, so he figured it would have to be at least 8 a.m. His watch was in the pocket of his jeans, and his jeans were on the opposite couch, and it was cold.

He pulled the sleeping bag around his ears, groaning, his bladder fit to burst. Well into November and it was freezing. Maybe he'd end up sleeping in his clothes for the duration of the winter. Pity he couldn't hibernate. If he lived in a caravan he might even not bother to wash. At least in Room 7 he could have a wash in the bath, even if the water was cold. That was important to him. Staying clean. His arse wouldn't be clean, though; a bad case of the squits during the night had seen to that. No bog roll either. Old newspaper had done the job instead.

He tried to close his eyes and go back to sleep, but his guts were still rumbling and he badly needed to piss. He shouldn't have told Terry about a SCOPE prototype that was trialled in Africa, driving villagers to murder each other when it went live. It was just more inexplicable butchery on the Dark Continent, with no suspicion falling on helpful development-minded Western telecomms companies.

Carl lay on the couch, gazing without focus at Terry's charcoal sketches of twisted gorse trunks and brooding headlands.

There were noises-off from the bedroom, which was more like a cupboard just big enough for a bed. Terry was up and about, belt buckle jangling, then a yawn. He came out of the bedroom, rubbing sleep from his eyes, tangle of straw-coloured hair sticking up and out and every way.

'How's it going?' he said, his throat dry.

Carl wasn't sure. 'I've felt better.'

'You get the squits?'

'Oh yeah . . .'

Terry smiled, drank some water. 'I thought Hendrik had ironed that problem out, unless maybe he gave you a bottle of the old stuff by mistake.' He sat down on the sofa, moved a pile of clothes aside. 'When you were out of it, when you were ill, there were a few cases of Delhi Belly. Hendrik didn't clean his fermenting gear properly.'

Rain came gusting against the caravan. Terry made sure the windows were closed properly. He tested the soil round his plants, gave a few of them a drink from a three-litre plastic bottle. Carl sat up in his sleeping bag, reached over for his fleece. Maybe Hendrik knew fine well he'd handed over the wrong bottle, containing the stuff that was shat out in the same state as it went in: liquid. You get the sense that he would enjoy that, giving someone the shits, laughing about it the next day.

Terry picked one of the potted cacti off the windowsill. It was squat and sprouted tufts of purple hair. 'Pal of mine was in Mexico and he brought back two of these for me. Peyote. Over a few years two became four. They're hard to grow, so I don't use it very often. Fucking wild though. All that doors-of-perception stuff, surfing the archetypes. You hungry?'

On balance, Carl figured that eating would do him good. He nodded. 'Some muesli and semi-skimmed will do nicely.'

'Only unskimmed cows round here, I'm afraid. How about an omelette with an optional slice of mutton?'

'Even better.'

'Coming right up.'

Terry put his prized peyote plant back on the windowsill and went to a cupboard, took out a camping stove and a Tupperware dish, lit the stove, and scooped some lard out of the dish. 'Alec John gave me this,' said Terry. 'Sheep fat.' He broke three eggs and mixed them in the pan.

'Another day in paradise,' muttered Carl.

From another plastic box, Terry took out four slices of fatty meat.

'What did you do?' said Carl. 'Before the redzone, I mean.'

'You're seeing it,' said Terry. 'I was here about a year – before.' He tore a rubbery cheese slice into pieces, dropped it into the egg, his thin face darkening. 'I was in a bit of trouble in London, took myself off to Glasgow, but the trouble followed me up here. Then I found out my uncle had died and left me his place.' He tried to smile.

'What kind of trouble?'

Terry cleared his throat. 'The wrong sort of chemical habits with the wrong sort of people. Nothing new in that. Anyway, everybody's got to end up somewhere, and we can't all be in the same place, so here I am.'

Breakfast was served.

'Unless you have a pressing engagement we can head down to my uncle's house,' said Terry through a mouthful of meat and egg. 'There's something that might interest you.'

•

Down the lush seaward slope, a two-minute walk along the headland path, stood a solid-looking stone house. Across the bay Adam and the boys were setting off from the boatyard, back to cut more firewood.

From the outside the stone house looked in reasonable

condition; the date 1934 was carved into the stone lintel. Inside, it was more or less unfurnished, with bare floorboards and bare plasterboard walls, watertight apart from a leak in the loft, said Terry. It had two bedrooms. The front room was full of junk, and stacks of black plastic bin bags, each one tightly wrapped with Sellotape, lined the walls. The committee would have taken the clothes and the shoes, but there were books and magazines, knick-knacks, photos, two TVs, a foldaway chess set, and a shitload of other stuff lying around.

'Have a look at these,' said Terry, tearing open one of the black bin bags. He took out a newspaper, handed it to Carl.

He held it reverently in his hand. 'Jesus.'

An old edition, yellow round the edges, dated almost nine years ago. Big pic on the front and HEATWAVE KILLS HUNDREDS along the top. Carl looked at the plastic bundles. He couldn't believe what he held in his hands. He lifted a few more, opened another bundle. The same, going back years.

Turning to page two in one paper he saw his own name under the heading WHITE RUST FUNGUS CONFIRMED IN SPAIN. He read the first paragraph: 'A total ban on all exports from Spain was in place today as the European Emergency Authority confirmed an outbreak of the white rust fungus in wheat fields outside Malaga ...'

'Twenty years' worth of newspapers in here,' said Terry. 'Right up till February of last year, three weeks before my uncle died. You could say he was a bit of a hoarder. Thought you might be interested.'

Terry went upstairs to empty the bucket that had filled with rainwater, leaving Carl to browse the bin-bag archive.

There were plenty of leaks in the pages of these newspapers. Insiders. Sources. Once, years before, the information flowed freely from numerous contacts. But then the stream dried to a trickle, a few drops still coming out. The insiders had too much to lose.

Carl checked the date on the front of one paper: four months before Glasgow became the third city under Civil Contingencies Enforcement. He used to go out then, socialise, go to the theatre, plays at the Citizens. He had a life. They tried to ban that play at the time, fuck knows if he could remember the name. It closed after four nights; didn't tour. Funding was cut. Official threats.

Eric. Lesley.

He leafed through some more issues, opened another bundle, stopping as soon as he saw the masthead and the headline's first word. He knew which issue he was holding; his first big scoop, the flats in the East End built on contaminated land. The same front page was hanging, framed, back in Glasgow on his bedroom wall. It may as well have been on the moon now. He unfolded the old newspaper and spread it out tenderly on the floor.

The date was five years before the privatised insanity of CivCon, when targets were plentiful and you could be sure of hitting one if you pointed your nose in the right direction.

For years this front page had hung in his room and he'd barely noticed it. Now he touched the dried-up, yellowing newsprint with his fingertips.

And then he saw it clearly. His old life was no longer invisible; it was present and alive in his longing for something that he couldn't return to. This was all he had been, right here, in 500 exclusive words, part of an award-winning series. How many articles had he written altogether? How many deserving targets had he harried over the years? His words, or rather the paper they'd been printed on, had become a resource of a different kind now. The paper was more important than the words. In fact, the words served no purpose. Truth was now measured in calories, and his investigations were all closed – spiked on thousands of SCOPE transmitters. Maybe the village would use the paper for something. It could still have a vital function to perform, like wiping arses or as bedding for animals. The committee would decide. Truth was now a full stomach and a warm room: the same as it had been before SCOPE, for many. No wonder people never wanted to know the truth he'd been trying to serve up, in steaming piles, on a plate. They had other things to worry about, like eating and paying the bills.

Carl tossed the old newspaper back onto the pile, the layered strata of his fossil life. It hadn't amounted to much. That was that. End of.

He went outside.

And there was the village, houses strewn along the edge of the northern headland; the viewpoint flagpole; guys on the pier; dark clouds brewing over the Atlantic. Out in the distance.

For the first time in a few weeks, he wished the pneumonia had finished the job.

He went round the side of the house to the shed. With a heavy nudge from his shoulder, Carl opened the door.

There was only one small window and the light was poor. The shed smelled of engine oil and creosote. As his eyes got used to the gloom, Carl could see a workbench along one wall and the guts of an outboard motor in pieces on the dirty concrete floor. Rusty saws hung on nails; a grass strimmer; a stack of old paint pots in one corner; oars, rakes and spades standing in another.

In a dark wooden chest he found literature of a different kind, also yellow with age like the newspapers. Internet printouts: women and girls of all ages and races, with their muscular male jockeys and sex toys. The detail was difficult to make out, so faded were the colours. Carl pushed the pile of loose pages out of the way. At the bottom of the chest was a grubby olive-coloured case of some sort, fastened by brown leather straps. As soon as he grabbed the case, he guessed what might be inside it.

It was a rifle — but only an air rifle. And he couldn't find any pellets. He held it in his hands, cold and heavy, took aim through the window at the boatyard across the bay. It felt good to aim at what he'd love to hit.

Brandishing his ammo-less peashooter he went back outside and back into the house to find Terry.

'You got any pellets for this?'

•

His hangover easing, Carl took the track at the head of the bay up towards the stalker's house. It was set apart from other houses, more in the hills than in the village. The noise of the biofuel generator made his brain hurt.

He knocked on the porch door. There was no answer. Peering through the dusty glass in the porch window, he could see walking-sticks in the corner, each one with a carved horn on the end, along with walking-boots, wellies and jackets. A barometer hung on the wall, and the framed photo of a woman. He knocked again.

No response.

Carl slung the air rifle over his shoulder again and headed back down the path. A dog barked behind him.

'Hello there,' said a voice from round the side of the house. A scruffy Border collie trotted round the corner. 'What can I do for you?' Alec John stopped. 'Oh, it's you.'

Carl unslung the air rifle, walked back up the shell path. The dog came trotting towards him, tail wagging. He took a step back.

'Hi. I found this in Cathal Sullivan's shed. Terry said you might have pellets for it.'

As he got closer to Alec John, Carl could see there was blood on his cheek, and on his forearms, and all over the plastic apron he was wearing.

Alec John took the gun and studied it. 'You won't get much with this popgun. Maybe more rats and crows than Cathal did. It's in good enough condition, though.' He walked around the outside of the house. 'I'm sure I'll have a tin somewhere.'

The stalker disappeared into a low-roofed concrete outbuilding. In the middle of the straw-covered floor, on a metal bench, the headless, skinless carcass of what Carl assumed to be a deer was splayed. Chains and hooks hung from a shiny metal runner that curved along the underside of ceiling beams and into a steel-lined cooler; saws and cleavers and knives glinted in the dangling strip light.

Carl tried not to gape at the remains. Pelt and waxy dermis in a pile. Hooves and head, minus the antlers, and a huge rubbery tongue lolling from a blood-crusted mouth. The smell of flesh.

Jess waddled in and stood, panting, near Carl. Alec John opened a few drawers and cupboards until he found three small round tins. He shook them. 'Here we are,' he said, prising the lids off. 'They're still pretty full.' He put the tins down on the trestle table next to the skinless, headless deer. 'Help yourself.'

'Thanks,' said Carl, eyeing the inside of the animal's ribcage. 'Is that an ordinary saw you're using?'

Alec John went back to work on the deer's hind-leg, sawblade rasping through the femur. 'Aye. A joiner's.' He smiled. 'Once upon a time, if we knew the hygiene inspectors were coming we would get a proper butcher's saw out for them to see – they were sticklers for that – but once they left we'd get this out.' He paused, the saw still at work. 'You look much better than the first time I saw you, up close.'

Carl couldn't meet the man's eye. 'Yeah,' he said. 'Getting there.' He picked up the tins of air-rifle pellets. 'Thanks for these.'

The stalker jagged a hook into the carcass, hoisted it up by a chain pulley, and pushed it along the ceiling runner and into the cooler. He shut the heavy metal door with a thud. 'You're welcome.'

Alec John watched Carl walk back down the track. After wrapping cuts of meat in old newspaper, the stalker put the parcels into big plastic boxes and loaded them into the trailer of his six-wheeled argocat.

He went back round to the front of his house, dog trotting at his heels, and opened the front door.

As always, his wife's smiling face met him in the porch – the framed photo an icon of her enduring presence.

18

'What the hell's he doing with that gun?'

George was standing at the kitchen window, watching Carl fire pellets at old tin cans arranged along the fence posts.

'Terry Sullivan gave it to him,' said Simone. She was gutting a pollock in the sink, slitting the soft white belly, pulling out the guts. Tail next, then the head, spine grating under the blade.

'Well,' said George. 'Trust that guy to have a gun.'

Father and daughter stood watching.

In total, Carl had about 300 pellets. After a few pot shots – without hitting a target – Carl did a quick calculation. How many pellets would he have to fire before he became reasonably proficient? How many would fly wide of their mark and be lost in the grass?

He lowered the gun and studied the line of five tins he'd placed on top of five fence posts. Perhaps he should rethink his target practice. If only there was some way to gather the pellets up once he'd fired them, so that he could re-use them. He looked around the garden for a solution and noticed Isaac sitting on the back step.

'Can I have a shot?' the boy asked.

'Maybe,' replied Carl. 'But I've got to rig something up first.'

Isaac wrinkled his nose. 'When can I have a shot?'

Carl ignored the boy and sized up two rowan trees at the bottom of the soggy garden. They were just the right distance apart. He went to the shed, Isaac on his heels, and dug out an old bed-sheet covered in crusted splashes of paint. He also found a length of rope and some string.

He rigged up his target range and pellet catcher. The tin cans were now suspended by string from the rope he'd tied to both rowan trees. Behind the line of dangling cans was the old bedsheet, staked into the ground so it wouldn't blow about in the wind. A sheet of plastic, to catch the falling pellets, was staked out on the ground with old tent pegs. His theory was ready to test.

He raised the rifle and fired. There was no satisfying *ping* of projectile on metal. But, he saw the pellet hit the sheet and, on inspection, he noticed there was a spent slug, intact, beneath the line of cans.

Bingo.

Pleased with himself, Carl loosed off a few pellets, then turned to offer Isaac a shot. But there was no sign of the boy.

He looked back at the house, saw Simone and George at the kitchen window, probably wondering what the hell he was doing shooting at tin cans in the garden. Should've asked about his little pellet-catching set-up before raiding the shed.

Simone had been playing her flute earlier, something by Debussy, Aeolian analgesic that must be resisted. Life has to be rougher than that.

He fired another pellet. There's always some fucking committee, or council or cabinet or conclave, he thought, enforcing and reinforcing their own particular worldview. People in authority were always giving you some spiel or other to justify their own positions. Whether it was shaman communing with ancestors or government ministers rhapsodising about fantasy futures, there was always a message to sell.

Ping.

A dangling can jerked on the line.

About fucking time.

'About bloody time,' muttered George at the kitchen window.

Isaac was sitting on the floor, wearing his visor and gloves, his little body jerking around as he played a game. 'Mum, is Carl going to be my new daddy?'

George rolled his eyes at his daughter.

'No, darling,' said Simone, 'he isn't.'

Isaac took off the visor and considered, with relentless logic, his next line of enquiry. Before he could ask his next question, Simone hopped directly to what she knew was the next phase of the conversation.

'Dad's in a place called Bristol, Isaac. You know that. It's very far away. I told you that before. And he's probably dead. I told you that as well. But we're all okay here.'

The brutal facts needed confirming, and reaffirming; repeating them was making the brutal facts stick in the boy's memory. It was easy for her to rattle off the salient points of the situation, even the one that involved her mother. If she just repeated the same phrases to Isaac as soon as he asked her a question, Simone could say the words like a mantra, and not have to think about their meaning. And that was no bad thing.

Soon, she'd have to tell Isaac something new, that he was going to have a little brother or sister.

•

In Room 7, Carl wondered how to disassemble the air rifle. Isn't that what people did, take guns apart to clean and oil them? Kneeling on the floor, he had the parts spread out on old newspaper. He was going to look after it.

At the head of the bay, beneath the bridge, there were rats in the rock embankment, so George had said. He'd also mentioned that he might be able to persuade Adam to take Carl back on the work crew. Carl said he'd think about it.

Well, he'd thought about it: Adam could shove his offer.

There was something satisfying about the feel of the metal and wood in Carl's hand; the snug fit of the rifle stock against his shoulder. And the *ping* of the cans! That made him feel good. Taking aim. Having an effect. When you don't have any real power, even over yourself, you'll take whatever fetishised substitute comes to hand. With a screwdriver and pair of pliers he undid the rifle's mid-point hinge and exposed the spring piston inside. He poked it with the screwdriver.

In a heartbeat, the spring shot out of the stock, whizzed past Carl's face, and cracked off the plaster wall behind him so hard that it also bounced up and hit the ceiling before landing on the bed. Instinctively, Carl dropped the gun and jumped towards the door. He stood for a second, then went to look at the spring, now three times as long as it had been when compressed inside the barrel. An inch-deep hole had been gouged out of the plaster where the spring had hit the wall. Carl picked the spring up, the oily metal spiral flexing in his hand. Better a hole in the wall than his skull.

He looked at the space in the rifle stock from where the spring had rocketed, tried to slide it back in, and realised it wasn't going to fit. There was probably a special tool to do that; a tool he didn't have.

He thought of Simone. So much for the tool he did have.

When would her bump start to show? Everyone else would know the truth when it did. Carl knew that she had seen him looking. She knew the pregnancy, or at least the size of her stomach, was making an impression on him. The information had registered. But what Carl was doing with that awareness he himself hardly knew. The baby was growing inside him as well. It might have been taking all Simone's nutrients and energy, but it was stealing his fucking headspace, the dark shadow of it moving across the sun, blocking out everything else that he needed to think about. In a few months' time the eclipse would reach totality, and there would be no more light.

Getting back up to the broch appealed again, briefly. But it was nonsense, trying to rebuild it. It was insane.

He put the rifle parts back in their soft leather case. Alec John might know how to put the spring into the barrel.

•

There had been something unpleasant in Room 14. New sheets couldn't hide it; illness and the scent of death haunted the room, and he was glad to be out of it. He washed himself in the bathroom, in a few inches of lukewarm water.

At the top of the stairs, a moment passed before he registered exactly what Isaac was doing. The boy was in one of the vacant bedrooms, number 4, boring a hole in the plaster wall with a screwdriver. Carl watched for a spell as Isaac removed a handful of plaster chalk, put it in a cup, and went off to the bathroom, where he added a splash of water to the cup from the bath tap. With a teaspoon Isaac stirred the mixture, looking very pleased with his morning's work.

Carl coughed. For a split second a nervous smile made Isaac cute: he'd been discovered, and it was time to turn on the charm.

'What're you doing?' said Carl, coming over and taking the cup out of the boy's hand. 'What d'you think your mum will say to that, eh?'

With a fair degree of venom, Isaac kicked Carl sharply in the shin and ran for the door. Carl dropped the cup of sticky plaster mix and it smashed on the tiled bathroom floor.

'Fucker,' he growled, clutching his shin.

Isaac bolted from the room, screaming for his mum. There were footsteps drumming up the stairs in response to the commotion.

'What the hell is going on?' Simone shouted from the corridor.

Carl opened his mouth to bellow the truth, then paused. 'I just dropped a cup of water,' he shouted back, his shin stinging. For once, the wee bugger had been wearing his shoes, worse luck. Carl stood blocking the doorway. He smiled at Simone.

'Sorry. I didn't know Isaac was up here and he gave me a bit of a start. I dropped the cup on the floor.'

Isaac was hiding behind his mother.

'Sorry about that, wee man,' said Carl. 'Didn't mean to give you a fright.' He smiled again at Simone. 'And sorry for swearing, eh? Shouldn't use that kind of language around a wee kid.'

'I'm not wee,' said Isaac, peeping round his mother's thigh.

'Of course you're not, darling,' she soothed.

'I'm not wee,' the boy repeated, eyeing Carl.

Carl shrugged, still standing in the doorway. 'Yeah, okay. You're not wee.'

Simone nodded, none too convinced by the explanation of what had happened. She looked at Isaac, then back at Carl. 'Pavel's coming round to play in a while,' she said to her son. 'Come on.'

'Oh,' said Carl. 'Don't bother cooking any food for me tonight, I'm going over to Terry's.'

For a second, Simone allowed her face to fall, then pinned it back into a position of fixed blankness. 'Thanks for telling me,' she said, shooing Isaac downstairs. 'You're a very polite and thoughtful man, I'm sure.'

Isaac was a cute kid – Carl could see that. He had all the right attributes for cuteness, which he used to good effect: cherubic smile, big brown eyes, tousled mop of sandy hair. But when he didn't get his own way, the kid could also be a temperamental little shit. Angel and devil. Or maybe Carl couldn't see the good, just the bad. People never really pay much attention to a kid that's sitting nicely or playing quietly.

George, as granddad, did his best to jolly the boy along, but there were limits to the guy's patience. Sometimes his temper would go and he would just snap, usually over something trivial. At other times George could tolerate the worst tantrums in the kid. The man was doing his best to deal with his own stuff, and he had bad days when he had no patience. It must make it easier for George, having his daughter and grandson to fill the void.

He set off for Terry's.

It was all fucked up. Right to the very edge of the redzone was 2.26 miles. Maybe he could live in a tent, high in the hills where no one except Alec John ever went. He could live there until the nearest SCOPE mast failed. That's what he would do. Then, when the masts started to stop working he would . . . What?

Walk another ten or twenty miles until he came to a dead village? There was bound to be another Inverlair out there, another prison shelter. There would be lots of empty houses, for sure. Desiccated corpses in their beds or slumped at the kitchen table. He could make his way south – a wanderer in the silence, following the masts as they packed in, until he got to the Channel; then he'd find a boat, or a magic fucking carpet to take him to the land of milk and honey.

For the first time since before his illness, he'd walked around the bay, and through the village, entirely by road. When he reached Terry's, and without really knowing why, Carl blurted out the truth about Simone.

'Christ, you didn't hang about there.'

Carl shook his head. 'It wasn't like that. It was strange. My third night here and she came up to ask if I wanted anything to eat, and it just happened.' He sniffed. 'We just wanted to hold each other, I suppose, then . . .' He shrugged. 'It sounds stupid . . . but it didn't feel like sex – real sex, I mean. Not with a spraysuit – not remote, but connected.'

Terry grinned.

'Fuck off,' muttered Carl.

A plastic Coke bottle was produced. Even in the dim light of the oil lamp Carl could see that it did not contain Coke. Terry poured two mugs of Hendrik and Maganda's cloudy home-brew.

'Actually, it doesn't sound stupid,' he said. 'I swam out to the buoy at Heron Point the day after SCOPE happened, after I'd run into the redzone as far as I could. Nose was streaming blood, and I just ran down to the water, stripped off, and dived straight in off the rocks.'

He adjusted the flame of the oil lamp. 'So what are you going do about Simone?' He flashed an edgy grin. 'You could always run away.' He coughed and started laughing; took another draw of his spliff and passed it over. 'God knows when I'll get my next shag.' Before the evening progressed any further, Terry thought it a good idea to check what he had for breakfast the next day. If the cupboard was bare he could cadge an couple of eggs off Maganda, but he saw there was some mackerel left and the bag of peanuts he'd found earlier. That would be enough. He could at least satisfy that appetite.

19

'It's funny, but you still expect to offer someone a cup of tea when they call on you,' said Alec John sheepishly.

Carl shrugged. 'It would be nice, I suppose.'

'Yes,' said Alec John. 'I gave the last teabag to Maganda yesterday to put on her veg; I must have squeezed a dozen cups out of it.'

Of course: Alec John was one of the lucky few, an essential worker.

'How many teabags do the committee give you?'

'Three a week. I think they're getting pretty low on supplies now.' He smiled at Carl. 'I've always been fond of a brew.' He lifted his cap and smoothed his greying hair back. 'I have to admit that I do miss it when I don't have it.'

Carl stiffened. 'If that's all you miss then you're doing well.'

Alec John went through to the kitchen. He'd witnessed too many traumatic scenes over the last few months, and now he knew when to stay silent. He rummaged in a cupboard, searching for a distraction.

While Alec John was through in the kitchen, Carl looked around the small low-ceilinged living room. The place was dark, with only a small window facing the bay. On the deep windowsill there was an old ice-cream carton, half full of loose change. A tea towel depicting Morecambe Bay had been draped neatly across one end of a drop-leaf table. Carl guessed that Alec John sat there to eat, alone at the window, looking out over the bay. Framed photos, some of them black-and-white, hung on the wall, which looked as if it could use a lick of paint. Above the fireplace a wooden mantel clock sat, its hands frozen behind dirty glass at twenty past two. Carl leant closer, but heard no ticking within. More photos next to it. Among the clutter on the dark wooden sideboard there was a toy car, a metallic blue Mercedes, still in its box.

'You don't strike me as a fan of toy cars,' Carl called through to the kitchen.

'It's a bit of a relic, that,' Alec John said, abandoning his search for an early lunch. 'For my fiftieth birthday someone asked me what my favourite car was. It was Allan Robertson's son, he left Inverlair to . . .' Alec John paused. 'Anyway, he turned up at the door on my birthday and said come outside and see your new Merc.' He laughed. 'And there it was sitting on top of a fence post.'

Alec John turned a log over in the open fire. Warmth flooded into the room as the wood's red-hot underside was exposed.

'Terry said you might want me to help you with something.'

'Well,' said Alec John, 'you've been using his uncle's old air rifle, so I thought you might want to spend a day on the hill, see how you are with the real thing.'

'What – shooting? Shooting animals?'

There was a glint in the stalker's eye. 'No, clouds – for the sheer hell of it.'

'Oh,' said Carl, abashed. 'Right.'

Alec John grunted, left the room. 'Come or don't come. It's up to you.'

'But I've never fired a proper gun. Never even held one.'

The stalker came back with a few gutted mackerel in a plastic bag. He put a blackened frying pan on top of the stove. 'You can learn. There's more to being a keeper than just firing a gun – a lot more, especially now that every animal matters to us. But that's nothing you need worry about for now.'

'Listen,' said Carl. 'I don't suppose you know how to get a spring piston back into an air rifle. It came out yesterday.'

'Aye, there's a tool for it, but I don't have one. I can make something that does the job, though. Did you take the spring out?'

Carl nodded.

Alec John narrowed his eyes. 'What did you use?'

'A screwdriver.'

'You're lucky you never lost an eye.'

Carl nodded. 'Bloody thing tore a lump out of the wall.'

Alec John uncorked a wine bottle and poured oil into the frying pan. 'Where would we be without Adam Cutler?' he said as the oil spat. 'Our Lord and Protector. Do you want some mackerel?'

Carl laughed. 'You're not his biggest fan then.'

A grimace was the answer. 'Always been a bit full of himself,' said Alec John. 'Thinks he's lord of the manor. Tried to suck up to the Arabs, whenever they flew in.'

'Arabs?'

'The estate owners, from Kuwait.'

'Did they like to shoot?'

'Oh yes,' said Alec John, turning the sizzling fillets. 'But they didn't have the patience to stalk for long or do a spot of fishing. They got fed up quickly. So it was five minutes in the chopper up onto the hill, half an hour to kill the beast, then down to the big house. It's no big deal to shoot a red deer when you've shot elephants and tigers.'

From a cupboard, Alec John took out a small yellow block of waxy polycarb and cut it in two. 'The committee let me keep this.' One wedge he placed on Carl's plate, the other on his own, along with some cottage cheese from an old margarine tub and the fish from the frying pan. 'Wasn't that kind of them?'

Carl agreed. 'Generous to a fault.' He cut a slice of polycarb. It was bland and rubbery in his mouth. And there was something about it he didn't trust. It was the last of the old man's supply. But it was carbohydrate.

As he ate, Carl noticed a framed photo of a young woman,

long-haired and laughing. An obvious question occurred to him which, in his former universe, he would have come right out and asked. But this time his curiosity, the habitual probing, slipped out of gear and into neutral. There was no article here. No need to probe. There was very obviously no Mrs Stoddart around the house, and there could be any number of reasons for that. There was no need to find out the answer right now, so he left the question unasked. They spoke about Glasgow and white rust. And about Howard and SCOPE.

Finishing his food, Alec John wiped his mouth and laid knife and fork neatly together on the empty plate. It had been difficult for them not to gulp the food down.

'I've got to go to the boatyard for more biodiesel, and to see if they've fixed the argocat.'

Carl grunted, finished his own food, felt warmth spreading in his limbs. 'What time do you want me to turn up tomorrow?'

'If the weather's half decent, about nine. We're well into November now so it'll be getting dark mid-afternoon, though we can't go that far into the hills any more.' He took the dirty plates through to the kitchen and plopped them in the basin. 'Casper said he'd have the argocat fixed by today.'

They left the house and walked down the track together towards the main road. Carl squinted at the pitched corrugated roof of a stone shed, surrounded by nettles and bramble bushes, that stood at the bottom of the track.

'Have a guess how old the roof is.'

Carl shook his head. 'Dunno – thirty, forty years?'

'My grandfather put it on, not long after the First World War. He got the corrugated iron second-hand from Glasgow.'

Carl eyed Alec John. 'Is that what you used to tell the tourists?'

'If they asked me, yes.'

'And it's really that old?'

'It is.'

'It looks in a bad way.'

'Well,' said Alec John. 'Round the edges maybe, but it's dry enough inside.'

'You never thought of putting new iron on?'

'No. Why?'

Carl shrugged. 'I don't know. Some people might say it doesn't look good.'

'And who was going to see it?'

Carl raised his eyebrows. 'The tourists?'

They turned down into the gorse and alder-lined lane towards the main road. 'If it was a shiny, new roof,' said Alec John, 'do you think the tourists would have stopped to take a photo of it?'

They reached the bottom of the lane.

'I'm going to see Terry,' said Carl.

'No bother,' said Alec John. 'See you tomorrow. Nine o'clock, or thereabouts.'

•

It was warm inside the caravan: the tiny solid-fuel stove didn't have to work too hard to heat the space, despite the chill. Using a steel ruler, Terry ripped out another page of Leviticus, rolled some leaf and a sprinkle of bud, glue-sticked dabbed along the edge, and it was ready to spark. 'D'you fancy being a ghillie, then? The hours are long and, at six extra spuds a week, the pay leaves a lot to be desired.'

Carl was scrolling through the comedy section of Terry's film files, thousands of them on the palmpod. He accepted a puff from the joint. 'He invited me out tomorrow. Didn't say anything about being a ghillie, though.'

Terry frowned. 'No? That's strange. I thought he would've.'

'Why?'

'Well . . .' He looked at Carl. 'He didn't tell you?'

'Tell me what?'

147

Terry flexed the steel ruler he held in his hands. 'He's got emphysema. The nanomeds were keeping it in check, but Dr Morgan says there are none left.'

'Jesus,' said Carl. 'He didn't say a word.'

'Without treatment, he'll find it harder and harder to breathe,' said Terry. 'Eventually, he won't be able to walk twenty feet, never mind up in the hills. The old guy always sidles in at an angle to things. He'll want to see what you're like before asking you outright.'

'Fuck,' said Carl, stunned. 'I had no idea.'

They were silent for a while.

Carl considered what Alec John had said and, more importantly, why the guy had made his offer in the first place. What was going on here? What was in the stalker's mind? Maybe Terry was wrong, and there was no secret trial period that might lead to a permanent position. Maybe it was all a mistake.

Carl wasn't sure he even liked the idea; it sounded like another random event over which he had no influence. He'd endured enough of those to last a lifetime.

'I don't know the first thing about being a gamekeeper,' Carl said. He squinted at Terry. 'There must be other guys here. Better candidates for the job.'

Terry shrugged, relighting his joint with a taper from the stove. 'Maybe so. But you're the one he asked.'

What to feel? Confusion, anxiety? But there was pride too. It wasn't the easiest combination of emotions for Carl to deal with. He stood up. He sat down again.

There was a knock at the door, voices and laughter outside.

'Come in.'

The door opened and a teenage girl popped her head round. 'Hi,' she giggled. 'Sorry to disturb the mood.'

Terry sat up. 'I can't possibly imagine what you lot are after,' he said. 'You guys finished that half ounce already?'

'No way was that half an ounce,' protested the girl. 'Graham's got a set of scales.'

'Has he now.'

She nodded slyly. 'Uh-uh.'

Terry opened a drawer where some cannabis bud was drying. He took out a thumb-sized section of stalk and threw it to the girl. She was pretty, with short black hair and dark eyes, wearing a ragged denim jacket.

'I'm surprised you lot didn't float across the bay to get here.'

The girl smiled. 'Thanks.' She put her hands in her jacket pockets and took out an egg from each. 'Don't say we're not good to you.'

'I'd never say that,' said Terry, accepting the eggs. 'Cheers.'

The girl rejoined her mates, and the group shouted and goofed their way back up the track to the main road. Terry shut the door, held the handle for a second. If Carl hadn't been so focused on Alec John Stoddart, he might have picked up the electric shift in the air.

'You think you'll make a go of things with Simone?' Terry said, handling the eggs he had just been given.

Carl snorted. 'You're kidding, right?'

'You know,' said Terry, 'I tried it on with her, just after I moved up.'

'With Simone?'

Terry nodded. 'Yeah. Tried – and failed.'

'She blow you out?'

'Completely. Reckon she thought I was bit of a Jack the Lad. That's the thing with some places: you get labelled, and you soon run out of options because of it.' He sighed. 'Unless you're prepared to settle down with anybody who's just as needy and desperate as you are.'

Carl pursed his lips. Where was this going?

Terry considered the two eggs the girl had given him. He set them down gently in a bowl. 'You don't have many options, Carl. That's for sure. And Simone's a nice person, smart – usually. Maybe you don't see much of that, but it's there. She's a looker as well.'

Carl shook his head, incredulous. 'I'm sure she's all of that, but ...'

'People are clinging on to each other,' insisted Terry. He picked up one of the eggs again. 'Everything's changed.' He was speaking almost to himself now. 'You've got to take what you can – know what I mean?'

Unsure of what Terry meant, Carl agreed, though, unlike the first time, this time he felt the electric shift in the air, the misalignment of personal signals. If only he'd been aware enough to realise that the tension wasn't focused on him.

Terry put the cracked egg he was holding down on the worktop and, picking up a tea towel, discreetly wiped the slime from his fingers.

August

20

The meeting didn't so much end at an appointed time as dissolve, a crowd of a hundred or so evaporating over the course of an hour, dwindling to a dozen stifled souls. Onlookers, really. There was nothing to discuss. There was no gradual adaptation, no consultation. People could only absorb what they were being told. Then the last dregs wandered away, confused, into the summer haze that warmed the bay. Necessary business had been conducted in near silence, with Howard Brindley in the chair, the guise of formal proceedings ensuring a hushed acceptance. Six days had passed, and the delta field was still impenetrable.

After leaving the meeting, Carl made his way down to the pier. It was a beautiful still evening. In another time he would have watched, in awe, the bright horizon of shifting silver, and the sunset bloody on rags of high cloud. He might have relaxed, at another time. How long ago was that?

From the end of the pier he looked back down the length of the village towards the head of the bay, at the people drifting home in silence from the meeting. Nothing existed around him. Everything appeared to recede into the distance – even what was close at hand. It wasn't a dream after all. It was here and now, and he was in the middle of it. It was real, zooming in and out of focus, sharp and raw and then diffuse, dreamlike. Is that what shock does? Is that how it works?

He looked around, amazed at what he saw.

Ropes and prawn creels and piles of rain-bleached netting. They looked real. Apparently, that was the case. They seemed to retain an everyday purpose. That was how the world worked: it was composed of little details, like roads and cities and living people.

Carl stood with his mouth open, but no sound came out. Brindley's words from the meeting were buzzing in his head. One moment he was able to understand what had happened – he could grasp it. Then he found it so ridiculous he felt like laughing.

During the meeting, Howard had seemed in control, dispassionate. He'd organised it all, compartmentalised his numb flock to ensure their survival; had assumed the worst – that the masts would prove as durable as their manufacturer had claimed and the signal would last two to five years. Maybe this time the marketing hype would be accurate.

Two joiners, two bricklayers, four mechanics, an electrician, foresters, an architect, those with livestock, a doctor, gamekeeper, a retired district nurse, fishermen, gardeners. In all, thirty-eight names were read out during the meeting. Those with essential skills were identified, as were the very young and the very old and those too ill to be of much use. George Cutler's job, as emergency committee chairman, was to record all the names and their allocated tasks; a technician who could keep the water treatment works operating; guys who could hotwire the forestry machines. Now that the electricity was off, they'd need to use the solar freezers in the community centre.

The name Carl Shewan had not been read out.

He made his way back to the hotel from the pier, just the gulls wheeling in the air and a dog trotting along the shorefront. Standing in the silent lobby, he thought he heard a cry from the hotel annexe, a woman sobbing. Maybe the waitress, Simone.

Her body.

Her smell.

His semen on the floor, where she'd walked away. No underwear. A dream of oblivion within a real nightmare.

In Room 14, he counted back to the exact time when the delta field sprang into existence, and adjusted the timer on his palmpod accordingly. The on-screen seconds counted. Six days, eleven hours and seventeen minutes.

•

Look at her photo.

Don't look at her photo.

There was the committee to think about, George reminded himself through the tears. Planning and organising to attend to. He looked at his wife's photo, properly, for the first time in years. Depending on where she'd been when this SCOPE system was switched on, she could well be dead by now. If she'd been sitting on her sister's couch sipping tea, then she might still be alive. How could she be dead? How? She'd been forced to sleep by these delta waves. It caught him again, all thought of his official responsibilities rendered nonsensical. Worse: obscene. George cried again, sobbing quietly into his hand, a strangled high-pitched sound that he forced back down into his throat. Confronted with words like hypothalamus, sinusoidal and entrainment, he felt impotent.

Brindley and that journalist from Glasgow, they'd known about SCOPE for a long time, especially Brindley – he knew what the risks were; the thing about the crystal filters and magnetic resonance. He'd even worked on it, the bastard. George dried his eyes with a hankie, blew his nose, and washed his face.

Maybe Brindley had done all he could to stop it. Maybe the same went for Shewan. And maybe the pair of them should be strung up from the nearest lamppost.

Look at the photo. Listen to her advice, her instruction. Right, love, I'll get on it straight away.

Downstairs, Simone had also just dried her eyes, blown her nose, and was splashing her face in the kitchen sink. Isaac was playing outside, in the sandpit, with Pavel.

'You okay?' said George.

Simone's voice was thick and uncertain. 'Fine.' She grabbed two steaming cups of black coffee and headed outside. George watched Simone and Fiona, sitting side by side on the bench, their kids building their worlds in the sandpit. It was normal. Nothing out of the ordinary. Why pretend at being normal? Because if you believe it for long enough then that's how everything will turn out. That's how to defeat pain and grief – exorcise them with the spell of the ordinary.

George grabbed the folder containing the electoral roll, and set off for the community centre. There was nothing ordinary about this situation. But he was the chairman. That was his role. He had to concentrate on whatever it was he needed to do.

•

Howard Brindley studied the PowerPoint maps projected on to the wall. The emergency committee, he knew, were looking for answers; guidance. First, he outlined a computerised food rationing system, then he set out the geographical context – the main hubs of Berlin, Paris and London marked in blue; SCOPE's rural network of masts in red – down to the Scottish scale.

'This is not an exhaustive map of SCOPE transmitters,' he said. 'It was based mainly on our company's register, and we were only subcontractors for the northern region. I managed to get some info from the east, from a contact I had there. Even in Scotland we didn't have the whole sector. And there are thousands of smaller nodes in towns and cities, in lampposts, on street corners, made by other firms.' He turned back to the map. Nobody was really taking in anything he said. The copper was doing his best to pay attention, but George and Councillor Matheson and that retired architect, whatever his name was, were zombies. 'As I was saying,' said Howard, his voice dropping. 'There will be other notspots, but where exactly I can't say.'

He paused. 'I think mapping the extent of our own notspot would be useful. The delta waveform fluctuates, so to have an average of several sweeps would be needed.' He looked around. 'And . . . it's good that the community centre has photovoltaic panels on the roof. That's . . . good too.'

'You said sweeps?' said Gibbs.

Howard took a mobile out of his pocket. 'Yes, this will plot the field intensity, a reading every fifty metres or so will do it. Once I've done, say, four sweeps around the bay, I'll feed the readings into the palmpod to give us a map of our safe zone.'

George clenched, unclenched his fists. 'Safe,' he repeated, looking around as if he didn't know where he was. Who was safe?

'Yes,' answered Howard. 'Someone might get too close to the field. If there are fluctuations then it could be dangerous. It would also be useful to know exactly how big a notspot we're in, and what that means for our resources, living space, and so forth. We can't waste time waiting for the masts to fail. I imagine winters can be pretty harsh up here.'

This moment had occurred to Howard, again and again, over the last few months. Here he was, telling shell-shocked people about SCOPE and how to organise for survival. It wasn't a concept any more. He was here, and the thing he'd dreaded had happened. And now he found that he couldn't just get on with it. He'd thought about this so often that it had become polished, like a lecture he could just rattle through. But instead of attentive students, there were broken people in front of him. His cleverness hadn't taken that into account.

If he'd acted sooner, a lot sooner, then none of this would have been necessary.

He brought the meeting to end, saying that was enough for today, and trudged back to Room 22.

•

The tide was out, exposing mudflats at the head of the bay. Carl crunched along the shingle beach, past a line of small boats that had been dragged above the high-water mark. Paint peeled and flaked from two of them, exposing old rotting wood. The boats looked neglected, forgotten about. He stood, looking up at a big house, half hidden by trees, patio doors and a veranda facing the bay. He heard footsteps crunching on the shingle.

'Hi,' said Howard softly.

Carl barely acknowledged the greeting. He patted one of the boats on the gunwale. It felt solid enough, but blue paint flaked off in brittle shards as he touched the wood. He rubbed the paint to dust between his hands.

'Listen,' said Brindley. 'I've been speaking to the committee, but I don't know what information they've actually absorbed and what's going over their heads.'

Out on the mudflats Carl spotted what looked like an old bicycle, its rusted frame swathed in seaweed. The sea was burying it, making the bike part of itself. He watched wading birds, long-legged and slender-billed, probing the edge of the tide. He tried to focus on what Howard was saying.

'Anyway,' continued Howard, 'I told them it would be a good idea if we plotted the delta field. You can help me, if you want. First of all, though, I reckon we should take a boat and see how far we can get.'

Carl roused himself, responding to the idea behind the words. He stood straight, attentive now. 'Of course – a boat.' He smiled. 'A boat. Why didn't I think of that?'

Howard shook his head. 'There are coastal masts north and south of here, and masts on the islands you can see on the horizon. I wouldn't bet on a clear passage out of here.'

'But it's a possibility, right?'

'Yes, it's possible, though where we can go I don't know.'

'Somewhere. Anywhere.'

'We *are* somewhere.'

'Somewhere else,' insisted Carl, his voice rising. 'Taking a boat is a great idea.'

Brindley pursed his lips. 'OK, I've put the idea to the committee, and George Cutler said his son Adam would take me out in his fishing boat. It's a bit rough today, I was told. Maybe tomorrow, if the wind drops.'

'Can I come with you?'

'Well,' said Brindley, 'if there are fluctuations in the delta field – sizeable ones – then being in a boat might not be the safest place. There may be refraction effects because of the tide. We might not be able to turn the boat round in time.'

Carl shook his head.

'I'll take that chance.' He was staring at Brindley, face to face. 'Take me with you.'

Brindley nodded.

Carl pulled a single cigarette from his pocket. It was bent and crumpled. He looked at it for a second. 'Do you have a light?'

Howard shook his head grimly. Carl looked at the cigarette again and put it back in his jacket pocket.

'You know,' said Howard, 'maybe here is as good a place as any to pitch up. Inverlair is one of the biggest notspots, that's why I came here.'

'Yeah, well,' said Carl, picking at the flakes of paint. 'I came here because of you. And, if it's all the same to you, I'd like to get the fuck out of here as soon as possible.'

•

It was after 11 p.m. and still daylight, the southern headland of Inverlair black against the glowing west. Carl could still see his hand in front of his face, the path up from the shore and the forms of the houses. There were stars in the darker east, a gentle salty breeze and each seabird so clear in the calling as their cries pierced the quiet. The hours and days were mounting up, and the rest of the world was saying goodbye. For all Carl cared, Adam Cutler's fishing boat could drop him over the side where he belonged, down among the devouring shoals. Better the CivCon sharks than here, where there was no normal terror.

21

From an upstairs window Isaac watched his uncle's fishing boat come back into the bay. He ran down to the kitchen to pass on the news. 'Uncle Adam is back,' he said, pulling a disgusted face. 'With more fish.'

George was hunched over the sink, hands covering his face. He was shaking.

'Grandpa?'

Without turning round George straightened up, ran his hands under the tap. 'I dropped something.'

'What did you drop?'

George splashed his face with water. 'Never mind. It's fine.'

Isaac came over. 'Is it cut?'

'No.'

'Let me see?'

'It's fine,' he barked, quickly drying his hands and face. He threw the dish towel aside.

Before the boy's shock became tears, George whisked him out into the lobby, the mask of tolerance restored.

Down at the pier, a group of people had gathered. George gripped his grandson's hand, figured that if the boat was back so soon it must be bad news. The *Aurora* ploughed towards them, throttle easing back and into reverse as it neared the pier.

The expressions of those onboard told the story. Engines idling, the boat came to a stop, backwash lapping against the pier's barnacle-encrusted legs.

'Just over three miles,' shouted Howard. 'We went as far south as we dared and worked our way west and north.'

George sagged, letting go of his grandson's hand. His voice cracked. 'Could you see any other boats?'

Howard shook his head. 'Nothing.'

The sea looked inviting to George as the *Aurora* was tied up alongside. The urge to jump off the pier took hold.

He felt a little hand slip into his, squeezing. The pressure roused him.

'Well, we know what we have to do,' George found himself saying. He spoke loud enough for everyone to hear. 'We sink or swim. That's the choice. We were told it a few days ago, now we're hearing it again – that's all. We're going to get through this – all of us – together. We stick with the plan that Mr Brindley told us about at the meeting. Tomorrow we'll start organising jobs and work crews.'

Fair enough, that kind of pep talk. But what George really wanted to do was jump into the boat and race it out to sea as fast as he could, regardless of the consequences and blind to the reason for doing so. Despite that, his words had come out in a firm and clear voice. He wondered how that had happened.

George walked away, gripping his grandson's hand a little too tightly. As he climbed the rhododendron-lined path, he tried to remember when, exactly, the hotel stopped being a thriving business and became a huge empty building that ate his money. The process had been gradual. Like a heaving late-night party, people had slipped away, imperceptibly, until there were only a few stragglers left to face the dawn.

Inverlair Hotel had gone way beyond being a drain on his resources, he thought. It had become a mausoleum, and he was the caretaker.

•

Carl and Howard started their first sweep of the redzone at the roadblock, on the north road out of Inverlair.

'We'll head down towards the sea first of all,' said Howard. He nodded inland, to the brooding massif of Ben Bronach. 'Then we'll move up there.' He studied his deltameter-cum-phone. 'Look, the reading at the roadblock today is weaker than it was when Gibbs put the roadblock up. We'll need a few sweeps of the bay to get an average.'

On the grassy verge, a fat bee bounced from stem to stem. Howard's plan seemed like a good one.

'It's lovely here,' Carl murmured, looking out to sea. 'It was pissing down yesterday and now it's like the Bahamas.'

They left the single-track road and walked down the grass slope to the rocky shoreline, then came back up towards the roadblock, Carl entering co-ordinates on Howard's palmpod like he'd been shown. Sheep and sturdy black-faced lambs scattered as they retraced their steps.

'Don't take this the wrong way,' said Carl as they reached the road again, 'but why didn't you go to the media about SCOPE? Something this big is hard to ignore, even with the PLC on our case. Someone would have published, spun it as a managerial issue. There must've been some way of getting it out.'

Sweat glistened on Howard's hairless head. He took off his jacket. 'I was a partner in a firm, GeoByte Services,' he said. 'Three of us in a management buyout. The other two were more finance and deal-making, but I wanted to stay in product development. It was my job to iron out the signal noise from other telecomms on the site-share. Anyway, I went to Len, one of the partners, a guy I'd known for almost twenty years. I told him the modelling results confirmed the resonance in the diarite filters when the transmitters were networked. So he said he'd have a look at my results.'

Howard cleared his throat. 'A week later he still hadn't got back to me, fobbed me off when I asked him about the resonance results. Then, when I was about to go to him again, we got a visit from the main contractor, their head of procurement no less, who starts talking about a new contract, a bigger one, *if* we deliver on SCOPE. And that's when things got difficult for me. I went to Len again, but there was no budging him. I could see what they were trying to do, the contractors, so I went to the Security Ministry, and another sympathetic hearing took place.

'Two days later there was a break-in at the science park, my hard copies of the modelling report were stolen, and all my back-up data – three months of research – was wiped. Flash drives, cloud accounts, everything.'

Howard looked straight at Carl. 'I guessed then that CivCon would be monitoring me so I couldn't risk any kind of contact with you. And anyway, what would you have said if I'd phoned you up ranting about SCOPE and its two-hertz harmonic that might send people to sleep as they were walking in the street?'

'I would have thought you were nuts. If you were lucky I would have checked you out and asked for proof.'

'And I had none to show you.'

They pressed on in silence, Carl dropping back a little, lost in thought. What Brindley had said was plausible enough to dispel guilt, culpability. Could he have done anything different?

•

A few days later they were halfway through a second sweep of the bay. The first set of readings had given a maximum safe distance of 4.2 kilometres from Inverlair Hotel to the edge of what everyone now referred to as the redzone. They were about 400 metres above sea level.

'These are the exact co-ordinates, no doubt about it.' He handed the deltameter back to Carl. 'The field strength is much weaker than it was on the first sweep. Down to 120 microtesla again.' He frowned at the readings.

Here was something. Carl grabbed at the floating feather of hope with both hands. Twelve days and maybe SCOPE was conking out already. Never mind two to five years. Sitting on a moss-covered rock, Howard wiped the sweat from his eyes, frowning over his deltameter. Insects droned and hovered over the stewing bogs. He screwed the top back on his water bottle.

'Both the delta field's magnetic and microwave components are still present, which means the nearest transmitter is still working. I don't know why the signal strength has dropped off. There can be temporary attenuations in a signal for all sorts of reasons.'

Carl's head dropped. 'So, it's just a blip?'

Brindley pulled at blades of long grass. 'I don't know.'

'Why not? You built the fucking thing.'

'Incorrect,' said Brindley, glaring at Carl. 'But I think you know that . . . I think you also know that SCOPE was more than an emergency communications system. You *do* know that, don't you?'

Carl set off back down the grassy slope towards the village. He turned round, walking backwards. 'Well, if there's one man who can tell the rest of us what SCOPE really was, it sure as fuck isn't me.'

22

Grief belonged in the past. He had no use for it now. George kept telling himself that. It was too soon, that was the problem, and if he'd been given to platitudes, he would have said that time is the great healer, or something along those lines.

When he was alone he felt naked before grief. It had reduced him to the core of what he was. It was testing him, interrogating the workings of his soul, responses that he had barely given a second thought to before. It was testing his stitches. Was he held together properly? Would he come apart?

He would endure, withstand the punishment, or he would disintegrate. For the time being, he'd let grief take him, but he knew there had to be a way out of it, a way of confining it, mostly, as an experience that was based on memory, not raw actuality. George kept telling himself all that but, for now, it was no use. Maybe one day he would find himself entirely focused on what he was doing: the past's ability to hurt him reduced to an intermittent and fading signal.

The bench was warm. George sat with his face to the sun, an empty space beside him that he could picture being filled by Alison. So many times she had sat there and he'd hardly been aware of her; now that she was missing, he could hardly take his eyes off the space she used to occupy, when the weather had allowed.

Simone and Isaac were round at Fiona's, so he had cried on his own, a trickle this time, rather than a torrent.

He'd noticed that his daughter wasn't letting him look after

Isaac as often as she had; whenever she went out she took the boy with her. Did she think he was incapable of looking after his own grandson? Through his grief, George felt a surge of anger. It fired off in several different directions: at Brindley and the journalist, at the bastards who dreamed up the SCOPE system, at his own daughter. Himself. Alison had been pissed off with his moods, his sullen sarcasm. If it hadn't been for that, maybe she would never have felt the need to go to Edinburgh for a break in the first place.

He tried to focus. There were important things to do now. The situation is what it is, he told himself, and now we have to think of the future, like Brindley said. What was that stuff he'd been talking about the other day? Drawing up work crews. Rationing the food according to age and sex and usefulness. Okay. Lots to be done.

George cocked his head at the sound of his son's fishing boat returning, engine throbbing. It was too soon. The other day they'd reached four miles out. He stood up, blew his nose and wiped his eyes, and headed down to the pier to meet the *Aurora*.

Carl shouted something from the deck of the boat but George couldn't hear him above the engines. Adam eased back on the throttle, and guided the boat alongside, nudging the rubber casing. It was low tide and the *Aurora* was well below the top of the pier.

'There might be a gap, a way out,' Carl repeated. He scrambled up the metal ladder to join George on dry land.

Brindley doused some of their excitement. 'It can't be more than a few hundred metres wide,' he said. 'Hard to tell if it opens into the Atlantic. And if there is any kind of fluctuation in the field strength the gap could close in around you before you know it. There are refraction effects to consider as the tide rises and falls. You'd never turn around and get out in time.'

Carl stiffened. 'You said it was possible.'

'Possible, but extremely risky. A channel that narrow. In a boat.'

Howard shook his head. 'And there's no way of telling how far it extends.'

'There might be a way out,' urged Carl. 'That's what you said.'

'Sounds like a death sentence to me,' said George. 'And where would you go?'

Carl glared at him. 'Anywhere. West coast of Ireland – Howard's friends went there. Or Spain.'

George considered the horizon. 'I wouldn't like to sail to Spain in a tiny boat like that – especially if I have to head north to start with to get into the Atlantic. And don't they have that white rust fungus pretty bad down there?' He glanced at Howard. The guy was talking sense. 'In any case, there are over a hundred people in Inverlair and only three small boats.' George shrugged.

'So we just sit here for maybe five years, is that it?' said Carl, unable to believe what he'd heard. 'Shouldn't we, er, actually try to get out of here? There isn't much food, in case you hadn't noticed.'

Brindley guessed that George was thinking the same simple question. 'We can cope with the food we have, so I'm told. But why should we try to get out of here?'

Carl was flabbergasted. 'Why?' He shook his head. There were so many reasons to leave this place. Or at least Carl felt there must be. But when he needed just one of them, to slap down on the table as a trump card, he found himself unable to summon anything that sounded convincing. The places SCOPE hadn't blanked out weren't likely to be any better off than Inverlair. Further away, say north-west Africa, there might be a good life waiting – if a ten-metre fishing boat could make the 2,500-mile trip; if it could find a way out of the delta field and through the mountainous Atlantic.

'I don't know,' he said quietly. 'I just thought . . .' He looked at George. 'Don't you want to try and get to Edinburgh, to your wife?'

For a second, emotion charted a charmed route in George's heart, around Cape Wrath and the Pentland Firth.

'You won't be able to get anywhere near Edinburgh, or any other big town, for maybe ten years – I told you that,' Howard said to Carl. 'That much I can say with virtual certainty because of how SCOPE is configured in urban areas. I told you all this.'

Carl repeated the phrase, making the point. 'Virtual certainty. Virtual. But not absolute.'

His eyes wide, Howard waved him away. 'Oh don't be so bloody stupid.' He strode away. 'Go on then. Go. Take the boat and see how far you get.'

'Oh no, he fucking won't,' said Adam, climbing up onto the pier. 'No one's taking my boat anywhere.' He looped a thick rope from the *Aurora*'s bow around a metal cleat on the quayside. His father tied the stern line.

'There's a spot of lunch waiting,' George said to Carl. 'Not much, but it'll fill a hole. Brindley's right, you know. If it goes wrong, it's a death sentence.'

The boat nuzzled against the side of the pier, plastic squeaking on rubber, wet ropes taking the strain. A big seagull, snow-white chest, settled on a railing beside the men.

'It would be a quick death, at least,' said Carl. 'And that's better than the alternative.'

Saying nothing, George strode back to the hotel.

In the kitchen, they ate in silence. There was so much to say, and so many questions to ask. But instead of risking conversation, which might begin painlessly enough, saying nothing was obviously the safer option. Conversation could expose feelings, and feelings were hard to control, so the unresolved pressure of not talking swelled within the room. Isaac watched all the adults distill their private pain.

Eventually, Brindley spoke. 'It's still early,' he said to Carl. 'So I thought we could take some more signal readings in the hills, if you want to.'

It was unbelievable. Carl resisted the temptation to hurl his plate of food against the kitchen wall. Here they were, sitting nice and cosy around the table. Simone was being civil to him. But she was a door that had been closed and locked. He felt like saying: it was only a shag, and not a very good one at that. And that wee Isaac was giving him the evil eye as well. Little shite.

He nodded at Howard's suggestion. 'Shall we make a move then?'

Carl took his plate to the sink and rinsed it under the tap. The water was warm, the kitchen uncomfortably so because the fire was lit. From the window, Carl looked towards the summit of Ben Bronach. They would follow the line of the fence to the burn, then meet the forest track. From there it was up past the old stones and onto the shoulder of the hill, following the ridge, heading inland across the headwater streams that fed the river. He knew the way by now.

•

'I don't know if I'm imagining it, but is there something between you and Simone?'

It was another warm day, and plump lambs dozed by their chewing mothers. Carl figured there was no point in denying it. 'We had sex.'

Howard didn't know what to say. 'Oh.'

'She gave me a hug – that's how it started.' Carl's voice cracked. 'It was just comfort – closeness, y'know?' He felt tears in his eyes and his face reddening. 'But it doesn't matter.' He shook his head, annoyed with himself reacting this way. He was all over the place. 'Embarrassment is a pretty pointless emotion to feel, given what's happened, wouldn't you say?'

The slope was getting steeper now, grass giving way to heather. Howard stopped for a breather, taking out a hankie to wipe the sweat from his face and head. 'Your guess is as good as mine,' he said. 'I could never work women out.'

•

Five hours later Howard was flat out on the bed in Room 22, his legs and back aching, his neck sunburnt. Thank Christ he'd taken a baseball cap with him, otherwise his scalp would be toast. He felt good, though; physically tired, but relaxed with it. It was their longest stint yet, and they were well on with the second sweep of readings. He lay for a while, fully clothed, staring at the ceiling. Maybe he'd ask Adam Cutler if they could venture out in the fishing boat again, test the gap in the redzone to the north. Staying active made people forget – and that was good. If people did useful stuff, then so much the better. That was the only thing to do now: work. Survive.

There was a soft knock at the door.

'Come in.'

The door creaked open. 'Hello,' said George, peering into the room.

'Hello there.' Howard smiled. 'I can't seem to move.'

The smile was returned, weakly.

'I thought you might appreciate a dram,' said George, his voice low. 'If you feel up to it.'

Howard heaved himself up against the bedhead. 'Whisky doesn't really agree with me, but I'll make an exception, on the grounds that it may have some curative effect. I'll have a wash first. Freshen myself up.'

Ten minutes later Howard appeared in the residents' lounge, just as George cracked the seal on a bottle. An oil-lamp burned on the mahogany coffee table. George handed Howard his drink and gestured to an armchair. 'Carl said he would join us in a while. I prefer it in here to the annexe, although that didn't used to be the case.'

Gingerly, Howard lowered himself into the chair. He raised his glass of single malt. 'Cheers.'

Without any real enthusiasm, George returned the toast.

After a mouthful of whisky, Howard smacked his lips and held the glass up to the lamplight. 'Liquid gold,' he said.

George took another gulp of his drink. 'You guys must be nearly finished the second sweep of the . . .' He gestured towards vaguely towards the window.

'Redzone,' said Howard.

'Is that what you've called it?'

'We've marked it on the map in the community centre in red pen. I suppose we can't keep calling it "out there".'

'No,' said George. 'I suppose we can't.'

They fell silent. It was quiet enough to hear the wick burning in the oil-lamp. George swirled his whisky round the glass, felt the fire in his cheeks. 'Do you mind if I ask you a question?'

Howard stretched his tired legs in front of him. 'No,' he said, taking a sip of whisky. 'I don't mind.'

George let go a breath. His words, so carefully rehearsed, were jostling for position. 'People . . . some people . . . are wondering how you ended up in Inverlair. Why you didn't leave the country altogether if you knew this was coming – that kinda thing.' He waited for a reaction.

Howard smiled. 'People are suspicious of me,' he said. 'A stranger arrives and a terrible thing happens. The stranger was connected to the terrible thing. It makes sense.'

George poured another round of drinks and took a mouthful. 'You know how people are.'

'And what do *you* think?'

'Well, you worked on this system, you didn't like what you found out, and you tried to do something about it. But I do wonder why you didn't leave the country – go somewhere safe, I mean.'

Howard sat back in his chair, glass resting on his belly, stockinged feet on a footstool. 'We were working on SCOPE – this is about seven years ago – and my company was hired.'

'You owned a company?'

With a wave of his hand, Howard dismissed fifteen years of his life as 'nothing major'. He told George most of what he'd told Carl. The whisky worked its magic, and he kept talking.

'Some people, a few, were well connected enough to buy their way out of the country. People who knew what might happen. But I didn't have enough money for the traffickers. Even if I had, I was probably pretty high on CivCon's watchlist at that stage, so exit-point biometrics would have been primed with every move I'd ever made and an image of every pimple on my fucking face.'

He glared, briefly, at George, a gulp of whisky souring his expression, his voice rough. 'That's what gave them the initial idea for SCOPE. You can change the way you walk, your eyeballs, your whole face, even your fingerprints.' He tapped his temple. 'But you can't change this.'

George looked puzzled.

'Brainwaves. The active Beta range, to be exact.'

A bit clearer: but George was still missing the bigger picture.

Whisky storming round his head, Howard spoon-fed him the ABC.

'If you took an EEG of your brainwaves just now it would record a waveform which is unique to you. Between twelve and thirty-eight hertz is the beta phase of brain activity when the brain is alert.' Howard tilted his glass. 'Though we're getting less alert with every drop of this. Everyone has their own exact frequency.' He tapped his temple again. 'In here. Each emotion – fear, anger, even anxiety – has its own signature.'

Smiling was not something George felt like doing. He looked at his glass, a regular poisoned chalice; every mouthful of anaesthetic was bringing his pain into sharper focus. Only oblivion cancelled it out.

He became aware of another presence in the room.

'Hi,' said Carl. 'I feel more human after a shower.'

'The man himself,' called Howard, twisting round in his chair. 'The man who sniffed it all out.'

George poured another three-finger measure of whisky, handing it to Carl.

'Howard was telling me more about SCOPE.'

'So I gather,' said Carl. Something they had both agreed not to talk about was now being talked about. He accepted the whisky and sat down. Howard grinned as he finished his second generous measure.

'So SCOPE was designed to track people,' stated George, puffing at the reflux in his gut. 'Is that right?'

Howard helped himself to another drink. He was dog-tired and well on the road to being plastered. 'To begin with, that was the idea, but it became much more than that, Georgie boy.'

'We agreed, Howard,' said Carl firmly, staring grimly at his drink. 'We agreed. Certain things, yes?'

'Is that a fact?'

Before Carl could answer, Howard stood up, his index finger raised. He tottered, steadied himself. 'The questions we have to ask ourselves are: how do you control chaos? How do you manage the slow-motion train-wreck of civilisation? Fear and surveillance – that's how you do it. Fear makes people accept what you're doing, and surveillance keeps the money circulating – European research grants and Security Ministry contracts for everything from behaviour-prediction software to non-lethal weaponry for our militarised police forces. Not as much money as there was before, but enough to keep some important wheels going round.'

Tired now, and drunk, George sagged into his armchair.

She got on a bus. Got on a bus and didn't come back.

Howard lurched forward, waving an arm at Carl. 'There were no people anymore, no individuals, at the end of it – only data to be mined, targets on a screen. Our digital trails were actionable intelligence for certain interests. We weren't users of technology any more – we were its subjects. Finally, the right kit came along, advertising total control.' He wagged a bony finger at Carl, grinning.

'But they weren't as clever as they thought. Oh no. Hidden imperfection got the better of them. Carl there, he knew all about that. He knew what was going on with SCOPE – but he was too shit-scared to tell the rest of us.'

Carl drained his whisky. 'Fuck off. Don't give me the you-did-as-much-as-you-could crap. You worked on SCOPE for years. You were part of the whole fucking anti-terror show. SCOPE was originally a tracking system long before it was mood manipulation.' He stopped, glanced at Howard, went for a refill.

'The perils of dual-use technology,' declared Howard. 'Scientists could believe that everything military also had a civilian use – for the benefit of society. That's how we could do what we did with a clear conscience, more or less. But we couldn't see the bigger picture, not on this one.'

Howard was talking to George, but George wasn't really listening. He was too busy remembering.

'That's what we could tell ourselves.' Howard glared at Carl. He jabbed a finger towards Carl. 'You knew.'

Carl stood up. 'Look, you prick, what was I supposed to say to my editor? There's this new government communications system that's really an attempt at mass fucking mind control ...'

George looked up, aware of the fuss, but unsure of what he'd heard.

Howard was swaying with whisky and fatigue. 'I'll let our roving reporter tell you all about that little secret, George. It's time for my voluntary grave.' He aimed for the lounge door. 'A government contract is a substitute for intellectual curiosity,' he intoned as he tottered from the room.

Nonplussed, George looked to Carl. 'What was that?'

Whisky downed in two, Carl poured another. He started pacing the room, silently cursing Howard, slurping from his glass.

He could tell George the truth. He could tell him all about brainwave entrainment through pulsed magnetic induction. He could tell him about extremely low-frequency psychotronics, charting its history all the way back to the Russians in the 1960s and the CIA's MK-Ultra programme.

He stood at the bookcase, the shabby edition of *Highland Animals* at his fingertips. Where was *Vipera berus* now?

'Fear and money, George, just like old Ike said,' Carl said at last. 'And one hell of a ghost in the machine.'

23

It was 5.50 a.m. and a pale September morning was leaching into Inverlair Bay and into the hotel. Being awake at night was the worst; there was nothing but silence and uncontrollable thoughts darting in and out of existence. That was when sadness and terror stood tall by the bed and kept her awake. So there was nothing to do but get up. She could grab an hour's sleep in the afternoon. There was always something that needed doing, and doing something, anything, was better than lying awake in the dark.

Her mother. That journalist. The baby she was going to have.

Simone pulled her dressing gown tight around herself, more afraid than cold.

From the window of the residents' lounge, she watched dawn break over the village, heard the birds in full voice, light spilling into the bay, the tops of the far headland ablaze in the early beams. There was nothing unusual about any of it: day beginning and day ending, on a spool that replayed over and over and carried her along with it. She was now moving through days filled with other people and the things that always needed doing. People still had their needs, and their appetites. She tried to rationalise, to absolve, and she wondered if Carl was doing the same.

'Mum,' she whispered at the windowpane, cold glass under her fingertips.

She heard a noise behind her in the corridor and turned from the window.

Howard stood in the doorway wearing a grey tracksuit, a glass of water in his hand. 'Oh,' he said groggily. 'I'm sorry, I didn't realise there would be anyone else up.'

Simone caught sight of a coin-sized stain near Howard's crotch. For some reason, this put her at ease.

'It's beautiful – but very bright,' he said, gesturing to the window, squinting at the daylight.

'Yeah,' said Simone, turning back to the dawn. 'It used to attract a lot of artists. The quality of the light, and the colours.'

Groaning, Howard slumped into the chair he'd occupied the previous evening. Christ, what an arse he'd been.

'Too much of your dad's whisky last night. It's never agreed with me. Think I was a bit of an arse.'

'You're not the first person to turn into an idiot after a drink.'

'I suppose not,' said Howard. 'I'm stiff as a bloody board as well. All that walking in the hills.' He winced. 'Sunburnt too.'

They were silent for a spell, the only sounds the seagulls and the clock on the mantelpiece. Stirring from the window, Simone said, 'Where did you live, before you found out about SCOPE?'

Howard didn't really feel up to a conversation. He drank most of the water in three gulps. 'Near Reading. Private estate. Part of a science park.'

'Did you have anyone, a family, or . . .'

He groaned again. 'A father with Alzheimer's and a sister in New York.'

Simone nodded. 'Sorry.'

'Yeah.' Howard looked pained for a moment. He didn't really feel like elaborating. 'Haven't seen my sister for years. We lost touch.'

'Sorry, I don't mean to be nosey,' said Simone. 'It's just that you sit at our table every day, but I don't know the first thing about you, apart from your job . . .'

'You've got other things on your mind,' said Howard. 'I'm sorry about your mother.'

Simone chewed her lip.

'I've heard your father mention Hannah. Is that your sister?'

'Yeah,' she said. 'She's in Norway working as a translator. Maybe she still is.'

'Maybe,' said Howard. 'They didn't have SCOPE there. It was installed across Sweden though ...'

Simone frowned, tightened her dressing gown around her. 'There's some tea. Would you like a cup?'

'Oh, yes please,' breathed Howard. 'That would be fantastic.'

When Simone went through to the kitchen, Howard picked up the empty whisky bottle and sniffed the smoky fumes. What an arse. What a loose-tongued vicious pain in the arse.

•

Carl waited on the pavement outside the hotel.

Okay, Brindley had said sorry and, yes, whisky brings out the demon in some guys, but he was a complete wanker for telling George about SCOPE, no two ways about that. With a bit of luck, George had been too pissed to realise what he was being told. Then again, maybe it was no bad thing if he did remember the previous evening, just so long as he didn't blame the obvious targets for not being heroic enough to stop it all. That's what they would've been if they'd blown the whistle on SCOPE: heroes. And not everyone can step out of the crowd like that, saying what no one else will say. Carl wondered if George would understand any of that. The risk and ridicule involved.

The hotel's front door squeaked open.

'You're keen to get started,' said Howard, without meeting Carl's eye.

Carl set off down the path towards the main road.

After a few moments, Howard caught up with him. 'I knew you knew what SCOPE was. I knew it. Listen, maybe it's no bad thing we told George.'

Carl snorted. 'No bad thing.' He shook his head. 'Do you realise that people are still wary of us? Do you actually get that? Some of them still think we had something to do with all this. And now George might be wondering why we waited three fucking weeks before telling him about the secret SCOPE upgrade. Do you want to get us lynched? These people are strangers.'

Howard shrugged. 'It won't come to that.'

A pick-up truck, piled high with logs, rumbled past them and turned into the boatyard. The driver was a heavy-set red-faced man in an orange boiler suit. He and his passenger jumped out, clattered open the truck's side-flap, and let sections of tree-trunk roll off, thudding onto the concrete forecourt. The driver eyed Carl and Howard with suspicion.

They passed the schoolhouse and skirted round the stalker's farm, leaving the bay behind.

Almost two hours later they reached the spot where the stream that fed the River Lair soaked away into the boggy uplands: fathoms of water-engorged peat that spilled and sprung their loads.

Howard consulted his deltameter. 'Twelve days ago, the delta signal dropped by 200 microtesla for a few hours. The signature was still there in the H-band, but a much weaker primary harmonic. Six days ago the same thing happened. And now again today. Some kind of pattern by the looks of it, every six days. I'll do a spectrum analysis later on my tablet, but I think we should wait here for a while, see what the main waveform does; there was marked attenuation for about four hours the last time it happened.'

Carl took out his palmpod and consulted the readings. As graphs, the signal behaviour was clear: there were dips in the primary signal every six days. But though each dip lasted four hours, their start times were unequal. First dip: 11.27 a.m. Second dip: 1.42 p.m. Third dip: 11.24 a.m.

'So the time now is eleven-thirty and the signal is going down. We could have almost four hours, or we could have two, or less or more.' Howard squinted at the sun. 'Not enough datasets to be sure.' There were clouds massing out at sea. Definitely a hint of autumn in the air. He looked across the bay to the fissured summit of Ben Bronach. 'We could perhaps try to get to that farmhouse today,' he said. 'It can't be more than four hundred metres into the redzone.'

Carl gestured across the bay. 'The farmhouse – behind Ben Bronach?'

'Yes.'

'It will take us well over an hour to get up there,' said Carl. 'If we wait another six days we'll know for sure.'

Howard shook his head. 'You said six days ago that some of the chickens at the farmhouse were dead. The automatic feeder must have broken or run out, and there isn't enough in the coop to feed them much longer. They might all be dead by next week.' He looked at Carl. 'Just think of it – we could probably carry half a dozen each, maybe more. Tie their legs together. More eggs. More flesh.'

'Yeah,' whispered Carl. He drank some water and stood up. Man brings food from hill. People would appreciate that.

'Okay,' he said. 'Let's do it.'

An hour and a half later, they were high on the ridge. Through binoculars, Howard studied the farmhouse in the glen. A few of the chickens looked very dead, and a few more looked close to it, scrawny and inert. He could see one, a hump of wind-ruffled feathers, pressed against the coop's wire fence, unmoving. The Land Rover had a flat tyre now and there was a ewe standing in the open doorway of the house, a former hunting lodge. The owner, or what was left of him or her, was probably lying in the house. Howard checked his deltameter, and they set off down the steep rocky slope.

As they descended into the glen the terrain gave way from rock to knee-high heather that made walking difficult. Hidden burns gurgled under hags of peat. It was hard going and they worked up a sweat. By the time they got to the farmhouse it was half past one.

'Jesus, Howard,' panted Carl. 'We're cutting it too fine, man.'

But Howard was already inside the hen-coop. 'Come on,' he shouted, chasing after a chicken that flapped clear of him. 'Give me a hand.'

After a few minutes they had grabbed and tied three birds each. And then the noise started, pricking in their skulls. They looked at each other, Howard with a panicky smile.

'Whoops.'

They bolted from the coop.

•

They were only 500 metres or so from the red marker stone that Carl had painted on their first sweep of the redzone. That was the distance to safety. But the ground was uneven, with hidden hollows and holes, sloping upwards to the mouth of the glen, and they had to hurdle through heather.

They ran with their feathery bundles of protein. After about 300 metres pain skewered Carl's temples, and his lungs were burning with the effort.

Fuck the hens.

He ran away from death, with every ounce of the strength he didn't know he had, and fell, semi-conscious, just metres from the marker stone, blood streaming from his nose.

•

Cold splashes on his face. Hard. Harder. Rain. Dark. Pain.

Carl sat up. It was pelting with rain and he couldn't see a solitary object or light, anywhere. Thrashing a hand blindly on the wet grass next to him he shouted for Howard, panic firing him awake.

He stood. His lungs ached from running. He was soaked to the skin, wearing nothing but a T-shirt and jeans. A gust of wind flung rain into his eyes as he began to run. He tripped and fell, braced himself for the impact, but there was only cold grass under his hands.

'Howard!' He tried to think. Howard had been behind him, running. They'd both been running.

Okay, okay, a bit of reasoning was required here. No need to lose the plot. Carl tried to visualise the glen in daylight: the red marker stone and the track that led from the farmhouse to the north road. If he walked and felt no pain in his head, he was safe, and if he hit the redzone he could about-turn and walk in the opposite direction. If only he could find the track, that would give him his bearings.

'Howard!'

There was no response.

'Jesus, man,' he wailed. 'Howard!'

He waited and shouted again.

After a few minutes, he knew he had to get under cover, out of the wind and rain. The nights were colder now, and longer. He knew he had to seek shelter. There was no question now of death being a viable alternative: he had to get back to the village. Wanting to stay alive, and the force of this impulse, took him a little by surprise. Dying out here, in the wet dark, was not an option.

Fuck that.

Edging forward in total blackness with his hands outstretched, it was slow going, and he was cold – dripping wet, blinking into the rain and wind, cursing, groping his way forward, afraid to take big steps.

He fell again. This time he wasn't so lucky, and smacked his forehead off a rock. He curled up on the sodden grass, nursing the point of impact and the percussive quiver inside his skull, tasting his own blood along with cold rain. After a few seconds, he lay back on the ground, the heavy drops cascading onto his face, into his open mouth.

Maybe he should wait until dawn. It couldn't be more than a few hours away. He could rest here.

Howard.

He shivered, teeth rattling. Was he going up the slope or down? Whimpering, he bit down on fear, head still ringing from the fall against the rock. He stood up again, edged forward into the black miles of steep hills and hidden streams, hands outstretched, feeling their blind way into the void.

Alec John found him seven hours later, barely conscious and huddled in a bank of heather, the groundwork for double pneumonia deep in his lungs.

December

24

At night he could hear the stags roaring out their challenges to other males. Procreation was everything, or at least insemination was, the urge that sprung open like a time lock every November. At this time of year, so Alec John had said, there was nothing but the urge. Stags were slaves to it. Everything, from fat deposits to the thickness of neck manes, was geared to besting their rivals and gathering as many females as they could.

Standing in the hotel garden, on a windless night, Carl could hear the snap of branches as they barged their way through the trees and bushes on the lower slopes of the hill. Brute power had the horn, and was looking for as many places to insert it as possible. But before that, there was the fear of violence to sow first. The urge to fuck was preceded by the urge to dominate. They were indivisible.

Out in the dark garden Carl shivered in the breeze. He zipped his fleece up and jammed his hands in the pockets. It had been a warm enough day, in the sun, but the breath of winter commanded the night air. His new room, number 7, was cold now, most of the time, as winter gales thundered in from the south-west, one charging storm front after another. Tonight there was a lull, and the few constellations that were now familiar to him stood out from the dense infinity of lesser stars.

Carl sat on the bench at the bottom of the garden, the smell of damp decay thickening the dark, until it got too cold to stay outside any longer. There was still a faint glow in the west, and it was amazing how people learned to cope in darkness that could no longer be banished with the flick of a switch.

He was getting used to moving around at night, sensing his way and what lay in the deepest shadows. Extra care was required on the stairs, however: that's where Isaac was in the habit of leaving bits of Lego, or worse, toy cars.

Carl stepped deftly up to the first-floor landing, where the moon waned behind the stained-glass window. In the room he set match to candle, took another swig of Hendrik's home-brew, and rolled himself up in the duvet. He lay, staring at the candle flame, in absolute silence, and thought about the day, and the days to come. Today, out on the hill, they'd crept up to this sleeping stag; its eyes were closed, jaws munching on cud and a thread of drool hung from its mouth.

'You can see how thin he is,' Alec John had whispered. 'He's run out – exhausted after all that shagging and squaring up to the others.'

They crawled through the heather for a while longer, elbows in the spongy moss, making sure to keep their arses down, until Alec John stopped. They were at the edge of a peat bank. Down below, and easily within reach, was their dozing target.

Alec John reached into his pocket, took out a coin and flicked it into the burn. The coin pinged off a rock before it hit the water, but the beast didn't move a muscle in response.

'Years ago,' said Alec John, raising his voice a little, 'in a different part of the estate, I saw one like that, fast asleep. He was a fourteen-pointer, and it turned out to be his last year as top dog.' He chuckled. 'I could've walked over to him and put the fucking barrel in his ear if I'd wanted to.'

He passed the rifle to Carl. 'Now's your chance. You won't get a better one. The rut's almost finished.'

Carl took the gun. He'd fired dozens of practice shots and now, maybe as close as he would ever get, here was the real thing.

'Remember,' whispered Alec John. 'Breathe easy, find the mark, and squeeze through it. Brace yourself, but stay relaxed.' He smiled. 'You know, I used to get a lot of Germans up on shooting trips. They're a hunting nation, the Germans, but there aren't enough animals in their own country to shoot. A lot of them were members of clubs and they all had medals, but they had never actually shot an animal. It was a big moment for them, to shoot a deer, and they were shaking.' Alec John chuckled. 'Half of them were so nervous they missed – more than once.' He considered the sleeping animal. 'So take your time, and relax. Regulate your breathing.'

Lifting his binoculars, Carl could see the saliva glistening on the stag's chin, long eyelashes glinting in the weak sun, closed eyelids, and the jaw muscles flexing, working, as the animal chewed. If Alec John was right, maybe he could walk down there, press the barrel of the .308 against the base of the stag's neck, and pull the trigger. Easy meat. His first kill. Protein for the committee to allocate, according to their affiliations. One squeeze of his finger would do it.

But it didn't seem right. The animal was asleep in the sun after getting its hole for the umpteenth time. If the beast had been active, alert, then he could do it easily, maybe, from this distance, though he wasn't entirely sure about that either.

He sighed. 'It doesn't seem fair,' Carl whispered. He squinted at Alec John. 'D'you know what I mean?' He shook his head, took in a breath of cool, clean air, his hands gripping the Ruger's walnut stock.

'That's just what I was thinking,' said Alec John, smiling. 'The time before, the one I just told you about, I didn't think it was right then, him just sitting there. He deserved a better death, I reckoned.'

'But we need the meat.'

'Well,' said Alec John, 'if we really needed the meat I'd say go for it. But the freezers are full enough and we'll need to save bullets.' He shrugged. 'Take him if you want. He's an easy target.'

Carl engaged the safety on the rifle. 'A fair fight, and all that.'

Alec John nodded. 'Come on then, let's go.'

Both men crept back the way they had come. The stag would sleep, recover his strength, and wake up none the wiser. There was still another season's peak performance ahead of him and enough strength to keep rivals at bay, this time. Then he'd be a target, sleeping or not, for a stronger power.

25

They had this game, the kids. Well, they weren't exactly kids. The guys were fifteen, sixteen, and one of them must have been six-two if he was an inch. The girls, one or two of them, looked like women. There was no beating about the bush where that was concerned; they looked older, though he could tell when speaking to them, the words they used, their awkwardness, and their concerns, that they were in transition. Gemma was fifteen. He knew that. He didn't know how old the other one was, but he guessed they were all about the same age. Terry could play the worldly-wise man and make them all laugh, and the boys, smart enough in their sullen way, were no real match for him in the one-liner department.

So, anyway, they had this game, the kids.

Terry had seen them come back down the road one evening. They'd pitched a tent down between the dunes, where they smoked his weed and messed about. He'd heard one of the guys snarking about not getting his blow job. It was their own private spot, their refuge, when they weren't required to work or account for themselves. Deprivation was making adults of them, drawing them into dutiful necessity and away from childhood. In their den, they could just chill out.

One evening they were coming back from their den and Terry was heading home on his bike, out of the saddle, desperate for the headland incline not to beat him in front of Gemma and her watching crew. They gave the old man a ribbing as he struggled up the road towards them. Thigh muscles burning, Terry stopped trying to turn the pedals, doing his best to act like he wasn't completely shagged out. As he got his breath back, he noticed one guy's white T-shirt had a splatter of red down the front.

'Is that your first shave, Hector?' he said, gesturing to the stain. 'You'll get the hang of it eventually, as long as you don't cut your throat first.'

'Hector got the flag record off Tony,' said Gemma brightly. At that, Hector started proclaiming his pre-eminence loudly. He'd clearly enjoyed a celebratory home-brew or two along with his smoke; his eyes were red and his voice hoarse. If he'd started to beat his chest and roar in triumph Terry wouldn't have been too surprised.

'Flag record?'

'In the redzone,' said Gemma, as Hector was thumped on the upper arm by one of his mates. 'He did a hundred and twelve metres before he had to turn back.'

Terry frowned, confused.

'He doesn't know,' said Gemma to her mates. 'Come and we'll show Terry the flag.'

At the roadblock on the south road they stopped, microwaves buzzing and clicking in their heads. Down the straight, level road – out in the redzone – fluttered a small yellow flag. 'Yellow's a positive colour,' said Gemma. 'Like in Buddhist countries they wear yellow. Red's so negative, you know?'

'So,' said Terry, mock-thoughtfully, 'the barrier isn't really a barrier, and by the power of positive thinking you'll make the redzone disappear?'

'No,' chirped the other girl, Annie. 'We're not fucking saying that.'

Terry looked down the road in disbelief. 'Let me get this straight: you run into the redzone, down the road, with the yellow flag. And how d'you get it back?'

Hector piped up. 'The challenger has to get it back.'

'You can have a rest though,' said one of the other guys. 'Before you try and beat the record. You need to have a rest cos of the nosebleeds.'

Some things that Terry had done in his life were inadvisable, to say the least. But running towards an excruciating head-bursting noise that would eventually kill you was not one of them.

Gemma brandished a wrist-phone. 'We get the distance from this. There's a pedometer on it. The flag's in a wee sack of sand so the wind doesn't blow it away.'

'Well, kids,' said Terry, trying to look impressed, 'that's certainly an inventive game you have there.'

'It's not a game,' spat Hector. The rest agreed.

'It's an ingenious challenge,' said Annie.

Terry smiled. 'With death the prize for the winner. If human ingenuity can get a man on the moon, then there's no telling what challenge we can meet, or where we can plant our poxy little flags of positivity.'

Gemma glared at him. 'Fuck you,' she said. She pointed down the road. 'You run out to that flag and tell us all about human ingenuity, with the blood pishing out of your nose because of SCOPE, or whatever it's called. What a brilliant invention.'

'Go, Gemma,' encouraged Hector.

At that, she quietened, uncomfortable with her power. There was a pause, as they all considered the little yellow flag, fluttering 112.56 metres down the single-track road.

There was an obvious question, so daft Hector asked it. 'Want a shot?'

For a second, the thought of taking off in pursuit of the course record actually crossed Terry's mind. It was soon put to bed. 'Nah,' he said. 'I've been known to try and swim across the bay when I'm fucking pished, but I don't fancy that, guys.'

'Pussy,' snapped Hector.

Terry glanced down the road again, unable to catch Gemma's

eye. He turned back to the boy. 'Maybe so, but you'll still be kissing my arse and saying sorry when you want a smoke.'

The group laughed, and Terry made his getaway while he could, his bravado intact. He found Carl in the caravan, stuffing a pipe with some dry leaf.

'You not out with Alec John?'

Carl lit the pipe with a taper, sucked in the smoke. 'He's not feeling too good, so we finished early.'

Terry poured some home-brew. Hendrik was confident, this time, that the demijohns had been cleaned properly, and that this batch would be less purgative than the last.

A couple of hours later it was dark, the wind on the move, surging and swishing around the caravan. The conversation turned to Howard, and the world before, and Carl's mood had soured. The same line kept running through his head: the machine gave us everything, then it took it all away. He wished he could stop thinking. Too much booze. Too much weed.

The wind-lamp brightened as the roof-mounted turbine whirled furiously in a gust, but the far end of the room, the tiny partitioned bedroom, a jumble of clothes and books, was in darkness. Carl felt tired, dead-beat, and talking about the past made him want to curl up, alone.

'I'm off,' he said.

Terry stayed sitting on a beanbag near the stove. 'Don't be daft, kip on the couch. What do you have to go back for?'

'I don't know.' He shrugged. 'Call it a homing instinct for somewhere that isn't home. Territorial urge.'

Carl shuddered at the thought of walking back to the hotel, groping along the road, afraid of where his next footstep was going to take him. The last time that had happened it had almost killed him, and his urge to leave the tiny caravan was stronger than the fear that it might. Carl stood, unsteady on his feet, and zipped up his jacket. It was black outside the window and he felt the wind give the caravan another shove. Maybe he should stay right where he was. He couldn't face feeling his way through total darkness, and if his wind-up torch packed in that's what he'd have to do.

'Right,' said Carl, his hand on the door. With light, he'd find his way. Opening the door, a fresh nor'westerly came diving in, fluttering curtains and paper, with the tide on its breath. The torch worked fine, its beam showing wind-tossed rhododendron and willow.

'Okay,' he said. 'See you tomorrow.'

On the road, Carl started to fret that the torch would stop working. A thick bank of gorse jerked in the wind and, for a second, Carl saw it as a crowd of onlookers jostling for a better view of this poor creature lurching past. He gave the charging handle a few more turns, but then worried that it might break because he had over-wound it. He was moderately pissed and fairly stoned – again. And the day ahead wouldn't be easier because of it.

The look on Howard's face, in the hen-coop, when he realised what was happening, what was about to engulf them. Call it a desperate smile. Whoops, I've just killed us. It all came back to Carl, no matter how hard he tried to keep it away.

Whoops. And then he was gone.

Carl kept the torch-beam focused on the road.

That's why people are afraid of the dark, he thought. They aren't in control, and they don't know what's in front of them or around them or where exactly they're going. An aversion to that level of uncertainty and powerlessness is hard-wired. Full illumination means freedom: people don't have to go to bed when it gets dark. Maybe Inverlair would reacquire that natural rhythm of responding to the night. It's dangerous to be in absolute darkness, with no possibility of light. Nothing bad can surprise you if the way ahead is clear, if you have a way of slicing through the unknown, making it visible and ordinary. Bad things hide from the light. He'd had light of his own to shine, once upon a time. Down the headland road he walked, curving round the loop to the other side of the bay, down past the shell of the old tourist information centre, blue-and-white signage bleached by years of rain. His torch-beam found the bus stop across the road from the copper's house: scorch marks from a vandal's gas lighter, graffiti on the few unbroken Perspex panels, Callum advertising buttfucking. Maybe Callum had no idea that his phone number and availability had been scrawled for all to see. Unless Inverlair was more relaxed that Carl gave it credit for. Offering sexual services in this way is common enough in Soho, so why not here?

Eyes. Silver-green. An animal, out in the darkness. In the woods near the bridge Carl caught the baleful eye-beams in the torchlight, then heard the hooves pounding and a quick thrash of leaves and branches as the animal bolted, making for higher ground through the gorse and bracken, out onto the open hill.

Carl burped, steadied himself, and lurched on towards the bridge at the head of the bay, through swirling scrap leaves, the river rushing underneath, its force dissipating in the salt softness of low tide.

In the south-east, as the wind surged through the branches, an electrical storm flashed, though it was too far away to hear.

Once he got closer to the houses, he could see a dim light from the PV batteries in a few of them. Electric lights were also on in the community centre. Probably the committee in there, cooking up more ways to expropriate some communal creature comforts. It's amazing how quickly dishonesty re-establishes itself, once officialdom takes hold and makes everything seem natural, rational and unavoidable. Food for the select few had been the norm, the last century and a bit notwithstanding. Normal dominion had been restored, after a reign of plenty.

Tomorrow there was the wedding. A dance in the community

centre to celebrate. Good for morale, he'd heard George say. Something to unite around.

Bollocks to that.

At first, Carl couldn't believe that there was going to be a wedding in two days' time. But now he figured that maybe George was right, and that it made more sense now, as a statement – call it a declaration of defiance – for two people to pledge lifelong fidelity to each other. The principle, he supposed, was admirable, even if, by all accounts, the bride-to-be had been having serious doubts before the redzone happened. The poor groom was clueless, apparently, and was telling everyone how love was eternal, and how lucky he was, even now. Especially now. Maybe the woman was right to play the percentages. Her options had narrowed, somewhat.

At the hotel's front door, Carl switched off the torch and stood there in the cold November black. The wind was really picking up now, and sleety rain started to spit on the windows and on his face. He felt a surge of remembered panic, fought to stay in control, feeling the hotel's rough exterior wall, the ordinary and safe under his fingers. In the pitch dark, he felt his stomach lurch, as terror gave him a squeeze to remind him of where he was and what had happened to his world, ninety-six days before. Maybe there was no redzone. Or maybe they were being imprisoned here, for some unfathomable reason. He turned on the torch again.

'They're not as clever as they think,' he muttered, climbing the stairs to forgetfulness, as quiet as any drunk can be.

26

There had been no-show from Carl today, so Alec John was out on the hill by himself. He'd seen the beam of a torch weave its way along the road last night, on the way down from Terry's. Maybe Carl wouldn't have been able to do much work today even if he'd wanted to come out: that home-brew was lethal.

From below the ridge, Alec John scanned Inverlair Bay with binoculars, out to the far islands and inland, across the moors to the jagged basalt teeth of the Needles, where the eagles nested. Further south and west was Glen Athar, where the nearest SCOPE transmitter stood. He knew it was there, had seen it on the map, though he couldn't see it. One day it would stop working, and they could see what was out there. It wouldn't be him though, not if the transmitter lasted the average of two years.

All was calm now, but the night before had been blustery. The bay was well sheltered, and Alec John knew that only a direct westerly gale could reach straight into it and do any real damage. Last night's wind had come from the north-west, brushing the last of the leaves from the alder trees near the road, pruning a few of the weaker branches. Doing its job.

He could see towards the south-east into the redzone, to the house of his former employer. Inverlair was sheltered from the north-west winds, but the sheikh's fourteen-bedroom holiday pile was not so lucky. It took a hammering in the winter. Maybe people would live in the house again, one day. It had stood for almost 200 years, after all.

Down at the community centre Alec John could see final preparations being made for the wedding reception. He shook his head at what he saw.

Bunting.

Can you fathom it? Probably the councillor's idea, or that stuffed shirt of an architect, Anderson. George would have gone along with it because he'd been so henpecked by his wife that he didn't have any thoughts of his own left. The good lady Alison said jump, and George didn't even have to ask how high. But he had loved her, and now she was no longer around to give him the orders he had come to depend on without even knowing it.

Alec John sighed, felt the tightness in his chest, his breath rasping, even when he stood doing nothing. George was doing his best, just like everyone else.

It was easy to forget that SCOPE had happened at all. Who, Alec John wondered, did he have to mourn? A few cousins in Glasgow and Canada; that was more or less it. He was sorry they were dead. Perhaps they weren't. But, in all honesty, he would have to say that he wouldn't be too upset if they were. To look at the world – the one he was used to – was to see nothing that different. It was just that he couldn't cross the estate like he'd been able to. Everything familiar to him was here, and everything from the first half of his life was strange and dead anyway, so there was no need to fret over it. It bothered him that he wasn't that bothered. He scanned along the village with his binoculars. There was activity at the boatyard. Washing on the line. Kids on their bikes.

'Bunting,' he said out loud. 'And where the fuck would you be going for a honeymoon?'

Looking at the hotel, Alec John could see George in the back garden. And there was someone else with a pair of binoculars, in a first-floor window. Carl was watching the hill.

•

There was a dusting of snow on Ben Bronach. Carl was at the window of Howard's old room, overlooking the back garden, with its clear view of the hills. This is the time of year when the deer come down to lower ground, Alec John had said. They'd even come as far as his back fence for food, not that there would be much of that this winter. What a racket the younger stags made at night now, crashing about in the trees, barging and bellowing. Showing off, like all young males.

There were wind-blown branches on the hotel's back lawn, and the leaves that had clung to the alder yesterday were now splattered all over the garden. Rain glistened on the grass.

George was out again with his rake and Carl watched him from an upstairs window. George would stop every now and again, stare into space and wipe his eyes, then carry on with the job. You had to feel sorry for folk like George. Married for years and then, all of a sudden, alone.

Nobody was really to blame for non-violent death, except maybe the person who died, but you could pin SCOPE down, attribute its malignancy to the nameless few. Blaming Howard was possible, though uncharitable: the guy had lost everything and the thing had killed him, far away from anyone that he might have called a loved one.

Was it unreasonable to blame himself? Could he have stopped SCOPE without any proof of what its real purpose had been? No. SCOPE's real purpose wasn't the sort of hypothesis to entertain for any length of time, not in a sane and rational mind that wanted to stay that way. In any event, minutes after the article had been printed, CivCon would have trashed the office and banged them all up for a Category 1 violation of the Emergency Order.

Carl lifted the binoculars to scan Bronach. He spotted Alec John looking at something with his own binoculars – the community centre, probably, judging from the direction he was pointing. Carl had heard they were even putting bunting up for the wedding.

He shook his head, wondering if that had been George's idea; the poor guy who was shuffling about in the back garden and who now looked every one of his sixty-four years.

Isaac ran out into the garden, followed by his pal from a few doors down. Simone and Fiona would be in the kitchen, talking about food, kids and the dickhead upstairs. It was a wonder his ears weren't ablaze.

He lifted the binoculars again to look at Alec John and saw that the stalker was looking straight at the hotel, and at him. Carl smiled and waved, before lowering the binoculars and heading downstairs.

Simone and Isaac were piecing a jigsaw together on the kitchen table when Carl came into the room. There was no sign of Fiona and her kid. Simone acknowledged Carl's presence by refusing to acknowledge him.

'I haven't seen one of those for a while,' he said. Simone clicked a jigsaw piece into place, picked up another.

'It's Grandpa's,' said Isaac, smoothing over the pieces that had been put in place, feeling the joins with his fingers.

'Does he like jigsaws?'

'He did,' said Simone, her eyes still fixed on the developing picture of a red racing car speeding round a racetrack. 'When he was a boy. This jigsaw is about fifty years old.'

Carl remembered jigsaws. He looked at Isaac and at the ragged outline of the racetrack, banners flying and crowds cheering. From out of nowhere, tightness took hold of his throat as he half remembered something from long ago.

'Oh,' was all he could say, a moist heat in his eyes. He turned his back and poured a glass of water at the sink.

'Let's go and see Grandpa,' said Simone. 'I think he wants to read you another story.'

Isaac shot out the door, delighted. Simone walked to the kitchen door, then stopped to make sure Isaac had run on ahead.

His back to the room, rinsing his mouth at the sink, Carl braced himself. Simone was watching him; he could feel her eyes on his back. She was gearing up for something big, and he could feel the weight in the air of what was coming.

The silence dragged on until it became obvious that he had no choice but to turn away from the sink and face her. Leaving the room would mean walking towards her, unless he went out the back door which, barefoot in a T-shirt and boxer shorts, would look pretty stupid.

He turned round, a glass of water to hide behind.

'I'm just waiting,' said Simone, 'to see how long it will take you to sit down and talk to me about what's happening.'

Downing the water, Carl wiped his mouth. 'You said you were keeping it,' he said. 'I don't know what more there is to talk about.'

'Yes,' said Simone quietly. 'I am. Wouldn't you like to know why?'

They stood there, the silence thickening again. There were no thoughts in his head and there were a million thoughts in his head.

He shrugged. 'What do you want from me? Shall we get married and settle down?'

'You're a funny guy – did anyone ever tell you that?'

Carl opened his mouth to reply.

'I want you to tell me how you feel about it,' said Simone, cutting him off.

'Delighted.'

Simone folded her arms. 'Probably as delighted as I am.' Her eyes widened. 'Do you feel happy, sad? Do you feel anything? Maybe you can't feel at all, and all you've got are crap jokes instead of real feelings.'

'Okay,' he raised his voice. 'I feel . . . sick. You happy now? I feel sick to think about being here and what happened and that there's a kid coming into this horrible fucking world because of me. There you go, now let's sign the register and jump in the limo. Let's call him or her something noble like, like, Gawain, or let's go all alternative and call it Sunflower or . . . I was thinking of mustard yellow for the nursery, with teddies . . . and rainbows splashed across the fucking walls.'

He stopped, aware that he was gripping the empty glass too hard and was brandishing it in Simone's direction.

'I hope being a total arsehole isn't inherited,' she said quietly. 'Isaac's a lovely boy, so I don't think it is. Because his dad was an arsehole as well.'

Her footsteps were quiet in the foyer, the fire door swinging open and squeaking to a soft close. Would she storm off to Fiona's? Unload on her? Would she throw him out?

Leaning over the half-completed jigsaw puzzle, Carl picked up a piece of red racing car. Something within him stirred, came to life. Shouting voices echoing from many years in the past, jigsaws fitting together under his concentration while his parents came apart. He gulped down another glass of water and went off to his room to wash. Face the day. All that shit.

In the reception area, a shaft of sunlight came through the frosted-glass window, lighting up the front desk. Carl went behind the desk, turned the guestbook to face him, its flat edge clearing the dust to reveal clean wood. He opened the book and signed in as 'Total Arsehole'. In the 'Number of Nights' column he wrote 'Indefinite Stay'. Three months ago he had signed 'Carl Shewan' for 'Three nights'. Now someone else had booked in, and there was only a passing resemblance to the other Carl Shewan.

On the shelf below the desk he spotted the ID scanner, an old model, like so many he had seen before in train stations and hotels and not paid much attention to. He took it out, the keypad and separate downlink processor, and laid them on the desk. After a bit of fiddling and forcing, he managed to prise apart the book-sized processor's plastic casing, exposing its circuitry. He squinted at the meaningless serial numbers and chip sets. Ingenuity, dexterity, made flesh, or at least memristors. Single-occupancy geeks or family men, who all had Government mortgages to pay off – they had made this, like they had made SCOPE and all the other kit that was needed to keep people safe from themselves. The people who had made the ID scanner were busy with their pieces of the puzzle. They only saw what was in front of them, the people who had been streamed into the only growth industry left, insecurity. They couldn't see the bigger picture.

Part of him wanted to crush the scanner under his heel, stamp on it, grind it into the dust. This gizmo should be obliterated, expunged from the cultural record: it was an aberration of nature. Instead of destroying it, he slotted both halves of the casing together again and put it back on the shelf. It didn't mean enough any more to bother with. The guys who'd invented it were just doing a job. It wasn't like they were guards at Auschwitz; they were just making little bits of rubbish, just as their training had shown them, and making precious money in the process. That was all. Maybe he should bury the fucking thing: HERE LIES FEAR – THE OLDEST TRICK IN THE BOOK.

He trudged up the stairs for a wash. The pressure in the tap was low again, and it took a good few minutes for four inches of water to dribble into the bath. He stripped off and climbed in, sat down in the cold puddle with his scrap of soap, removing the worst of the grime and stink of days. Cupping water over his head, the cold shock woke him up. His hair had grown to a soft crew-cut now and it needed cutting again. His beard was back. But what was the point in shaving? Why bother trying to look the way he used to look? Maybe he should start to sketch, like Terry, to forget who he was, to focus on something else that would eat up some time.

An hour later he was sitting up at the broch, watching, through binoculars, the crowd at the tiny church. He'd exhumed only two stones in the last week.

There was no minister or priest down at the church, so P.C. Gibbs, as the nearest thing, was joining together in matrimony the happy couple. There would be speeches. Looks like the local councillor is doing the honours: plastered in make-up, even now, hair solidly lacquered. It was scarcely believable.

Scanning along the bay, he saw Alec John was down at his house, spreading some scraps for the hens. Winter was coming and they weren't laying quite so often now. But Gibbs, and one of Cutler's mob, would still be round to collect; so said the Year 1 plan in Howard's survival strategy, and by Christ the committee were not going to deviate from it, in public at any rate. There was no chance of him pulling strings with George on anyone's behalf. Given Simone's condition, George was likely to use those strings to strangle him.

27

Carl had joined Alec John up on the hill; both men glad to avoid the wedding.

Within an hour, Alec John whispered, 'Down.' He pulled Carl by the sleeve and they lay still among the banks of heather.

'Over there,' Alec John said, pointing. Propped on his elbows, he raised a small pair of black binoculars.

Carl could see nothing.

'The wind's in our favour. Come on.'

Alec John crawled ahead and slid into a soft mossy gully. 'We'll have to wait, he's on the slope.'

'Can we not get any closer?'

'It's not that,' said Alec John, peering over the edge of the gully. 'The slope's rocky and it's too steep. If I take him there he'll roll all the way down and get smashed to bits. Bruised meat isn't very appetising, and he'll be harder to cut up. The slope's too steep for him if he goes further on . . . He'll come back, if we wait.'

'For how long?'

'Until he comes back.'

Twenty minutes later there was sign of movement. The stag had been eating the juiciest patches of grass that were hard to reach. If he'd fallen, it would have been the end of him, but the reward was rich, undisturbed grazing. With autumn curdling the air, it was worth the risk.

Alec John inched backwards into the gully. 'He'll come on a bit and then hopefully stop once he's more exposed. He'll want to check around for a bit before heading down into the glen. We'll take him then, with a bit of luck.'

They watched the stag come closer, picking his way along the ridge, wary of every sound and smell. He stopped.

'Just a bit more,' said Alec John, his eye to the rifle's scope. 'Another few metres will do it.'

'Is he too far away?'

'Ten years ago I might have, but I'm not too good at that kind of range any more. I can hit him, but that's not good enough. He could be miles away by the time he dies.'

They waited.

After what seemed like an age, the stag finally walked on towards them. But he soon stopped again, his nose in the air. He turned to face the long curve of the glen, and stood, almost side-on to the gun.

Alec John jerked as he fired, and the crack nearly deafened Carl. The stag's legs buckled and he collapsed as if his feet had been swiped from under him.

Carl rubbed his ear. 'Jesus.'

'Ha,' said Alec John. 'Now that's not bad, not bad at all.' He clambered to his feet, pulled what looked like a stopwatch from his pocket, and strode away.

Something was dead, thought Carl as they rushed towards the animal. A huge living creature had been shot dead, right in front of him, and it all looked so ordinary, so workaday. Alec John was more interested in his pedometer.

'Will you look at that?' he said, stopping right next to the stag. 'A hundred and sixty-four metres. It's been a good few years since it was one shot from that range.'

There was no obvious hole in the deer, but then Carl figured that the exit wound would be on the other side. Still, there was nothing on the chest or head. He stooped to look at the beast, the mound of breeze-ruffled, brown-grey fur, and the staring eyes.

'Where did you get him?'

'Base of the neck. Severs the spinal chord and windpipe. I couldn't get a heart shot, and I knew he was turning for home. We were about to lose him.'

Alec John laid his rifle on the rough grass and took off his wax jacket. From the inside pocket he pulled a sheathed knife, a silver seven-inch blade with a plain black handle.

'We have to bleed him first,' said Alec John. He knelt by the animal's side. 'Find the breastbone, you're over the aorta, and then ... in you go.'

Alec John worked the knife a little and then pulled it out. Like a bottle of wine on its side, the blood poured out onto the grass. 'That'll take a few minutes.'

Carl felt his knees weaken. 'I didn't know ... Do you have to do it up here?'

'Of course.' Alec John squinted at him. 'I thought you said you weren't squeamish?'

'Not when it's ... meat, no. But this is different. A few minutes ago this was alive, eating and walking around. Now it's dead and we're sticking knives into it.'

At Alec John's insistence, Carl helped to manoeuvre the carcass onto its back. The stag was a good eighteen stones.

Finding his mark, Alec John set about the next part of the process. With a sound like tearing cloth, the knife was dragged along the deer's belly, opening the hide from dick to sternum. Taking great care, next he unzipped the fine membrane that encased the viscera.

'This is life,' said Alec John. He rolled the stag onto its side, and a coil of tubing slopped out onto the rough grass.

'All I can see is blood and death.'

'That's where you're wrong. This is life.' He pointed in the direction of the village. 'Our life. This is what's true now.' He continued to work the rest of the guts loose, switching knives to one with a curved blade.

'People have lived around the River Lair for thousands of years. It's only recently they started going to the supermarket. This is back to how it was. Help me or don't, but realise that.' He started to clean the knives with handfuls of grass. 'You might, in the middle of January, after a few months of fish and turnip. Now, you stay here, and I'll go and get the argocat.'

Alec John left Carl alone on the damp hillside with the dead deer and a pile of steaming organs.

•

Everyone was pumped up. There was a frenetic energy inside the community centre: the release of tension through vicious enjoyment. The bride and groom had long since departed, leaving a few revellers to warm themselves with dancing, home-brew and the few bottles of wine George had conjured from what he had previously said was an empty cellar.

Carl left the community centre, the sound of riotous fiddle, guitar and clapping following him into the fresh air. That kind of traditional dancing he'd never been able to master, and he certainly wasn't in the mood to try again. It was difficult for Carl not to view the whole event, both the ceremony and the dance, as some kind of hysterical, hallucinatory episode.

The night air was cold, and it sobered him up. The rain was on, just spattering, not the horizontal stuff of the week before. He'd had too much to drink. Should never have had that whisky either. Time to blow home.

'Home,' he said to himself. Pissed again, home to Room 7. Not to his flat with all his own stuff, with lenses and other distractions and fighting the good-but-pointless fight. In a way, he still yearned for CivCon, and food riots, and Eric arguing with the PLC. All that business had kept him alive and kept him thinking. Now he had nothing to think about except that past.

As he headed back to the hotel, he didn't see the couple skulking around the side of the community centre. A girl was giggling. Carl swung round, focusing on where the noise had come from, but there was no sign of anyone. A fading sign above the doorway read: AUXILIARY HIGHLAND RATIONING CENTRE 102. Maybe George and the committee would get round to a renaming ceremony to boost morale. That would be another item discussed, and another step towards the new normality.

He sucked in some cold, salty air to clear his head. Crossing the road, he leant on the seafront railing, nothing but the cold sea-night in front of him.

He didn't want to pick up a gun again. He didn't want to learn how to shoot deer, to have something die at his hands. Never mind sins of omission – he wouldn't go on with learning how to shoot and slicing animals open, and that was that. It was sickening.

Alec John would have to be told in the morning. Giving him a hand was one thing, but no way was he going to put a bullet in anything. Thanks for the offer, but no thanks.

Inside the community centre, the music started up again. Feet stamped and hands clapped, noises that indicated enjoyment. Not everyone, though. There were a few who wouldn't dance, who sat in corners, grimly sipping the rations the committee had released for the occasion. There were folk who hadn't turned up at all, not because they didn't like the bride and groom or hadn't been invited, but because they thought having fun wasn't right. Isn't that what some religious zealots thought, anyway?

Carl's dead editor had liked to dance.

What a colour piece I've got for you here, Eric, Carl thought. The resilience and resourcefulness of a community pulling together. Leadership in a time of hardship. It's all here. He spat into the sea. And just as much bullshit as you'll find anywhere else.

He stood on the pier for a while then went back along the shorefront, leaving the lights of the community centre behind. An owl hooted. Carl felt hungry.

There were footsteps behind him on the road. He turned.

Someone was there, coming closer in the darkness with the light behind.

'That you, Terry?'

The silent figure came closer without speaking.

Carl waited for a response. 'What're you creeping about for?' he said, relieved.

'Just heading home,' said Terry.

'Likewise. I've given up. Pretending to have fun is hard work.'

Terry walked away into the dark, switching on his torch. 'See you.'

'Yeah,' breathed Carl, watching the narrow beam of light move away along the shorefront. 'Yeah,' he said. 'Mañana.'

The ticking clock was the only sound in the dark hotel lobby. Carl stretched out his hand to feel the wall and the doorway to the residents' lounge, brushing his fingers over the framed photos. The place still smelled of fried fish from dinnertime. As he felt his way into the kitchen, he almost forgot to curse the darkness; he was getting used to moving about like this at night.

The wind was picking up now, pushing at the windows in gusts, getting stronger. Maybe it would clobber the hotel like it did the other night. Carl stood in the darkened kitchen. There was bound to be some fish, maybe some of that mayonnaise George had made, and a few bottles of lime-green fizz to wash it all down, if there were any left.

Standing in the lobby, Carl heard voices in the street, and footsteps running past the front door. A guy shouting, sounding none too pleased about something. Then silence. Some drunken rumpus. Ordinary aggression. He fumbled his way to steal more of George's booze.

•

Tongue: the wrong size and dust-dry. Throat: painful proof that

211

he had, in fact, vomited until there was nothing else inside him to come out. Sitting up caused a bowling ball to shift position inside his head. At least there was no sign of puke anywhere near the bed, or on the bed, or on him.

Let's hear it for the committee, and their morale-boosting largesse. The wagon he'd been steering more or less on the straight and narrow was well and truly off the road now. Mixing different types of booze will do it every time, except there wouldn't be a next time, for a long time.

Alec John was expecting him today, though there was flexibility as far as clocking-in was concerned. Clouds were dark over the bay and it looked like it might rain. Maybe a hurricane would arrive and give him reason to lie, inert and suffering, for several more hours. He was going to call it a day with Alec John anyway. Enough with blood.

Tongue and throat demanded moisture. Carl sat up, groaning as the room spun and his head pulsed. Maybe he could ask at the community centre for some paracetamol. This time, the committee might take a kinder view of self-inflicted pain, given that its own generosity had been the cause. They might break out the painkillers. Maybe Terry would do him a fried egg. Eggs were good for hangovers – in the absence of any synthetic remedy.

With sledgehammer intensity, there was a sharp knocking at the room door.

He jerked himself upright, wished he hadn't, and quickly checked to see he was decently clothed, rubbing his face and smoothing his hair.

'Come in.'

It was Alec John.

'I didn't expect a personal wake-up call,' said Carl, swinging his feet onto the floor. He steeled himself for what he had to say.

Closing the door, Alec John stood, grim-faced. 'Something horrible happened last night,' he said. 'To Terry.'

Carl's hangover loosened its hooks. 'What do you mean – horrible? Is he okay?'

'Well, I heard different versions of what happened, but . . . it looks as if he's lost an eye.'

Carl mouth fell open. 'What?'

Alec John nodded. 'He's at Dr Morgan's now.'

'An eye?' Carl searched for his shoes. 'For fuck's sake. I saw him, I think, after the reception. What happened?'

'No one's sure. There was some kind of scuffle. It was pitch black and they ended up in the pine trees near the old bus stop. Casper says it was a branch.'

'Casper? You mean it wasn't an accident?'

Alec John shook his head, without any real conviction. 'I don't know the details.'

Carl pulled on his shoes, all trace of hangover purged by adrenaline. 'A fucking branch? Come on. Did Casper attack him?'

Alec John shrugged. He looked at Carl. 'Casper's cousin, this girl, Gemma, said that Terry raped her.'

Carl stopped tying his laces. He looked at his left shoe. The sole was starting to come loose near the ball of his foot. Maybe someone would have the right kind of glue to fix it, or any kind. Maybe there was some kind of plant resin . . .

'Who says it was rape?'

'The girl.'

'Any witnesses?'

Alec John squinted at him. 'Not as far as I know, no.'

'Right,' said Carl. 'So this girl says she was raped by Terry. There are no witnesses – but Casper attacks Terry anyway.'

'She's not known as a liar, Carl.'

'No one is. But everyone lies.'

Alec John got to his feet. 'I'm only going by what I hear. Terry's a nice guy but . . .' He shrugged. 'I don't know. These are . . . different times.'

Carl finished tying his shoes and grabbed his jacket. 'Yeah,' he muttered, opening the room door. 'But maybe not that different after all.'

•

Treating injured drunks wasn't that unusual for Dr Morgan, and she'd seen a lot worse than this during various stints in A&E. But it had been a long time since the last bad one in Inverlair, maybe three years or so. There was always booze involved and nearly always a fight between young men, though girls could be just as bad. And here it was again: the same ingredients in the same bloody mess, even after all that had happened. The disease had erupted again.

Dr Morgan gave Terry another shot of diamorphine. Not much left now. The orbital muscle in his right eye had been all but severed; sclera and cornea were in shreds. She pulled off her bloodied latex gloves and opened the pedal bin to drop them in.

She stopped. Maybe it wouldn't do to be so fussy about hygiene any more; there was probably no infection in Terry's eye, so the latex gloves could be saved, cleaned, for another time. She threw them in the sink instead.

The doorbell rang.

'What's happened to Terry?' asked Carl, as soon as Dr Morgan opened the door.

'He's resting,' she said. 'He's in shock, so it's for the best if he gets some sleep.'

'Is it true? Has he lost an eye?'

Dr Morgan hesitated. She considered inviting them inside, decided against it. Before she could answer, Carl said, 'Was it a knife?'

'I'm not sure,' said Dr Morgan, folding her thin arms. 'It could have been anything. Whatever it was, I had to take the eye out. I couldn't see any wood fibres, but that doesn't rule out . . .'

She smoothed her greying hair. 'It was something sharp, that's all I can say.'

Carl sighed. He glanced at Alec John. 'Can we see him?'

'You can,' said Dr Morgan. 'But please don't wake him up. He also cracked a couple of ribs, and dislocated his right shoulder.' She stiffened. 'I've also examined the girl, Gemma. P.C. Gibbs will interview her soon.'

'How is she?'

Everything was overlapping. Due process had no chance in this situation ... Carl and Terry were friends, and Dr Morgan's examination would, ordinarily, have formed the case for the prosecution. Yet here was the prime suspect's associate asking how the victim was.

Dr Morgan shook her head and closed the door.

28

From within the broch's low walls, Carl watched the village. A roiling bank of cloud was swelling out over the Atlantic, threatening. It was bitterly cold, and he'd not put on a jumper under his Gore-Tex. Just his luck if he fell ill again. His lungs had been clear for weeks now. He wouldn't want to clog them up again with a cold, or worse.

With his binoculars, he saw Gibbs walk round to Gemma's parents', then to Dr Morgan's, and then round to Casper's house.

Different rules. That's what Gibbs had told him, making all the right noises about procedure and a thorough investigation. And then what?

Maybe the girl wasn't entirely blameless. He remembered the glint in her eye when she came round for Terry's dope . . . maybe it had just got out of hand. It felt plausible. But he felt uneasy with the thought. If Terry had raped her, he must be punished. That's what should happen.

Simone. How much interest would she expect him to take? What did she want? Carl couldn't conceive any answer that would make sense to him. There's nothing, physically, to be done about any of it, he figured. The other day she had asked him if he wondered if it would be born healthy or not, or if it would be a boy or a girl. He was finding it difficult to care about any of it.

She was having his kid, he wasn't about to run away anywhere, and there was zero chance of a relationship. All the salient facts covered, and there was no need to keep going over them.

'Different times, different rules,' Carl said out loud, blinking as the Atlantic air surged over him. No white boat was going to come. Howard's friends – what a fantasy that had been. No matter when SCOPE packed in, he would remain adrift and unrescued, and there was no point in believing anything else. He was a refugee.

Down in the village: a figure near the boatyard, just a glimpse of form. Carl lifted the binoculars again, but the person was now inside the boatyard. He cursed his wandering attention.

Maybe the figure had been a paunchy fifty-year-old copper on his way for a friendly chat. Maybe it was justice, hot-footing it to apprehend a lynch mob.

This is life, Carl thought. This is what's true now.

•

'Are you going to charge any of us, Mr Gibbs?'

Work came to a halt in the boatyard. Gibbs managed, just about, to project a gruff professionalism from inside his uniform. Cutler's greeting had made a civilian of him, but Gibbs ignored the provocation.

'Terry Noble lost an eye last night, Adam.'

'That's careless of him. We'll help him look for it.'

One of the work crew suppressed a snort.

'I would like to ask a few questions,' said Gibbs, who leant against a workbench with his arms and feet crossed. 'Just to clear up a few loose ends. Surely that can't do any harm.'

Adam nodded to himself, scuffed the ground with his work boots. Casper and the other guys exchanged glances, said nothing. Apparently deep in thought, Adam studied the concrete floor, considered the rafters and the tin roof.

Gibbs waited.

'Suppose,' began Adam at last, 'just suppose, that none of us want to answer any of your questions, then what?'

The men looked at Gibbs.

'That might mean you've got something to hide.'

Adam nodded. 'Would it now.' He fell silent again, then went over and continued to load ten-gallon biofuel drums onto a trailer. The first drum crashed down heavily on the trailer's metal floor.

'You sorted the chain on that saw yet, Gav?' said Adam.

Gav was in his mid-twenties, gold-stud earring; blond streaks in a mop of scruffy hair. He smirked at Gibbs. 'Fully operational, boss.'

Everyone except Casper went back to work. He didn't look too pleased with the situation.

'Come on, Brian,' said Gibbs quietly, dropping the nickname. 'Just a few questions.'

Casper pursed his lips. 'I didn't do it,' he said, frowning. 'I pushed him, I think. That's all . . . I was pissed.'

'Don't let him confuse you, Casper,' shouted Adam. 'That's how these bastards work. None of us want to answer any questions, Gibbs.' He stepped towards the door. 'If you want to pull us in, why don't you phone the nearest station for back-up?' He grinned, and went on with his work. 'Looks like it's all down to you, Cuntstable, and if you don't mind, given the circumstances, I don't think any of us are going to come quietly.'

Gibbs moved towards Adam. 'You're being very stupid, Adam.'

'Leave him,' growled Casper.

'There's fuck all you can do about it, Gibbs,' shouted Gav, tensing himself. He picked up a spanner.

Exasperated, Dennis groaned. 'Oh, for fuck's sake, behave yourselves.'

Everyone ignored him.

Adam smiled at Gibbs. 'Gav's right. We're busy here, so why don't you go and hassle the Dutchman for his eggs – impound his grass plants while you're at it. Now there's a real criminal for you, Constable, a real menace to the community. I assume you'll be arresting Terry Sullivan for rape, once the doc's finished patching him up?'

Outside, through the open end of the boatshed, only the birds and the sea made their noise. Gibbs would lose what was left of his authority if he backed off; yet there was no way he could handle the three of them. A dignified exit was the only option.

'This is not the end of the matter,' he said gravely. 'There will be consequences, guys. And I'll be having a word with your father, Adam.'

'I'm a bit too old to get my arse slapped, Mr Gibbs.' Cutler turned back to his work. 'Carry on.'

29

There had to be a chance. His son and the grandkids were in a village in Buckinghamshire. Maybe there, too, was a notspot. There was always a chance. They were in the countryside, maybe far enough away from a mast or a town. Maybe they were all okay and the boy just wasn't able to get in touch. Maybe they were alive. Gibbs tried to believe it.

On the computer screen, the slideshow of photos kept scrolling, though the accompanying soundtrack had been muted. Music could always push those buttons, switch the emotions off and on. Gibbs heard his wife come through the front door. He turned off the computer, picking up his needle and thread again as he wiped his eyes. Ellen appeared in the living-room doorway, watching her husband for a moment. Her hair was greyer, thinner now, and her face was lined; she looked years older in just three months.

'Have you told anyone yet, about the girl?'

Gibbs carried on sewing. 'No,' he said. 'I'm going to fix this first. I noticed the pocket had come loose earlier.'

He glanced up at his wife. 'Do you think I should still wear it? I mean, do you think there's any point?'

Ellen considered the uniform spread out on the table, knew that the confrontation with Cutler the other day had shaken him. 'If you feel you have a right to fill it.'

Gibbs put down the needle and thread. 'Does it make sense any more?'

Ellen touched the uniform. 'Maybe it makes more sense now than ever.'

'I've got a gun, of course.' He felt his wife hold a breath, then relax.

'A gun ... what an excellent idea,' she said. 'Casper's got one too, and I'm sure Adam Cutler does as well. Why don't you go and shoot it out with them? I'll come along and cheer you on.'

'I don't know what to do, Ellen. There's no easy ...'

There was a loud knocking at the front door.

'Now that doesn't sound very friendly,' Ellen muttered wearily. 'I think I know who that might be.'

•

Up at the edge of the redzone, Carl had felt his resolve waver. Could you still cling to the old idea of the law taking its course? But now he felt angry again, and Gibbs's frosted-glass front door took the brunt of it.

'I want to know if you intend to arrest Casper for what he did to Terry,' he said, as soon as the door opened. 'If you're not, I want to know why. No more excuses. I'm not leaving until you tell me what you're going to do.'

Gibbs took Carl into the living room. A glass of Amaretto was offered.

'It's been sitting in the cupboard for years. No one likes it.'

Carl refused.

'So,' said Gibbs, 'you'd like me to arrest Casper – all six feet four of him – by myself.'

'I'll come with you. Maybe we can get one or two other guys.'

'Maybe,' said Gibbs, inspecting his patched uniform by the light of the window. 'Casper's in his mum and dad's house. They might not take too kindly to seeing their son carted off – and to where? There are no cells in Inverlair.'

'We can lock him up somewhere. I don't know ...'

Gibbs nodded. 'Maybe we can. Casper's dad's in his sixties but he's still a big fit man. Maybe his mum will weigh in as well. Do you think we can handle the three of them if Casper doesn't want to co-operate?'

'We can get others to help us.'

Carl wished he'd taken the offer of a drink, even if it was disgusting. He unzipped his jacket. The list of options all seemed to lead to painful, if not impossible, outcomes.

'Who should we ask?' continued Gibbs. 'Offhand, I don't know of anyone who would volunteer to tackle Casper and his old man, never mind Cutler and Gavin Marshall.'

Carl sat down in the soft armchair, staring straight ahead at the space in the corner where a TV had once stood.

'Now d'you see the problem?' said Gibbs. 'If they all stick together, we'll need at least five or six other guys to help us. Do you really want to start all that? A posse?'

'Do you have a gun? I've got one now.'

Gibbs stiffened. 'Don't be daft. Yes, I have a gun, but so does Casper, a shotgun, and I wouldn't be surprised if Adam Cutler had one too.' He looked around the room and sighed. 'They're just ordinary guys, Carl. There's nothing bad about them. Cutler's full of himself, but Casper . . .'

'Has Catharine Morgan examined the girl yet?' said Carl.

'Yes.'

'And?'

'That's none of your business, Mr Shewan.' Gibbs put his hands on the windowsill, looking out.

There was a rain shower on its way into the bay, a fine haze drifting over Heron Point and the headland.

Clearing his throat, he studied his meaty fingers, splayed out on the sill.

'Seems it was consensual, to begin with, then Terry went a lot further than Gemma wanted. Casper is her cousin, and he found her crying, and not exactly sober. You can imagine how someone like Casper reacted. She told Dr Morgan all that earlier today. And Dr Morgan told me.'

Sleety rain slapped its first dabs onto the living-room window. In normal circumstances, Terry and Casper would be facing jail sentences. But the actual scenario, the chain of offence and revenge, was playing out in fast-forward. Carl could see it, understand it – accept it, even – until anger got the better of him. Terry had been disfigured for life, and there was nothing to show that he was guilty beyond reasonable doubt. He thought of Gemma, caught up in the moment then unable to stop it, and he felt revulsion at what Terry had done.

Carl zipped his jacket up, unsure of his next move. Gibbs told him about the confrontation with Adam at the boatyard, and Carl felt his anger and frustration rise again. Adam and the rest would make fucking mincemeat of him. He knew it. As he headed out into the squall, action and reaction formed a plausible truth, one he felt obliged to accept.

30

A few days later, a strong wind swung to the north-east, and it turned colder, drier. Clutching the deltameter, Carl trudged back over the northern ridge from the furthest edge of the redzone. One day, the signal would not register. One day, the horizon would recede, and he would be able to travel further than 2.26 miles. Right now, he would happily have left this hole of a place and never clapped eyes on it again.

He'd read somewhere about the fear of a north-easterly wind, back when the Vikings were doing their stuff as the latest incarnation of invincible power. A north-easterly pushed the Scandinavians where they wanted to go, across the North Sea, and they didn't need to waste so much muscle-power rowing the few hundred miles. Such a wind meant big trouble for the locals.

Folk would have seen the longships from up here, the first masts rounding the headland. Now there was terror for you, having that lot slide into view. What would he have done? Fight or flight? Where would he have run to? This would have been home, in the bay, with domesticated animals and shelter and family, so the men would stay and fight. And get slaughtered. Plenty of eyes gouged out in those days. Enough grief and death to go round. No scarcity as far as they were concerned.

He felt the nip of a wind that was pushing the clouds south-west, clearing the sky for night frosts. Three and a half months ago the land had looked like a green Mars. Now it was more like the real thing: barrens of brown, grey summits of scalped winter rock, ochreous mattresses of bog. The Vikings were welcome to Inverlair. They could have it.

In those houses without photovoltaics on the roof, or solid-fuel stoves, it would now be turning very cold. The community centre would be warm though, with bunks laid out for those who needed them. Maybe the winter wouldn't be that cold. Maybe everyone would survive; even the oldest ones who chose to stay in their unheated homes.

Dr Morgan said Terry was fit enough to go home today as the skinplast had taken. His cracked ribs were bandaged. Now all Gibbs had to do was let him. It wasn't as if he was going to run away, and Carl doubted he was a danger to anyone. All Terry had to do was walk home, along the shorefront, past the hotel and the community centre and the boatyard, a gauze plaster over his eye announcing to everyone that the rumours were true. They would assume he was a rapist. Maybe they'd lynch him from one of the ash trees at the graveyard. Then they could just drop him straight into a hole in the ground.

Gemma was full of herself; cocky and whip-smart. But when it came right down to it she was only a girl. The rules couldn't be that different; some of them had to be kept. They had to be. It couldn't just be the appetites that ruled. There had to be safeguards, a veneer of measured responses. There had to be control.

As he made his way down from the broch, picking up the forest track behind Alec John's, Carl remembered what Terry had said a couple of weeks ago, a conversation that had started off about sex, but which had strayed onto more emotional ground. To begin with it was sex and hunger – where people are most like animals. The worst was hunger, Carl had said, because you can go without sex for ages. Party World avatars more or less gave you the same thing anyway, if you had all the kit and the lenses and enough money for your own spraysuit. Hunger, on the other hand, was a different beast altogether. People could turn nasty if they were hungry. A day would do it: four missed meals, wasn't that what they said? Kill their own mothers for a slice of toast then, most folk would. He'd seen it happen. Well, maybe not mothers, but at Kelvingrove, before CivCon took over security at the rationing centres, he'd seen kids get elbowed out of the way for a few slices of bread by fully grown men.

So, there they were, talking about sex and death. Terry had been sitting stoned in the caravan in front of the tiny stove. He'd been talking about how people were clinging to each other and how that daft marriage was still going ahead, even though he'd heard the bride-to-be had been on the verge of calling it off before the redzone happened. Obviously, the groom was none the wiser about any of that. He was delighted, the sap, talking about how love and life have to go on. A nice speech, by all accounts. If only he knew how close he'd come to being an ex-fiancé.

'Maybe you can't blame the woman for reappraising her situation,' Terry had said. 'Her options are kind of limited now, unless she wants to shack up with a meathead like Casper or Gav. Instead of doing that, she's making the best of a bad situation.

'What's your least worst option, Carl? And what's mine? We both have to think about that – because we're men, not monks, you know what I mean? As long as we've got enough food to keep us alive, and a roof to keep the rain off, the other big appetite will need satisfied, sooner or later. That much never changes. Maybe you could be with Simone, I don't know. But what about me? What are my options in the female department?'

He should have taken the hint then, and at other times as well – those little silences and awkward moments between Terry and Gemma. Maybe the normal rules didn't apply any more. Maybe it was okay for a thirty-three-year-old man to have sex with a fifteen-year-old girl. Perhaps it was time to get back to a more basic version of human behaviour. Was nature that perverted? Did the Vikings worry about the age of consent?

There would be no legal ramifications, that much Carl was sure about, unless Gibbs decided to pick the easy target this time and arrest Terry for underage sex. Somehow, as Jess bounded across the field to meet him, Carl doubted that would happen. Gibbs, he figured, would probably prefer to forget all about the whole thing.

A coughing fit told Carl that Alec John was in his workshop. He didn't appear to be doing much, just moving things around. Carl watched him through the window, listlessly moving to and fro, picking up tools and opening drawers.

Without turning around, Alec John said, 'So . . . you're back.'

'Well, only to say that maybe it's not working out. Maybe I'm not the right man for the job.'

'Is that so? Why d'you say that?'

'The gralloching, I don't know if I can do it. And . . . the other day, this huge animal was alive, and then it was dead. I don't know if I can handle doing that.'

'So you'd rather not eat venison, or grouse?'

'I can live without them. Look, I've been thinking about what happened to Terry, and what he did. It's . . . brutal. It sickened me.'

'It is brutal, yes. But the world can be brutal sometimes. You can hide from that or you can accept it.'

'I'm not hiding from it.'

'Of course you are. Your job was hiding in the shadows, and now you're out in the open and you don't like it. You need something to do, something to occupy your mind. If you can think of another job besides this one that's more useful, go right ahead – knock yourself out.'

Alec John wiped his hands on his padded checked shirt. 'How's Terry?'

Carl picked an adjustable spanner from its place on the wall, feeling its cool weight in his grip. Alec John had gone to the trouble of drawing a felt-tip outline around each tool. Every one had its allotted place from which to hang.

'Dr Morgan said he was well enough go home,' replied Carl. 'Gibbs said he could go home.'

'Has he spoken to Terry about what happened?'

Carl shook his head. 'He tried to, but Terry wouldn't say a word. I don't know what happens now. I don't think anyone does. I wonder if we should go and see him.'

Alec John stiffened. 'He might have raped that girl.'

'He might have, yes. But the only thing we know for sure is that he's been scarred for life.'

Alec John said nothing. The two men set off down the track to the main road.

'One day, maybe sooner rather than later, I won't be able to do this,' said Alec John. 'The doctor told me that herself.'

'I thought she couldn't say for sure?'

Alec John shook his head. 'The timing of it, no, no one can be sure of that. But without the medicine it'll come back. It already has.'

Carl glanced at him as they walked. 'Not bad enough to keep you indoors though.'

'No, not that bad. But I can feel it all the same, even on the lower slopes now, never mind the ridge. A shortness of breath that wasn't there a few months ago, before . . .'

They walked a little further along the main road, crossed the bridge at the head of the bay, the river in spate beneath it.

'There must be other people, better suited to it,' said Carl.

'There are. But it would benefit you the most.'

'I'm not ready for it.' But even as he uttered the words, Carl knew how weak they sounded. He wasn't ready for a lot of things. Stuff like tolerating the disfigurement of a friend, and the perpetrators getting clean away with it. He thought of young guys in Glasgow, getting killed in gang fights, and the coppers hardly bothering with a proper investigation, even if CivCon actually told them the murder had happened.

'Suit yourself,' said Alec John.

They walked past Cutler's boatyard and there was nothing doing, no sign of activity at all. Maybe folk knew that Terry could go home today and they didn't want to have to look at him. You'd think someone would come out, though, someone who cared to see how the man was feeling. Perhaps Terry had sacrificed the right to any such display. People could slake their curiosity from behind their fucking curtains.

Carl knocked on Dr Morgan's door. She answered, her face set hard, and told Carl and Alec John not to expect too much from Terry.

'He's still in shock,' she said. 'Post-traumatic stress, I'd say, though I can't be sure. He doesn't speak much.'

She led them through to the sitting room. Carl couldn't help but stare.

'All right, mate,' he said quietly to Terry, who was sitting, slouched, on a hard-backed chair, fingers splayed on his thighs.

After a second Terry looked up at the voice. 'Hi,' he said. There was something he wanted to say, but he wasn't sure what it was or why he should say it. He looked at the ceiling, down at his hands. No clues there. There was a pain in his eye. He was wearing a bandage. There was a reason for it all that he wanted to forget.

'Is there any more tea?' Terry asked Dr Morgan. 'Maybe they want a cup of tea.'

She nodded.

'They gave me half an ounce, so I should be able to squeeze another few cups out of it.'

Nice gesture from the committee, thought Carl: a few cups of tea for the inconvenience of losing an eye, the dependable fixer-upper that can soothe away all the bad things in life. He accepted the offer anyway, as did Alec John. Dr Morgan fetched the cups and teapot on a tray. Barely moving, Terry sat, head bowed.

After an awkward half-minute, Dr Morgan asked, 'Any luck with the deer today?'

Alec John took a quick breath. 'No,' he said, repositioning his baseball cap. 'Not today. They're mostly in the other end of the forest now, the part we can't get into. Maybe they're getting wise to where we can go and where we can't. Think I'll try out towards the Needles for a spell, give the forest a rest.' He glanced at Carl. 'One of us will, anyway.'

Carl tried to sound as upbeat as he could. 'So, will you be allowed to come home today?'

Again there was a wait while the question registered with Terry, winding its way towards an answer, which then worked its way mouthwards. Terry looked at Carl, and Carl wanted to look at Terry. But when you're looking into someone's face you generally scan across both eyes, the other person doing the same, and there shouldn't be just one eye, wide and wild, staring back, bandages over a raw hole where the other one should be.

Carl looked away.

'Yes,' said Terry. 'I, um, Catharine . . . Dr Morgan says that . . .' He nodded to himself, knotting his dirty-nailed fingers together. 'She says that. The copper says that. So that's what happening. I'm good to go.'

'Good,' said Carl, standing up.

Suddenly Terry sniggered, became alert. 'Fucking cyclops now, eh?'

The others exchanged glances.

'Bang goes my tennis game. You need binocular vision for that gig, eh? It's all about depth perception. Parallax. Still be good at pool though, because I always close my right eye when I take a shot. Save a fortune on lenses as well.' He sniggered again. 'Worse things have happened, eh? Worse things.'

No one knew how to react.

'Mine eye has seen the glory,' echoed Terry, snorting with laughter. He lapsed into silence while the others gulped their tea.

One their way out, Carl saw Simone and Gibbs walking towards the surgery. He waited for them, skipping the pleasantries when they reached the gate.

'Did you speak to your brother?'

'Yes,' said Simone, her voice flat. 'He had nothing to do with it.'

'Is that what he told you?'

Simone gave a slow deliberate nod. 'Yes. That's what he told me.'

Carl grunted. 'I'm only asking.'

'As I said the other day: if you grow a pair of balls – remember those? – you know where to find me if you want to talk about anything else that might concern you. Anything at all that might affect the way you live your life in any small way.'

'You don't even fucking know me, for fuck's sake,' hissed Carl.

Simone cocked her head. 'No, I don't – but I know your kind.'

Before Carl could answer, or ask what she was doing visiting the surgery, Simone went inside with Gibbs.

He refocused on what needed to be done. He could fetch Howard's car. If it would still start and its tyres weren't flat, he could get it out of Hendrik's lock-up and drive Terry home in it. That would mean no grand parade past all the houses. Better for Terry if they took the car home. But then Carl figured that those responsible should be forced to take a good fucking look at what they'd done. Did they think justice, whatever that meant, had been served?

31

Next day, Carl tried again with Gibbs. But the due process of law wasn't about to process anything.

'Gemma told Casper she'd been raped.'

'So that makes it okay? Taking someone's eye out and scarring them for life?'

Gibbs's eyes narrowed. 'I didn't say it was okay, Mr Shewan. It's very bloody far from okay. But there are different rules now, and I can't do anything about those. These are the hard-and-fast facts of life, I'm afraid. I thought you'd have grasped that by now. It is what it is, and there's nothing either of us can do about it. I'm sure as hell not going to start anything with Casper and Adam and Christ knows who else. We've been through enough. We've probably lost our son.' His jaw tightened, working on a pulse of angry grief. 'How do you think Liz would react if these bastards beat the shit out of me, or worse? Get a grip, man, and leave it alone. Perhaps you should spare a thought for a fifteen-year-old girl, rather than the man who might have raped her.'

Swallowing hard, Gibbs bit his lip and took a step back inside his porch. 'We've had enough pain to last a lifetime. You help yourself to more, if you feel up to it ... And it sounds to me like Gemma was groomed – supplied with drugs – by your fucking *mate*.'

Gibbs slammed his front door. It had been over three months since the redzone had sprung up. Now Inverlair was right in his face again, as hostile as any microwave cannon.

•

'I can't believe there was no one else who'd do the job.'

'Well, there was maybe one or two. I was giving it some thought, before . . .'

'Right.'

They walked on.

'So no one else will do it?'

Alec John screwed his face up. 'Well, I wouldn't exactly say that. I just thought that maybe you needed it more than most. Especially when you took the air rifle apart without a spring compressor.' He laughed.

'Very funny,' said Carl. 'But I was lucky the spring didn't take my eye out. And then Terry, you know? Whether it was deliberate or not I don't know, but it's odd, don't you think?'

'I'm not sure about that,' said Alec John. 'Maybe you're reading too much into it, over-thinking things, but maybe that's an occupational hazard with you. I think you're missing an opportunity up on the hill. I can feel my lungs getting worse and I need a decision. I need to take someone else on, if not you, then someone else.'

'No pressure, eh?'

'Yes, pressure. I'm not blowing my own trumpet, but this is an important job. You might not find it very pleasant, but you'll get used to it. It's also better than getting stoned all the time.'

Carl laughed. 'Hey, don't knock it until you've tried it.'

'Oh, I've tried it.'

'Eh? When?'

'A long time ago, before I came back here.'

'When was that? How d'you mean – came back?'

'You're a nosey bugger, aren't you?'

They passed through the forest-track gates and onto the road.

'Another of my old habits,' muttered Carl.

Alec John grunted, his heavy boots clumping on the tarmac as they rounded the bay. 'Well, since you're interested, I was twenty-seven at the time. My father took a heart attack, a bad one, so I came back, yes, almost forty years ago now.' He chuckled. 'I've tried a few things, for sure. Even after I came back, for a time.'

'What did you do before you came back?'

'I was a crane operator on a seismic survey ship.'

'Really?'

'Yes.'

'And your dad, he was the head gamekeeper here?'

'He was.'

Carl felt a tightening in the air. 'I thought . . .' He changed tack. 'Where were you a crane operator?'

'Where?'

'Aye.'

'All over. Oil companies, mainly. It was good in those days.'

'Good pay?'

'Yes, plenty of work in those days, before we drained the planet dry. We did some deep-water stuff off Angola, Spitsbergen. I spent a year in Baku, in the Caspian.'

'Really?'

'You sound surprised.'

They stopped at Terry's gate. What could Carl say – that he'd assumed Alec John had been born with heather sprouting from his ears? He fumbled for an explanation. But Alec John had moved on.

'How's Terry? I should come round more, but after being out with you on the hill, I'm tired.' He shook his head. 'It's a piss-poor excuse.'

'No, it's not.' Carl rubbed his face. 'He's okay, physically anyway. But it's affected him – there's no doubt about that. He doesn't say much and then he talks a lot of garbage, to be honest. Ideally, he'd get counselling . . . something.'

'Has he said anything about . . . that night?'

Carl sighed. 'It happened. They both had a bit to drink at the reception, went for a walk along the shore, started snogging and

234

then ... it went too far. He said he felt horrible after doing it and he just wanted to get away from the girl as quickly as possible.'

'And so she went to tell Casper ...'

'No,' said Carl. 'Casper found her crying, by the side of the community centre. She told him what had happened.'

They were quiet for a spell at Terry's gate. Then Alec John brightened as he changed the subject. 'Do you see how important it is to stay low to the ground when you're crawling, especially your arse and your head?' He laughed. 'And will you try and remember: when you get the chance, go for a crow with the 10-bore, or a rabbit – that's why you've got it.'

Carl looked sheepish. 'Sorry. I forget.'

'You mean you don't want to,' said Alec John, a stern edge in his voice. 'You're going to have to make your mind up about that. Always take a crow if you can – that's the rule. You stick to them or you're no gamekeeper, it's as simple as that.'

'The poor old crow,' said Carl. 'Just trying to survive like everything else.'

Alec John shook his head firmly. 'They're vermin,' he said, shouldering the .308. 'I'll see you tomorrow, if you're still interested. I'll show you which areas to burn in the spring for the grouse. But you have to tell me one way or the other. Are you in or out?'

Carl said goodbye, watched the old man walk down the road towards the head of the bay. He was definitely slower now, less able, and more reliant on the argocat to get onto the hill. It was such a lurching uncomfortable ride that Carl would rather walk.

He went through Terry's gate and part way down the track. He stopped among the stand of alder where the earth and treacly leaf-mulch smelled of rain. This end of Terry's caravan had no windows. White smoke emerged from the tin chimney and vanished in the breeze. One-eyed Terry, who had stopped washing himself and was now mute – when he wasn't spouting gibberish – was in there.

Carl waited among the trees for a minute. Then he turned and walked back up the track. If he went quickly he would be at the head of the bay, beneath the big trees at the bridge, and Alec John wouldn't be able to see him walk back to the hotel.

•

From the window of Room 7 Carl watched Simone and Isaac set off on a visit. Down in the lobby he had been able to listen to her playing her flute through in the annexe, standing transfixed by the sound until it stopped. Then he'd hurried back upstairs to his room. It was the first time he'd heard her play, though he knew she did.

There was still no sign of a bump – when exactly did a woman start to show? But she'd put weight on, and there were hardly any in the village who'd managed to do that. As a pregnant woman she'd be getting extra food, according to Howard's system. Simone's right to calories was inviolable. Maybe they'd worship Howard as a god, as their saviour, in years to come. No. That was unkind.

Miscarriages happen in a high number of pregnancies. Carl had read that somewhere. But it was still there, no doubt about it, and pretty soon there would be no hiding it and then it would be a case of: here's this little baby and ooh and ahh and before you know it he's actually caring for it. That was the ever-changing world, making up new rules just as you're getting used to the old ones. He grabbed his jacket and rucksack, intent on heading out and up as far as he could, and he grabbed the 10-bore. Perhaps the time had indeed come to get rid of some predatory vermin.

Instead of heading straight onto the hill, Carl made his way along the edge of the northern headland, along the shoreline, past the roofless stone ruins of the old herring stations. There was nothing but time for him in Inverlair, an open-ended sentence stretching ahead. He might not even want to leave when the nearest base station failed. He shivered at the word: institutionalised.

What were the golden rules inside a prison? Watch your back. Keep out of trouble. Accept each day as it comes. Do your time. Keep active. Then what?

Howard had said that the masts would pack in within a few years. But approaching the cities and towns would take longer. SCOPE had numerous urban nodes, embedded in lampposts and on top of bus stops, so Howard had said, and they were all harvesting power from countless micro-renewable sources. SCOPE was a blanket of silence, with only a few small holes in the fabric. Years would pass before those holes got bigger, merged, then people would move back, recolonise; maybe they'd be non-Europeans. Carl smiled as he considered a racist's reaction on that prospect. Repatriation may no longer be an enforceable policy response.

Fissured cliffs of shale loomed ahead as the worn path beside the herring stations gave way to rocky shoreline. It took him over half an hour to travel along the base of the northern headland, over a jumble of rocks, and in that time the sky had darkened. A shower was on the way, but he had on his waterproofs, so he'd be dry. He sat down for a spell, an outcrop acting as a windshield, picked up a dark pebble and turned it over in his hand, staring up at the shale cliffs. The book in the residents' lounge had said this was the right kind of place for ammonites. Inverlair was littered with fossilised remains. He put the stone in his jacket pocket and sat there, staring at the waves.

The memory of a dream came to him. He was eight or nine and he dreamed he was standing at the living-room window looking out and up, terrified, at the bright sky, from which lasered a single, massive eye, watching him. He knew it was God's eye, up against the keyhole in the clouds, an unblinking all-knowing intelligence. And God, for whatever reason, wasn't pleased with what he saw. Carl remembered the dream because he'd had another one like it last night, only this time there had been no one eye in the sky, judging him, like when he was a kid.

But there was still something watching him, in the empty dream-streets of Glasgow, at Heron Point, or out on the hill, an invisible intelligence probing him, analysing him. Carl got the feeling that whatever it was hadn't quite made up its mind. A judgement would come, but there was still time for him to influence the outcome by adding to one side of the scales, or by taking away from the other.

In his new dream there was no god's-eye, only himself, and nothing obviously awry with the world apart from the fact that there was no one else in it. The streets were the streets and the sea was the sea. Yet his dream-self this time knew that something was present, undeniably so, something that was under the sea and in the wind-creaking trees at night and behind a thousand untenanted windows. It was in all those places, and in none of them. It might be God, or time, or death, or life. Something eternal, anyway.

He remembered a conversation with Howard, about SCOPE.

'There were people in the National Emergency Authority, officials who knew about black projects, who opposed SCOPE once they found out what it was designed to do.'

'So what did they do about it?'

Howard took a deep breath, resigned to the telling of it. 'They raised their concerns through the proper channels,' he had said.

'And then?'

'They were told that everything was in order, or that their concerns were being addressed.'

'And the opponents of SCOPE were happy with this?'

'Some of them were, yes. The ones with families to feed, mainly.'

'And those that weren't?'

There was a long pause as Howard looked out of the window, at the shifting light on the hills. He kept it simple. 'If they pressed too hard, they either died in accidents or killed themselves, or just disappeared.'

He looked directly at Carl, searching for the realisation that stopping SCOPE had been impossible. There was too much money and power behind it. And Carl had been made to understand the risks Howard had taken to warn people, to warn him.

Ammonite in hand, Carl shook himself at the thought of Howard, stood up and set off again for Heron Point, picking his way over the rocky shoreline, stooping every now and again to pick up an interesting stone or shell. He could see it now, see how it was going to be with the committee and Gibbs and Adam Cutler. It hadn't been designed to end up that way – he was sure it wasn't intentional. But the people who were running the operation, who were applying Howard's survival system, could enforce their will, if that's what they wanted. The law of unintended consequences had struck again. There was always a god's-eye, of some sort, trying to control how people behave.

The shoreline came to an end at the base of a spur that jutted from the headland, and he had to take an old sheep track that zigzagged up the rugged grassy slope and onto the headland's heathery peak. After climbing for a few minutes he stopped to look back. Through binoculars he could see a flotilla of ducks, close in against the shore. He'd seen geese head south the other day; maybe the ducks were doing the same and had just stopped for a rest.

He lifted the 10-bore. There was nothing pestilential about roast duck. If he crept back down the path he could fire down on them from a range of about thirty metres. With a bit of luck, he could chalk up another species on his hit list. They were just targets at the other end of a lens. Necessity dictated that he view them as nothing more. A man can behave like a machine, can act on what needs to be done, and there's no need to for conscience to come into it.

Isaac, cocooned in his hooded coat, looked up from his sandpit as the gunshot boomed around the bay. With three litres of home-brew inside him Terry slept on his couch, not hearing anything, except the dream-shouts of his pursuers, and the crying of a girl.

32

Christmas. He'd heard a kid, a girl of about five, say the word the other day to her dad, but the guy didn't know what to say in response. Others had mentioned the idea since then, mainly adults prompted by their kids whose kids had told other kids, and so on. What can you say when your son or your daughter asks about Christmas? Sorry, it's been cancelled. Maybe parents should say it's no longer appropriate to celebrate, or how there are no more toys because of what happened. Carl wondered how SCOPE and the redzone had been explained to curious young minds. Dad tells me X. A pal tells me Y. Put all the stories together, and the kids might end up concocting their own version of the truth. They might grow up believing any number of implausible reasons why the world became the way it is.

Christmas had once been toys – the bigger and noisier the better. Carl could remember a few of those must-have big-ticket items coming his way. Like a lot of parents back then, the amount of money his own had spent on presents was inversely proportional to the amount of time they spent with their kids. He remembered one girl in his student days, beautiful, brittle as sugar glass; her dad swam in Middle Eastern oil and he threw cash and presents at her, though he hardly ever saw her. He'd sent her a brand new top-line computer that had sat in the hallway of their shared student flat, boxed and unopened, for a week or more, until the Fairy Princess could be arsed to have a peek inside.

There had been money to spend and then, quite suddenly,

there was no money to spend. Cue stress and marital difficulties. How come it always seemed to be the guys that walked out?

The sharp, still world of frost and clear skies had given way to wind and rain, sluicing against the window of Room 7, but it was still very cold. On days like this there wasn't much he could do out of doors. He could see that now and he no longer had any real urge to go squelching around the hills repairing a Stone Age broch. Eventually, figured Carl, every animal, human or not, learns to accept captivity, though that doesn't mean to say there's no corner of hope. That nugget of hope can be kept and taken out every now and again and looked at, like a lover's photo in a locket. Then you close it up, put the nugget back in your pocket and get on with the grind.

He lay on the bed, fully clothed against the cold, a scarf around his neck. The other day Isaac had shown him some crayon drawings, and it made him half-remember his own offerings as a kid. What had his own dad said when faced with a page full of his son's scribbles? Maybe he said, 'Brilliant, son, well done.' Maybe he'd been genuinely enthusiastic about stick men with giant clubbed arms and tiny drainpipe legs, or big yellow suns and multi-coloured dogs with all their legs down one side. That response was possible, but Carl doubted that his own father – business going tits up, money worries mounting – would have been remotely interested in his son's early artistic endeavours. In any case, he couldn't remember any such encounter, traumatic or otherwise, with any degree of certainty. But he could remember snippets of arguments, sure enough, and to be honest, his dad did have a point. An ocean of liquid wealth had suddenly dried up, leaving a patchwork of puddles for little fish like him to gasp and flap in. It was almost funny. Servicing the insecurity industry could have given the man a good living, yet he'd turned his back on the Navy to buy a seafood restaurant in Leith. A little fish right enough, cursing his luck and the big ideas of his wife.

As Carl lay on the bed smoking a spliff, he got the feeling that Isaac had not been happy with his critique of his drawings: obviously a single cursory 'nice' just didn't cut it. But what can you say about stick men? You have a real eye for composition, young man. No. But the kid clearly thought his drawings were good enough to impress. Maybe Carl should have gone along with it by making generally encouraging noises, even though the felt-tip scribbles were just the basic elements of people and things. The kid was okay, once you got used to the fact that he was just a kid, and a confused one at that. They get hurt without understanding why.

Carl could relate to that. At least Isaac was past the shitting and crying stage. After a while, when Carl spent long enough in his company, he could see that there were thoughts in Isaac's head that were worth knowing. And they're honest, kids – they can't lie. Not when they're young.

Bugger it. Carl was stoned and cold, it was pissing down outside, and he was hungry. He checked the time. Pretty soon, Simone would be out around the village, helping to check on the older folk to see if they needed anything at the same time as George liked to read to Isaac sitting by the residents' lounge fire. Carl could creep into the kitchen and help himself to whatever food was available, just like old times. His habit was being fed: there was usually a bowl of something left out for him. It was better that way, better than sitting round the table, stewing in thick silence. George had said they'd write 'Carl' on a plastic bowl and leave it on the floor.

George, he'd noticed, had developed quite a skill for making him feel guilty for eating their food and for dirtying their sheets. Whenever someone in the village was ill, he would always refer to Carl's pneumonia, and slow recovery. Maybe the old prick reckoned on bully-boy tactics, just like his son: if you don't come to some kind of arrangement with my daughter, then we'll stop feeding you and we'll kick you out into the cold. Anyway, Carl had started to sneak down in the afternoons, about two o'clock, when no one was in the kitchen, as well as late at night. Looping his scarf around his neck, he padded downstairs, two pairs of Terry's socks on his feet.

The bowl of food was there, laid out for him in the still-warm kitchen. No name was on it, so far, and the bowl was on the worktop not the floor. Mutton and turnip stew. He grabbed the bowl and headed back upstairs to his room. When he'd finished, he sparked another joint, and lay back on his bed, the ache in his empty stomach drifting to the background again, though it was always there.

Rain on the window. Music from his palmpod. Tetrahydrocannabinol in his bloodstream.

The old is dead, and there isn't going to be any miraculous resurrection.

'It's nothing to do with me,' Carl had said to Isaac. 'Everyone crying and your granny leaving and not coming back – that wasn't my fault.'

But even as he'd said the words, part of him said yes, it was his fault, and yes, he could have made a better effort doing something to stop SCOPE. And there was Terry, sitting over in his caravan, not washing, smoking Hendrik's blow as soon as he woke up, if he slept at all. It was hard for Carl to watch that, even though he'd only known the guy for a while. Terry was lonely, and he needed a friendly face.

'Maybe they'll finish the job,' Terry had said, slumped in his chair, one day, wreathed in smoke. 'Adam and the rest will come for me one night and do me in.' He'd looked up at Carl. 'Now they don't have to worry about the consequences.' Terry laughed. 'Like CivCon, or the Gestapo. A knock on the door and the bastards'll black-bag me in a dawn raid and whisk me away. Shoot me in the quarry this time rather than slice my fucking . . .'

'All right,' Carl had soothed. 'I don't think that's on the cards somehow.'

'Why not?'

Carl was silent for a moment, watching Terry flick his ash, tap-tap-tapping the joint on the rim of the ashtray, waiting for an answer. Tap-tap-tapping, even when there was no ash to flick. On edge.

'Why would they come for you?' he said at last.

Terry shrugged. 'Maybe they got a taste for it. Who could stop them if they came though the door, right now? You?'

Squaring up to Casper, let alone the rest of the boatyard crew, wasn't a prospect that Carl could imagine turning out in any way other than badly – for him. Maybe they did have a taste for it, and were enjoying flexing a bit of muscle, going round to polytunnels and greenhouses and hen-coops to see if people were hiding food. Enforcing Howard's system.

'You're just being paranoid,' said Carl. 'Besides, you said you couldn't remember what happened.'

Tap-tap went Terry's spliff on the ashtray. Tap-tap-tap . . .

'I can.'

They'd looked at each other.

'It's coming back to me, the more I try to remember, little snippets, in the dark, getting shoved around, and then the moonlight on something, flashing, a blade, you know, glinting in the moonlight . . .' Terry's voice broke, and the joint trembled in his hand. 'And, uh, then I was screaming and I, uh, could feel . . . I didn't meant to . . . I didn't . . .' His hand shook as he raised it to his eyepatch.

Carl felt the colour drain from his face. He pursed his lips. 'You sure?'

Terry sniffed. 'Yeah, I've been thinking about it, sitting here. I've remembered.' He gave a short laugh. 'Not much else to do but think.'

Now that he thought about that conversation, he wasn't sure if he trusted Terry's account of losing his eye. Can memories be recovered like that, after some blanked-out trauma? He sat up, went to the bathroom to splash cold water on his face. A knife glinting in the moonlight – how very cinematic.

There was a possibility, sure there was, but then he thought it might be a false memory because Terry wanted desperately for it to be the way he said it happened. To give matters their unvarnished truth, Terry might be lying. But he hadn't been lying about not using violence on Gemma. The rumours said Dr Morgan confirmed that the girl and Terry had sex, but there was no sign of force.

It was wrong. How wrong? Was the crime one of degree, of measuring initial intent, or was that just fudging the issue?

Carl tried to imagine someone being inside him when he did not desire it. When he wanted it to stop. What was he doing with Terry anyway? How could he associate with such a man?

He looked at his face in the bathroom mirror. The beard kept him warm, as did the hair on his head. There was no room for style or fashion any more. He'd forgotten why he'd shaved it off in the first place. There was only the simple truth of keeping warm in the winter. Maybe he'd shave it off for summer, like they did to sheep.

He set off for Alec John's. At least he'd spend today inside, learning how to saw a carcass, how to slice it into cuts and joints of meat.

It nagged at him, Terry and his flash of clarity. There was something about his way of telling it, something that wasn't obviously either a lie or the truth. Call it self-delusion. Was he supposed to spread the story around? Was he supposed to tell Simone?

He turned off the main road, just round the head of the bay, and walked up the gravel track to the stalker's farm.

He had to have the facts to stand up a hunch, and in this case his hunch was giving him trouble. There was no evidence to swing it either way; there had been no sign of broken glass or a knife in the trees in the clearing, just thin, sharp branches, sticking straight out from every conifer trunk. In daylight it was a pain to walk through; in the dark, and running, it would have been dangerous.

January–April

33

The sky cleared, and the temperature plunged. Two Celsius was the best the brief, crystal daylight could offer; by night it was sub-zero, down as low as minus eight. Clear skies meant crunching grass below and the full catalogue of constellations wheeling above, Orion rising in the east, where the ionosphere flashed and crackled every now and then to SCOPE's electric dance.

As dawn broke, a light wind rose. A mile above the stirring village a parachute opened, a silver cylinder suspended beneath it, glinting in the early sun. The canopy of white nylon drifted inland on the breeze, away from Inverlair, and sank silently out of sight.

Simone could hear Isaac humming to himself, as he thudded, one deliberate step at a time, down the stairs. Granddad would be down there, lighting the fire, wrapped in his dressing gown, with his balaclava on. He would probably tell Isaac off for coming downstairs without wearing any socks. Simone lay on her side, the duvet pulled up to her ears. At least she wasn't vomiting any more, that was something, and Dr Morgan had said everything was fine; everything, that is, except life in general. Simone tried not to think of her mum; tried not to picture what would be left of her after almost four months lying wherever SCOPE had sent her to sleep. There was her son to occupy her thoughts now, and the baby in her stomach, and her dad and her brother and other people to think about. They were here, and they were alive. Simone kept telling herself that she had to focus on the present, and that thinking about what had happened served no purpose. It would drive her mad if she let it.

What was she going to do?

She started to cry, her mother not present to make things right, to comfort and cuddle and nothing more, no, nothing more ...

A crust had developed on her vulnerability, and no man would be allowed to penetrate it unless she, in full conscious realisation, wanted that to happen. She would keep her guard up, especially now, and her persona would bar the way to those who deserved exclusion. No outside force, no man, was going to make her feel bad again.

It was obvious to her that Carl was either incapable of opening up or unwilling to try. She lay there, wrapped in the duvet, staring into space. Fatherhood, to Carl, was just a frightening word with unpleasant connotations.

She hoped that her brother had told her the truth about Terry. It had been difficult enough to raise the baby subject before, to make it real for Carl, and now there was a reason for him to dislike her even more: Adam. She tried to see the justice in what had happened to Terry, but she found it impossible. He was a sad and lonely man.

She felt nauseous again, and her breasts were tender. Pregnancy was real enough for her.

At the same time that morning Carl lay in his own bed, fully clothed and hungry, trying to figure out how to start the day. He mustn't stop washing just because it was easier and warmer to get into bed at night with all his clothes on. An effort to keep clean should be made, bollock-freezing water or not. He wasn't going to stink like Terry. Days like this made him yearn for a coffee, a splash of Irish in it, just to keep out the chill. And carbs. Even the synthetic shit they used to hand out at the rationing centres. He would take a slab of polycarb right now, and a bucket of coffee, to kick-start his system. He was tired. Everyone was tired.

Something would happen, something that would make his spirit soar. There had to be that in life, an end to the staleness and sameness and discomfort.

This is how people used to live, he thought, his eyes fixed on the ceiling. They survived, cold and hungry, most of the time. Probably much worse back then, when there were no polytunnels or chest freezers or photovoltaics; no duvets or taps. And now an echo of the past had returned, making life what it had been for most of humankind's existence: a struggle. Nature used to dictate that there was less of everything in the winter, including warmth. And now the power of seasonal rationing was back, tightening its coils around Inverlair for the long cold squeeze, until spring.

He sighed. Why did she keep pushing him? She could be asking questions about SCOPE or Alec John or Terry one minute, then the next she'd ask about his own parents and the conversation, inevitably, would turn to children and the child that was on its way. He wasn't going to get pinned down like that. It was too much like losing control, and he'd had enough of that over the last thirty-eight years to last a lifetime.

In a minute he would fill a sink of water in the en suite, scrape together a film of soap from somewhere, and have a wash; then he would go and do something. In a minute he would do all that. Start the day. Perform an allotted task. He was starting to get the hang of things. Some of it disgusted him; the reek of steaming innards from a gralloched deer, or a snared rabbit, mouth full of its own blood. At least he was only answering to Alec John, not the committee – the self-appointed good shepherds. Maybe everyone needed that kind of authority, doing all the planning and organising.

The committee had stepped into the breach and were now enforcing Howard's survival plan, tweaked with their own sly modifications. Maybe that's just what happens: those who get to call the shots pretend that everything is okay and above board, while the folks at the sharp end just accept injustice as natural, so long as it isn't waved under their noses. Even gouging out eyes as punishment could be tolerated.

Maybe he should tell the rest of the village about Adam Cutler's food rationing stitch-up, and maybe enough of them would listen. But then what? Hold out the begging bowl and watch it get filled to the brim by a repentant committee? That sort of admission of culpability had never happened before the redzone, so why should it happen now? People look out for themselves; it only takes the right circumstances for the mask to drop, for people to regress to growling over a fresh kill.

•

Sunlight came streaming through the crystal-coated birch and into Alec John's living room. The sky was cloudless and the early afternoon had a piercing light to it. The day would darken in two hours, but for now it was blue around and above the frosting bay. Hungry birds – siskin, Carl thought – were squabbling in the leafless trees, oblivious to him walking past, crunching up the shell path.

Alec John was in his favourite spot, sitting at the window with a blanket round his shoulders and another over his knees, dozing, but not asleep. As Carl watched through the window, Alec John, his closed eyes dark and his skin stretched pale over the frame of his skull, grimaced and turned his head. But there was no respite from the discomfort, and the man's gaping mouth struggled to inhale what his lungs could barely use. This is how it would be, from now on: Alec John's breathing would get quicker and shallower and the lack of oxygen, once his emergency tank ran out, would mean even walking to the toilet would be a struggle. Without regular injections of nanomed to fight the good fight, his heart would soon no longer be able to pump oxygenated blood to his lungs. This disease had been exorcised by inexplicable magic – in Alec John's case administered five times a year by Dr

Morgan. But now it was creeping back, repossessing its human host. Undoubtedly, emphysema would bring a few friends along, and they'd all have a wild old time in their Highland retreat. They'd do their best to devour it.

Carl watched Alec John for a while. He couldn't help but think of Eric and Leslie. Did they die together? The question kept occurring. He shuddered at the image of a Glasgow filled with desiccated corpses, in beds, cars, offices and streets, lying where they'd collapsed, bones picked clean. There would be other notspots and, one day, he'd drive away and find them.

Carl went inside the house. 'Hello, it's me.'

Alec John stirred at the sound. 'Hello there,' he gasped. He coughed, spat into his hankie, a trace of blood and sputum clinging to his grey-stubbled chin. He lifted the face mask, took a few deep breaths, and sat up straight to focus on his visitor.

Carl noticed the bowl of soup, untouched, on the drop-leaf table. 'George will take that personally,' he said.

Alec John shook his head. 'I must have nodded off.' He straightened his back against the armchair, smoothed his thinning grey hair into place. 'I had some of the soup, and the bread – say thanks to George.'

He glanced at Carl. He was showing the evidence. Food? Keep my strength up? Look, Alec John was saying, I am nothing but skin and bone. I am already dead. One day soon, a shortage of oxygen will put me in a coma or give me a heart attack, and no amount of soup is going to stop that happening. He took a few sips of water. 'You have it.'

'Have what?'

'The soup.'

Carl hesitated. 'No, keep it for later.' He put another log in the stove. 'Heat it up whenever you're hungry.'

He stood at the fire for a moment, looking at the framed photos on Alec John's mantelpiece. Mother and father in black and white, wife and nephew in colour. The clock ticked and Jess panted in her basket.

'That thing the fishermen saw come down the other day, it's definitely a capsule – Russian, I think.'

Alec John brightened. 'Really? How do you know it's Russian?'

'I saw their flag painted on the side,' said Carl. 'It was too foggy yesterday to get a good look. There's a parachute attached, but it's too far into the redzone. Must have been dropped from very high up.'

'There could be all sorts inside, stuff we need.'

Carl nodded. 'They would've dropped important stuff – medical supplies, high-energy food maybe. But we'll have to wait a good while to reach it.'

Turning back to the window, Alec John said nothing more. Carl took the bowl through to the kitchen.

'Is Terry still the same?'

Carl pulled up a dining chair, turned it around, and sat with his elbows resting on the back. 'He's been okay for the last couple of weeks. He's started carving animals into logs, even into trees. They're amazing, really detailed.'

Alec John drank some more water, brighter now. 'Do you think he'll snap out of it completely?'

'I think he is. Part of him seems glad that he's been punished for something he's done wrong.' He looked at Alec John. 'He did have sex with that girl when she didn't want to. It was rape.' He paused. 'He's getting some odd ideas into his head though. Keeps going on about Celtic myths and old religion.'

Alec John sighed and shook his head. He kept his eyes fixed on the scrawny patch of hazel in the garden. 'Well, it was wrong, what he did, though not wrong enough for what happened to him.'

'Well, there are different rules now. That's what Gibbs said: different rules.'

'I suppose there are,' said Alec John, clasping his pale white hands together. Then he looked up at Carl, fixed his eye for second. 'Different rules.'

He took a breath of oxygen. 'Did you put the strychnine down for the stoats?'

'Yes.' Carl smiled. 'That American woman, the one who latched onto Adam, she was pretty horrified. Called it barbaric.'

There was a twinkle in Alec John's eye. 'Maybe she won't want any grouse then – if the stoats and crows leave us any. Did you check the Larsen traps up below the corries?'

'Yes.'

'And?'

'Two hoodies.'

'Good.' Alec John relaxed into the armchair again, licked his paper-dry lips, and collected his thoughts. 'In the corner,' he said gruffly, gesturing. 'You may as well have it.'

A gun in a leather case stood in the corner of the sitting room. Alec John had several guns, but Carl recognised the case. He picked it up, smelled the linseed oil on the cracked leather. He opened the straps and took out the Ruger.308. It was Alec John's own rifle. Not one of the .22s or a shotgun, but the man's weapon of choice. The magic meat stick, handed down from father to son.

'You may as well take it,' Alec John said.

Carl felt the gun, hard and cold, in his hands. 'This was your dad's.'

'Aye, and now it's yours.'

On the tip of Carl's tongue there hung a question, more a consideration, really: he wouldn't ask if Alec John was sure about giving the gun away, because that would mean raising the possibility of its rightful owner never firing it again. And that, they both knew, was probably the truth. He put the .308 back in the case and closed the silver buckles. Alec John said nothing, waved his hand to dismiss any protest.

'Thanks,' Carl said softly.

Pursing his lips, Alec John resumed his vigil with the crisp winter scene outside his window. What had to be done was done.

'You'd better make them count,' he said. 'There aren't too many left.'

'I'll pick my targets.'

Carl stoked the fire, turning the log so that some heat would flow into the room. Once the sun sank, the temperature would drop quickly.

'How's Simone?'

There were a variety of responses to this question, covering simple lies and complex truths. Carl opted for the simple truth. 'I don't know.' He cleared his throat. 'We don't really talk, or see each other that much.'

'Why not?'

'Well, because . . . because she always wants to talk about her condition, you know. I mean, what does she want? For us to settle down and pretend to be a happy family? That's not going to happen.'

'How do you know she wants that if you never talk to her?'

'What else is there to talk about?'

Alec John let out a short laugh. 'The fact that she's pregnant and you're the father?'

'But we know that, so what is there to talk about?'

'How the hell would I know? And you won't know either unless you talk to her. She might be terrified at the prospect of having another kid.' His face darkening, Alec John turned back to the window. 'You're going to be a father. That's something you should be thankful for.'

Carl snorted. 'Right. A kid is exactly what I need. And exactly what Inverlair needs.'

'Maybe it is.'

'No,' said Carl. 'It's not.'

Alec John reached for his oxygen mask and took a few puffs.

He was quieter when he spoke again. 'My wife died of a brain haemorrhage at the age of thirty-one. She was in the post office down the road when it happened, buying stamps. She had a bit of a sore head, I said goodbye to her that morning, went out as usual, and when I came back, the doctor at the time and the postmistress were waiting for me. Every day I think about her, even now.' He wiped his nose with the back of his hand. 'We couldn't have kids. It was my fault, and now here I am. You see, no matter where you go or what you do, you'll always be a father. There's no getting away from that.

'I never met anyone else after my wife died. I suppose that was my choice. But you don't have a choice now. It's all a question of what you do with the knowledge. I don't believe any man can just ignore his child and if he does, well, it'll have some effect on him, sooner or later.'

Sermon over, Alec John looked out the window, clutching the oxygen mask on his lap.

Carl got up and put his chair back under the table. He zipped up his waterproof jacket. 'I don't know,' he said, standing there. 'I don't know what to do.'

Staring up at him, Alec John settled the blanket round his knees. 'That's okay. It's fine not to know. But at least think about it.'

Carl shrugged. 'I shouldn't have upset you.' He turned to leave. 'I'll see you later.'

Alec John smiled. 'So I'm firing blanks as well as live ammunition, eh?' He turned back to the window. 'I'll be up and about tomorrow to joint that carcass, so you can watch how it's done again. You're still making a bloody mess of it.'

At the head of the bay, down on the main road, the shadows were already hardening as the icy night reasserted itself. With the sun up, there had been a hint of warmth in the air, an easing. But now, at just after 4 p.m., the cold was clenching again. At some point, perhaps in a day or two, the air stream would swing to the south and the clouds would come back and the temperature would rise. It would start raining again. This was the wisdom of those who had been here for far longer than he had. There were those who could see the bigger picture, who could see beyond the transient discomfort of a cold snap. They could read the secret signs that were invisible to everyone else, the subtle cues that suggested what was to come.

Carl had been good at that – the sense of what lay beneath the surface, finely attuned to the hidden language of true intentions. If he paid attention, maybe he could make it work – being here. He could get through this, whatever this actually was, by learning a skill. That's the way he had to look at it: learn what needs to be learned and then get on with it, keeping out of everyone's way in the process. It worked for Alec John, that kind of approach. Every man has dreams of power. It's how he reacts to powerlessness that defines the kind of person a man becomes.

Climbing the main road up the southern headland had warmed him up. Cold air clawed at his lungs, steaming hot billows into the cold. His stride slowed at Terry's gate, but quickened again, and he pressed on towards the roadblock. A little further and he stopped, just short of the painted boulders, feeling SCOPE in his right temple. Today might have been the six-day pulse, but it was too late in the afternoon to know for sure. Besides, he didn't really want to know about the six-day pulse any more. It was a deadly hope, and a false one.

Running. Running from the low-frequency wave that was breaking over him, and that was killing Howard. And then the darkness and the rain and the realisation. All of it came back to him if he let it, but there was no need to let it because he was moving forward into some kind of future. It was happening. He could see he had no choice. The alternatives were worse, on balance.

The deltameter showed the delta field was, if anything, a little stronger today.

The useless sun was slinking away back into its hole and there was fuck all for him to do but become proficient in something, the capacity to shoot and walk and watch that had fallen into his lap. He stamped on an ice-filled pothole, causing a crack, but not breaking through. His primary task was now maximising the supply of protein obtained through the flesh of dead animals. Those animals, in the main, had to be shot. The man who'd performed that task, dutifully, for almost forty years was more or less incapable of walking any distance, and he, Carl, had stepped into the role. He put the deltameter into his inside pocket and turned back towards the village. As the light dwindled behind the southern headland the shadow of night started creeping around the bay. Round and round the limits of its orbit, the world turned and the day went on into cold star-filled night. Carl lifted the binoculars, took a last look across the bay. There was that big fucking thug Casper, dumping more logs from the pick-up. The guy doesn't even bother to knock now, just marches straight into people's hen-coops or polytunnels, sees what there is, and loads up the trailer with plunder. There was no need for violence; he took the food because people believed the committee had a right to it. Yes, Carl could see the sense in Howard's system, in having a committee to ration everything – but fairly. This system wasn't fair. When is it ever?

George still enjoyed a whisky: the perks of the publican, perhaps, but surely conduct unbecoming for the chairman of the emergency committee.

Across the bay, Carl could see Casper talking with Adam and another guy. They could take over, he thought. Inverlair's own emergency authority could run the place in whichever way they chose. It was their choice. Gibbs couldn't do a thing about what had been done to Terry, and the committee wanted to smooth the whole thing over. Move along now, nothing to see here.

But there must be a consequence, a punishment. The evildoers must get what they deserve. Isn't that what happens?

Carl watched the men across the bay. Big dumb Casper and his little emperor. There would be a punishment. He would bide his time and then, when the right moment presented itself, enact his own version of justice.

Simone entered the binoculars' field of vision, dark orange scarf wound against the cold, a striped woollen hat down to her ears. He watched her say hello to her brother and the other two but not stop. She walked past the shorefront houses, past the boarded-up craft shop, Carl following her progress. She was pretty enough, and he liked her. There was nothing wrong with her, and maybe he'd accept the way things were, but then again maybe he wouldn't. There must be something left – some choice that he still had the power to make. Simone stopped at Dr Morgan's cottage.

Part of Carl hoped for the worst.

•

'This is a great little lamp,' said Dr Morgan. 'Remember that big power cut a few years ago, the first big one? My nephew gave me this for Christmas.' She switched on the lamp; it had a slender conical base topped with a wire-and-paper shade. 'Leave it on the windowsill to charge during the day and you get a good three hours of power at night ... Can I offer you a refill?'

Simone raised her dark eyebrows, an empty cup in her lap. 'Please, that tea was nice and fresh.'

Dr Morgan went over to the fire and lifted a pan of steaming water from the embers. 'Wringing out the last few drops,' she said brightly.

It occurred to Simone that tomorrow was the day for handing out tea and coffee rations. At this point in the week, a teabag would have been wrung out a few times to make a brew, by most people.

She watched the cups being refilled with hot water, steam rising as the cold ceramic was soused. She knew the food-rationing situation was wrong, but the fattening foetus inside her had its own needs, imperatives that she had to obey. And it was only a cup of tea, after all.

They sipped at their cups by the fire. Even though her face was warm, Simone could feel the chill at her back, where heat ended and a cold house began.

Delicately, Dr Morgan raised the subject of Carl, and Simone tried to make light of the situation. While talking, she became conscious of the fact that she was defending him, so she wound up the conversation with a shrug. 'There's not much I can do about the situation. We'll just have to see what happens.'

Barring any mishaps, one thing was certain to happen, and she was over halfway towards it, or towards *her*, as Dr Morgan's test had just confirmed.

34

On a bright spring day the lamb is born; and on the same bright spring day it dies.

Carl was too far away to help it. Through the binoculars he could see birds, bigger than crows – ravens, maybe – taking up position around the mother; one was even perched on her back. They were all waiting.

The sheep stood to give birth, its hindquarters thrusting towards the ground, mouth open, head tilted upwards, as a sausage of pliable waxy life unplugged itself from the birth canal and spilled onto the ground. Then the birds moved in.

Carl lowered the binoculars, his lips dry. The lamb was seconds in the world, and now it was out of it. Months to make, and all that energy, from sunlight to grass to foetus, was now being pecked back into death by the ravens. That, surely, was the point. The ravens had to live – they had as much right to life as the lamb, or as little claim on it. He could run over there now, take up a good position, and probably kill one of the birds, let it act as a warning to the others. The lamb would still have its eyes pecked out, but he could even the score. There would be no justice in it, because the birds weren't doing anything wrong, as such; it was simply that killing them helped keep death away.

Carl walked along the ridge, cutting down the track and into the boggy saddle between the peaks, inland from the head of the bay. There was warmth in the air, so he took off his baseball cap and unzipped his Gore-Tex to the navel. On a day like this it was good to be alive. He wasn't about to rush anywhere to waste a bullet.

The ewe had needed to give birth there and then, out in the open, just one dumb brute struggling by itself to produce another. The birds, too, had no choice – killing and eating a just-born lamb, fresh from the oven, was a simple risk-free way of eating. People talk about the facts of life, but it could just as easily be the facts of death. There was no escape from either, though there were rules of engagement.

Alec John had a choice: the moment of death was now in his own hands, thanks to Dr Morgan and 150mg of diamorphine. By controlling the 'how' he could control the 'when' and, thus, the 'where'. Death might be the strongest animal, but, if you're lucky, there will be time to tidy up before opening the front door to it.

At least Alec John could cut short the pain, any time he chose, though staying alive was becoming harder every day for him.

'Howard said between two and four years, but he also said the nearest mast might fail tomorrow,' Carl had argued. 'When it does, we can get the stuff you need, the nanomeds.'

Alec John had gone along with that, to begin with, but now pain and permanent immobility were proving too much. The fight to stay out of bed – which he saw as a step closer to the grave – was all but over. Most days Alec John couldn't make it into his clothes, or a chair. Even if the nearest mast failed tomorrow, it might not be enough to open the way to the next town, and the nearest doctor's surgery would not necessarily have the right kind of medicine. They both knew it was ridiculous to think otherwise.

Up on the ridge, Carl scanned along the shoreline with his binoculars, settled on Terry's caravan and then on Hendrik de Vries and his wife, who were fussing around in and out of their polytunnels. She paid regular visits to Terry, probably just to check on him.

On this side of the bay Simone and Isaac were in the back

garden, putting logs in a basket. She had her padded jacket on. It hid the bump but made her look twice as big.

There was no white boat on the horizon. And there never would be.

Just like Alec John, it could be any day now with Simone. One going out of the world and one coming into it. But at least the ravens wouldn't be waiting for either Alec John or the baby. Carl watched Isaac help his mum with the logs, watched how they acted together, the little actions that revealed their intimacy. Then he lowered the binoculars and began the long, hard climb up to the crown of Ben Bronach. After a spell, he veered left towards the gully and the river. Two days ago, when the weather broke, he'd taken an older hind here. He'd gralloched her with inexpert hands, still using the gut hook to detach the hot innards, blood-warm slime and intestinal tubing, scooping it all from the body cavity and onto the rough grass. For Alec John, such an activity provoked no reaction; pinched disgust was the best Carl was able to manage, even now. At least he no longer vomited.

Now, two days later, there was nothing of the hind's guts to be seen except a little dried blood and tufts of downy fur clinging to the heather. Who knows how many animals had fed off the remains? Maybe the guts had made the difference between life and death. A crow might emerge, alive, from the winter because it had eaten its fill here. That crow might kill a lamb. That lamb wouldn't grow up to produce more lambs. The struggle for flesh was open and constant.

•

Dr Morgan was relieved. This looked like a straightforward pregnancy. 'The head has engaged. BP's fine. Everything's normal.' She smiled at Simone.

Simone pulled up her jogging bottoms. Isaac was cackling out in the back garden with Pavel and Fiona.

Normal. That was a good one. She tried to smile at Dr Morgan, puffing and heaving off the bed. 'Thanks for coming round.'

'I was passing anyway. Just checking on Mrs Mackay.'

'Is she not well?'

'Oh, she's fine, a tough old bird that one. But her house is all electric, and it's been bloody freezing in there, though we're into spring now. She's in her eighties. It was minus two in Mr Cameron's bedroom when they found him. He was seventy-seven. And without treatment, the Armstrong boy's leukaemia will kill him in a month.' She rolled the latex gloves into a ball. 'Just another day at the office.'

Simone started to put her trainers on, but she was too big to reach down easily.

'Here, let me.' Dr Morgan crouched to finish the job and tie the laces. 'How does the father-to-be feel now?'

Simone considered her answer. 'I think . . . I think he's resigned to hanging around.'

'What does that mean?'

'Well, he'll give it a go, I suppose.'

'There's a big difference between giving things a go and being resigned to hanging around, yeah?'

Pulling herself out of the chair, Simone pressed her fingers into the small of her back. She grimaced.

'He doesn't have kids, does he?'

'No,' said Simone.

'Did he have anyone special before, do you think?'

Simone watched Isaac out in the garden, climbing up the ash tree with Pavel. They were both laughing. 'No,' she said. 'Though I think there was someone a while back. She had an abortion and the baby wasn't his. He eventually found all that out.'

'He told you that?

'Yes.'

Dr Morgan nodded, satisfied. 'He must have lost someone.'

'As far as I can make out, his boss was the most important person in his life,' said Simone. She waddled into the en suite bathroom and closed the door.

Claire Morgan wanted to say that Simone reminded her of her own daughter. There was a photo of Simone's mother on the bedside table. The natural links had been severed – for both of them – and she should say the thing she felt moved to say. Your mother and I are about the same age; I had a daughter too.

She should draw the comparison, build something, and Simone should do the same. Only good could come of it. Her Nancy was gone and so was Alison Cutler and …

The toilet flushed. Dr Morgan gathered herself.

'You know these spraysuits?' asked Simone.

'No,' said Dr Morgan. 'Are they for swimming?'

Simone smiled. 'No. It's mainly guys that use them. Stuff called neurogel. You bought a nebuliser and sprayed the gel on at home. There were also these contact lenses.'

'Porn, you mean?'

'Well,' said Simone, 'I suppose you could say that. But it's more than porn. It was like living with someone, if that's what the users wanted. It was for lonely people, I suppose.'

'Well, there are plenty of them still around. Did Carl have one, a spraysuit?'

'My dad seems to think he did. They were talking a while ago, before … before Terry.'

There was a sharp crack against the windowpane, as the first nugget of hail pinged off the glass; within seconds the shower swept in at full pelt. Simone watched as Isaac, Pavel and Fiona rushed giggling to the back door, holding their faces.

'Does Carl still blame Adam for what happened?'

Simone nodded, feeling exhausted all of a sudden. She sat down heavily in the bedroom's only comfortable chair, her breath condensing in the cold spring air. 'He thinks Dad could've done something about it, though I don't know what he had in mind. I mean, what could Gibbs have done anyway? Locked him in a cellar? I just get the feeling Carl wants Adam punished, somehow. He wants some kind of justice. But I say: what about justice for Gemma? If Adam or Casper get locked up why shouldn't the same thing happen to Terry?'

'And Carl can't get what he wants,' said Dr Morgan to herself, then louder, 'so things are complicated between you two.'

As quickly as it had started, the hail shower passed.

'I think they always will be,' said Simone, closing her eyes, her pale lips trembling. She tried to smile. 'We didn't have the ideal start, you know. I suppose I should be a little more . . . understanding.'

'Why?'

'He's used to the city. He doesn't belong here. The world for us maybe isn't so different; for him it's changed beyond all recognition, and everyone he knew in Glasgow is dead.'

'True,' said Dr Morgan. 'But it's been nine months, just about. Maybe it's time he started to accept the situation.'

'That'll happen, eventually,' said Simone, surprised by how confident she sounded. 'Even if he could leave here tomorrow, there isn't really anywhere for him to go any more.' She sat up. 'I'm not expecting anything to happen between us. I don't think I even want it to. I'd just like him to acknowledge this.' She patted her distended belly. 'And accept the possibility that being a father might actually mean something.'

Dr Morgan would have liked to talk more, but the sound of thumping feet and voices in the hallway helped decide the issue. She got smartly to her feet as Isaac and his pals burst into the room with a story about a dead bird they'd found in the garden.

'Sounds like a greenfinch,' said Dr Morgan. 'Birds get disorientated sometimes – no one knows why – and they fly into windows, into the glass, and break their necks.'

Ornithology by osmosis made her reasonably certain it was a greenfinch. If it hadn't been for divorce, she might have been an expert on birds by now. He'd always loved birds.

•

Terry's feet were on the windowsill, dust from sawn plasterboard on his boots and clothes, and in his tangled brown hair. There was old newspaper spread all over the floor of his uncle's house, not much furniture in the rooms, and everything smelled of new paint. The smell of past normality and the freshness of the future, each room a different colour, right down to the floorboards. A house of moods, and a room for each one, so said Terry.

'So, the trick is not to be afraid,' he said, taking another suck on his spliff. 'Open your mouth and your heart and your mind, and let the stuff just pour out of you. Say what you are moved to say. Take that first step towards not feeling stupid, by feeling stupid.'

Carl sat on the floor, against the wall. He grunted, too convinced by Terry for comfort. He didn't like the way everything was being smoothed over. The scars of knee-jerk justice were plain to see; the word rape conjured images of frenzied, feral violence. The truth of both was hard to fathom.

SCOPE was an invisible glacier, just another expression of force. But now he was in a place where forces had overpowered choice. Glaciers don't have the urge to dominate the rocks they grind to rubble. There's no other mode of being for half-mile-thick ice; grinding rock is what it does. It was the same with stags. They can't choose what they are; they can't resist the actions they are compelled to perform. They are their actions. That's what defines them.

People aren't just vectors of blind force. They can choose. It wasn't just a case of subjugate and inseminate.

Just for something to say, Carl told Terry about the crow in the Larsen trap, up on the moors. The bird had gone crazy when it saw

Carl approaching. He'd stood quietly, watching it from a distance. After a while the crow stopped flapping and clawing at the wire cage. It had been hard to tell if the thing was afraid; there was no trace of emotion in its gleaming black eyes, head cocking and bobbing, alert. To save shotgun shells, Carl was supposed to use the metal gripper to grab the bird by the neck, if he came across one still alive. Thus pinioned, the crow was then to have its brains stamped on.

'But I shot it instead,' said Carl. 'And I blew the bloody Larsen trap to bits as well. I felt sorry for it – even though they take grouse eggs and go for the lambs. It was just a young one. Alec John said the older ones know not to go near the traps. The death of a few crows teaches the rest not to go near them. It's like every so often they need a reminder of how to stay alive. A sacrifice. It was just trapped there, helpless, in the cage. I mean, I know it's a pest, but you're killing something that's just trying to stay alive, same as you are. Anyway, I made a choice, and it's been a while since that's happened.'

Terry passed Carl the joint. 'Everything is entitled to its share. Somewhere along the line I think we forgot that. We wanted it all for ourselves.'

Carl took a single draw from the spliff and passed it back. He shifted his weight on the hard floor, uneasy. 'Different rules now, in lots of ways, I suppose. But there are still some that carry moral force.' From this angle, and in profile, and with the light from the window hitting him straight on, Terry's eyepatch wasn't visible. But every so often, as people do when they're talking, he'd turn his head, and Carl would see the patch. Off had come the surgical gauze that Dr Morgan had supplied, and in its place Terry had drawn an oversized eye onto a triangle of pliable white plastic. He'd sewn a red glass bead onto the patch as an iris. The effect was disconcerting.

'I saw Gemma today,' said Terry.

'What do you mean – saw?'

'She looked terrified, then turned bright red, then looked as if she was about to burst into tears. She said sorry and ran away.'

Terry put the joint down in the ashtray and got up from the wicker chair, his red-bead eye matching the look on his face. He started measuring another sheet of plasterboard.

•

In the old quarry Carl watched sand martins swoop and frolic over the lagoon, shooting into their holes in the quarry wall, then bulleting out and up, dipping and circling. Spring is here, and this is how these birds behave. He watched them for a spell, at the centre of the sand martins' wild wheeling orbit, until he forgot what had been on his mind. As afternoon lengthened, he turned and walked back along the main road and up the northern slope of the bay. Near the red-boulder roadblock he stopped. The *Aurora* was close inshore, just sitting there in the calm sea. Through the binoculars he could see Casper fishing astern and Adam, shades on, dozing in a deckchair.

And then it took hold of Carl. The idea of what to do next got him like a heart shot.

He raised the binoculars again, his pulse quickening. The *Aurora* must be a good 200 metres offshore, apart from one spit of rock, where the distance was maybe half that. He could get down there in ten minutes if he moved quickly.

He ran down the uneven grassy meadow to the bottom edge. Crouching behind a fence, he cased the best route. What the fuck was he doing? Before he could find an answer, he set off again, running stooped to the gate that led down to the shingle and the rocks, slipping on the bank of high-tide seaweed as he rushed down to the foreshore. If he kept to the north side of the spit of rock the *Aurora* wouldn't see him, and when he got to the point he would be close enough to . . .

He splashed through rock pools, the .308 slung across his back, until he got to the cover of the spit. Maybe Adam and Casper had been fishing for hours and were set to go back to the pier. As he clambered over the dark rocks, the plan snowballed in his mind; each problem was met with a solution.

Afterwards, he could run back to the ruins of the herring station, grab the old dinghy and oars, row out to the *Aurora*, drop the anchor, and shove the bodies overboard. Then he'd head back to the boat, sink it, and tell everyone that he came across the *Aurora* aground on the rocks.

Afterwards. After what?

The further out the spit he went, the wetter the rocks became and the deeper the water. Once or twice he slipped and nearly fell in. Under his breath he started singing, softly, 'Set my people free, free, free, set them free' over and over again, barely aware that he was even doing it.

His heart was racing, lips dry, and he could feel his hands and legs starting to shake.

And here he was. And there they were, close enough for a shot. He caught his breath, peeping round the rocks every now and again.

Free, free, set them free . . .

It was a perfect spot: the rocks were arranged so that he could adopt an ideal firing position. Even the barrel of the rifle would have a shelf on which to rest. The earth and the tides had provided for him in his hour of need. It was preordained.

Free, free, set them free . . .

As he raised the rifle he found that his hands couldn't stop shaking. His heart was pounding in his throat and, even above the crashing surf he could hear it in his ears. Every time he tried to settle into position it would happen, his body shaking and his heart hammering against his ribs.

Adam dozing in the sun, shades on. Take Casper first in the

head, then down and to the left as Adam roused himself and – *bang*. He'd be doing everyone a favour.

Free, free, set them free.

Carl set the gun aside, and with a trembling hand wiped the sweat and snot from his face. He laughed to himself, unchambered the bullet, and turned away from his position.

He held the rifle in front of him to look at it, one hand gripping the rubberised stock and the other the barrel.

This gun was older than he was and it had never taken a human life. He'd had it all of five minutes and was already planning to do exactly that. Is that what he was going to do with the gun Alec John had bequeathed to him? Bloodlust wasn't part of the inheritance, surely. He could block that signal, if he put his mind to it. A man isn't a machine that can set conscience aside.

He put the rifle back into its case. It's easier, at the end of a telescopic sight, but not that easy. Adam was safe to throw his weight around until someone else threw it back at him. Let him sleep in the sun, saved for another day. Uncle Adam. The Big Boss.

Laughing softly to himself, Carl made his way back along the spit, through the foreshore rock pools, and back up to the roadblock. The *Aurora* was motoring back towards the bay now. He watched it approach the pier, throttling back.

Calmer now, his pulse back to normal, Carl made his way to Alec John's. Shooting animals was power enough.

Change had been thrown over him like a cloak of lead. The more he struggled under it, the heavier it got. Maybe if he stopped struggling, the future would lie lightly on him, and possibility would begin to flower once again. Lead would transmute, become lighter than air.

Jess came scrabbling down the shell path as soon as she heard Carl's footsteps. He stroked her, which set her tail to a joyful thrashing. Every time he saw Dr Morgan in Alec John's house he assumed the worst: that the old man had decided enough was enough and it was time to go.

'Well?'

Dr Morgan was in the sitting room, heating some milk on the range. She stirred the pan, ordered Jess into her blanket-lined basket. 'He's okay,' she said. 'He's got something to think about.'

'What d'you mean?'

'It's good news, maybe.' Dr Morgan brightened. 'I found a nanomed in the surgery. It's less than two years old. It wouldn't slot into the applicator as normal, so I just stuck it in a drawer ages ago.'

'Can you use it?'

Dr Morgan nodded. 'I think so. It's a fiddly job getting it into an ordinary hypodermic, that's why I didn't use it.'

Carl clapped his hands. Jess jumped out of her basket and gave a short bark.

'That's fantastic.' His enthusiasm waned when he saw Dr Morgan's expression. 'What's wrong?'

Warm milk was poured into a mug. 'Well,' she said, 'if he takes the nanomed in one go his lungs will be restored, almost, to the way they were. He'll have three good months.' Dr Morgan glanced at Carl. 'And then, unless the nearest mast fails – and assuming we can find more nanomed when it does – he'll have to go through all this pain and discomfort again.'

Carl sat at the table and stroked Jess at his knee. Death wasn't going to decide this one, not entirely.

'What does Alec John think?'

'He's not sure. I could give him it in two lots. He'd feel a lot better than he does now, but not well enough to go into the hills. He'll have a few months if I split it in two.'

Dr Morgan went through with the milk, Carl following her, to the end bedroom. 'He's asleep,' she whispered.

Propped on a bank of pillows, Alec John slept with his mouth open, thin hands splayed out on the duvet, ancient at sixty-six. His breathing was fast and shallow.

'I thought he'd be asleep,' said Carl softly. 'He can't sleep through the night so he dozes through the day.'

'Are you up with him at night?'

'Not often,' said Carl. 'He hates it when I come in. He was sitting in the chair the other night.'

'Really?'

Carl nodded. 'Yeah. He was just sitting there, both hands on his walking-stick, like he was just about to get up.'

'Did he?'

'No. He was back in bed half an hour later. Is there a drop of rum in that?'

'Yes,' said Dr Morgan with a smile. She walked back through to the stove with the cup of milk. 'You can warm it again when he wakes up.' She poured the milk back into the pan and put the lid on. 'You're very attentive.'

Carl shrugged. 'He's done a lot for me.'

Dr Morgan rinsed the cup under the tap, dried it, and hooked its handle on the stand. She picked up her jacket and put it on. They both stood there.

'In about two days' time, I would say, your daughter is going to come into the world.'

Carl pursed his lips. 'I'm staying. Whatever happens. Even if the masts failed tomorrow, where would I go?'

'Good,' said Dr Morgan. 'If you hang around for long enough, you might even try to make the best of it.' She buttoned her jacket, picked up her case, and patted Jess goodbye. Closing the front door, she was off, scrunching down the path.

Evening came down just as the low cloud lifted, fresher air sweeping in off the Atlantic, warmth in the spring air. Carl sat in Alec John's sitting room, by the warm stove, listening: to the old clock on the wall, logs settling in the grate, Jess breathing in her basket, the wind outside moving through the hazel.

He sat for a long time, drifting between regret and uncertainty, watching the wind at work as it roused the awakening earth.

New Life

Carl stopped the argocat and crept down into the open depths of the glen, keeping his eyes fixed on the middle distance. He had an idea what to look for now; the telltale signs and likely whereabouts of what he was driven to find.

After half an hour, he found it.

Crouching, Carl sank into a bank of heather. A single hind, quite young, was grazing down the slope close to a stream. As if sensing she was being watched, the hind lifted her head and scanned the higher ground. Carl dipped his head, waited then inched upwards until he could see again. She was thin, and clearly not pregnant. She'd come through the whole winter without being impregnated, which was rare, and was on her own, separate from the rest of the master's harem who were across the glen near the forest. He heard Alec John's voice telling him what a gift this was, winter-thin or not.

The lie of the land was such that Carl had to double back a little to the stream that rose on the sodden slopes. It was in spate, and the sound of rushing water would help mask any noise that he might make in his approach. The hind was a good 200 metres away, too far for a kill shot.

Following the stream down into the glen Carl crept along its hunched banks of rock and thin grass, stopping close to where the water slowed and opened out across beds of gravel.

There she was, down below, a fair distance away. There was a better way to come, he could see that now. But this was as close as he could get by following the water. Settling into a comfortable firing position, Carl sized up the target.

The hind was head-on so he would have to wait. It took another ten minutes for her to change her stance. Now they were ready.

Just above and to the left of the hip joint. That was the spot.

Now there was the slowing of breath, the emptying of mind; the universe packed into a square inch of grey-brown fur, the dead centre of extinction, where the energies of death and life were interchangeable.

'Thank you,' Carl whispered as he held his final breath, squeezing the trigger on the exhale. Twelve stone of deer dropped where it stood.

He clicked the distance function on the deltameter, and started off down the slope. Carl watched the figures mount. He touched the barrel of the .308 to the hind's staring eyeball. There was no response.

The reading said 137 metres. Alec John was right – Carl had a talent for this. In a different life, he could have made the Olympic team, but this was his truth now. He found the animal's carotid and plunged the knife home, indifferent to the blood that gushed out onto the grass. Carl had learned to live in this world. A truce had become uneasy peace. Back when it mattered, there had been different work that needed doing, and he'd done it until long after it became a pointless urge. After years of doing this other work, he'd realised there was a river of shit whose flow he was powerless to arrest. He'd take the odd bucketful, just to show people that what they were being told was pure water was, in fact, tainted. Septic with lies. But there was plenty more where the bucketful had come from. The river never stopped.

Wiping the lock-knife on his trousers he closed it and put it back in his jacket pocket. He watched, impassive, as the hind emptied her blood onto the new grass.

He had eighteen bullets left for the .308.

His work now was pure.

•

That evening he lay on the bed in Room 14 and looked at the ceiling. Paint was flaking from the cornices; and there was a dark stain from an oil-lamp that long ago burned by the bed while he burned and sweated in it. The room smelled of dampness now, or maybe it had always smelled like this and he had just never noticed before. On this bed and in this room. With sunlight in the window, shadow creeping along the wall, and that bloody painting. There had been no escape from any of it. But Boat At Rest hadn't run aground. And neither had he. Afloat, in one piece, but with no great voyage ahead.

Carl became aware of a presence in the doorway.

'Did you go somewhere?'

It was Isaac.

'Yes,' said Carl, lying on the sheetless mattress with his hands clasped behind his head.

'Did you go for a walk?'

Carl sat up. 'Yes,' he said. 'You remember Alec John?'

The boy said he did.

'Well,' continued Carl, 'he died, two years ago today, so I went to the graveyard to pay my respects.' He glanced at Isaac. 'Do you know what that means?'

Isaac said he did.

Sighing, Carl got off the bed.

'Are you going away?'

'It's not far,' said Carl, closing the window, securing the clasp. 'It's just a' – he searched for the right words, wondering how the boy might react – 'a little holiday. That's what people used to do. Take holidays from . . . themselves, sometimes.'

'Have you fallen out with Mum again?'

'You could say that.'

'So, you're going back to the other house.'

Carl nodded.

'Oh,' said Isaac.

'It's not far,' Carl repeated, and smiled. 'It's where Alec John used to stay. He gave me his house. Do you remember?'

For a split-second Isaac looked utterly dejected. 'All right,' he said, brightening in a flicker, fizzing from the doorway and down the stairs, whooping, 'I remember, I remembeeerrr ...'

Carl went down the hallway to room seven, and sat on the bed for a spell.

They'd been doomed, him and Simone, from the outset. Instead of all the preliminaries, like getting to know each other and living together, they had gone straight to pregnancy. Hardly an ideal beginning. They had never learned to be a couple, just the two of them, so being parents was just too difficult.

He picked up his bag, feeling the radiator for warmth, and went downstairs.

Oh well.

In the residents' lounge, George and Isaac had their game visors on and rifles at the ready. Sound effects – squawks and explosions and barked orders – boomed from the wall-speakers.

Carl left them to their mission and went on one of his own, to the kitchen.

'Is she asleep already?'

Simone was at the sink. 'She was tired today. Her last teeth are coming through and she didn't sleep well, not that you'd know anything about that.'

Carl shifted in the doorway, saying nothing.

Stains were scrubbed, angrily, from clothes, and the seconds ticked by.

'Where did you get the soap?'

There was no emotion in Simone's voice. 'A bottle of shampoo from the Mackays. A Christmas present they never used.'

In the sink, his daughter's clothes were taking a damn good

pounding. There were things that could be said, if he wasn't careful. He almost said them.

'Go on then – piss off.'

'I'll be round tomorrow,' said Carl. 'If that's okay.'

'Don't put yourself out on our account.'

Simone threw a rinsed-out sleepsuit down on the draining board. Who was this irritant taking up space in her kitchen?

'Oh, just go away, will you? Clear off to your pied-à-terre and do us all a favour, you self-centred arsehole. Off you go and enjoy your nice easy life.'

She stormed into the garden with an armful of wet washing.

'I'll see you tomorrow then?'

'Don't bother,' shouted Simone from the hall. 'We're emigrating, on the next luxury cruise-liner.'

Outside, the day was dry, though there was a haze of low cloud wisping over the headland and round Heron Point as Carl walked along the road. He said hello to the folk who were out. Some days he could pass the boatyard and not even think about the guys in there. Today wasn't one of those days. Part of him enjoyed glaring at Cutler or Casper whenever he encountered them, but the place was silent today. No swearing and shouting, no grinder shrieking against metal. The biofuel generator wasn't even running. He heard footsteps, light ones, hurrying behind him.

'Hey.'

'Hey,' replied Isaac.

Carl apologised for not saying goodbye, and they walked on.

'You were busy killing aliens with your granddad. Does your mum know you've gone out?'

Isaac nodded. 'It isn't aliens – it's World at War: Battle of the Bulge. I'm the Germans, and I'm winning.'

'Really?'

'Yeah. I'm in Ostend now.' He added casually, 'It's a town in Belgium.'

'Ostend, wow. That's bad news.'

'But I'm winning!'

'Well, in that case, Gruppenführer, go for it.'

'I am winning . . . but Granddad's visor is going fuzzy.'

'Oh. Can you not swap about to make it fairer?'

Isaac screwed his nose up. 'Nah. He gets the fuzzy one.'

They walked on, around the head of the bay, talking and laughing about nothing in particular. Climbing the track to the house, Carl stopped and picked something up off the ground.

'Here's your knife, you wally.' He handed the penknife keyring to Isaac.

'Brilliant,' said the boy, delighted. 'We couldn't see it the last time.'

'Sometimes you can't see things for looking. Then one day, when you aren't looking, you find stuff that was lost.'

Isaac opened the two-inch long blade and tested it. 'It's blunt. Will you sharpen it?'

Carl shook his head. 'It's sharp enough.'

'Will it cut into a deer, through the ribs, into the guts?'

'No,' said Carl, smiling. 'Not that you'd want to cut through ribs anyway, and not into the guts.'

They walked up towards the house.

'Will you show me?'

'Show you what?'

'How to cut through the ribs.'

'What is it with ribs? Leave the ribs alone.'

'You don't cut the ribs?'

'No.'

'Will you show me?'

'Show you what?'

'Where to cut into a deer and how to do all the cutting. You can still do all the shooting, if you like.'

'Gee, thanks. But you shall go to Oxford, young man, get

debagged, sent down, then take over at the old man's firm. No cutting ribs for you.'

'Oxford – is that a place?'

Carl stopped walking. A lump came to his throat as he looked down at the boy. Oxford may as well be on the moon; the outside world was just a concept, unknowable and unreachable. In all probability, Isaac would reach adulthood before having the chance to get within ten miles of Oxford, or any other town for that matter. The thought stuck in Carl's throat.

'Yes,' he said quietly, picking up the pace. 'It is a place.'

There were kids down at the shoreline, one of them carrying what looked like an oil drum.

'It's Pavel and Kieran,' said Isaac. 'We're building a raft.' He bolted back down the track, then turned and shouted, 'Bye.'

Carl raised his hand.

Sometimes he got the yearning for a cup of tea or coffee. People had become dependent on caffeine, of course, and some couldn't function until they'd had at least two strong hits in the morning; it would be nice, though, just to get a little lift every now and again. Thinking about good coffee, he looked up the slope to Ben Bronach, and along the dark line of the basalt ridge, and tried not to think about what he had to do today. Isaac was keen to learn, so that was good. Carl went inside. Maybe he should trim his beard.

Sometimes his heart felt so heavy, like it would sink down into his boots. Sometimes the old pain would take hold, and a black awareness would come over him. But he made it pass. It took effort, to shake off the mood, though these episodes were rare now. As memory pressed down on him, he would rise to meet it, strong enough to bear the weight. There was no reason why he couldn't exist like this way for years. It was possible. It could be done. For so long as he could imagine an end, when something better would arrive, he could go on without too much trouble now that he had acquired a way of living.

But that kind of thinking only took him to one place.

Clearly, it wasn't going to work out with Simone; it was Alec John's anniversary; the Oxford thing with Isaac; and earlier on he had thought about Howard and Eric; it was a witch's brew of all the negative stuff. But then there was his daughter's smile of recognition, her soft, pink feet in the cot as she slept; that was like mainlining an antidote to misery.

That kind of thinking took him to a better place. If she were lucky, she would grow up with all the good stuff that a parent can give to a child. Everything grows from inheritance.

There was also a carcass in the cold store, waiting to be butchered, some weed in the house, and a 1,000-film cine-viewer that someone had lent him. The accessible half of Inverlair estate could do without him for one afternoon.

In the upstairs bedroom he'd already prepared the essentials: fresh white sheet pinned flat to the wall; heavy dark blankets pinned and taped to the window, a big comfy chair, and speakers in the corner. Now all he needed was the stepladder from the shed.

A problem presented itself.

The best position for the ladder and cine-viewer was behind the comfy chair and against the bedroom door. The door would have to be closed to keep out the light from the landing, and that meant that if anyone came into the house they'd come upstairs, maybe without him hearing, and barge into the room. In all likelihood, the bedroom door would push the ladder over, and that was not good news for the cine-viewer sitting on top of it.

Simple: he'd lock the front and back doors so that no one could come in.

He fetched the metal folding ladder from the shed. As he turned the key in the front door of the house, he stopped. Locking a door. Turning a key. Keeping something out.

'What the hell,' he muttered, turning the key. He needed some time to himself, some harmless escapism.

He bounded upstairs for three hours and eight minutes of *The Fall of the Roman Empire*, Alec Guinness giving good stony Stoic Emperor. Marcus Aurelius wasn't afraid, if you believed his *Meditations*. Maybe the fear simply hadn't made it into print, and all that the emperor left to posterity was a carefully polished image of himself, redacted in all the right places and purged of all weakness.

About two hours into the film, Carl heard a banging from downstairs, at the front door. He groaned.

'Pause,' he said. A two-metre wide, impossibly beautiful Sophia Loren froze.

'Coming,' he shouted. 'No need to break the bloody door down.'

He should remain stoic, accept with equanimity the fact that his film, his time off, impulsively taken, had been interrupted.

It was Old Bead-patch himself at the door, and Carl felt his anxiety return.

'Didn't see you head up to the ridge today,' said Terry. 'Thought you might be ill or something.'

'No,' said Carl, leaning on the door jamb. 'Christopher Plummer is up to no good.'

Terry looked blank.

'Watching an old swords-and-sandals classic. *The Fall of the Roman Empire*. Alec Guinness plays ...'

'... Marcus Aurelius,' said Terry. 'The passing of an empire. It happens. Now we can start again.'

Carl nodded, one hand on the door handle, closer to closing it than to throwing it wide in welcome. That much he made obvious.

Today, Terry's eye patch was orange with green beads. Earlier in the week it was white beads on black. Maybe the guy really had made one for every day of the year, like Carl had heard. He'd have come from the village hall, where his young flock gathered to hear their shaman's drug-fuelled gibberish.

'Will I leave you in peace, brother?'

'No offence – but yes,' said Carl, keeping his voice level, his eyes scanning the horizon. 'It's been ages since I've had a bit of downtime. Absolutely ages.'

'That's not a problem,' said Terry. 'Are you staying here now?'

Carl ignored Terry's sudden grin. 'For a while, at least.' He bristled, feeling he should downplay the significance of his living arrangements. 'We'll see what happens.'

Jess waddled up to the door, nudging Carl's legs.

'Right,' said Terry, his wry amusement fading. He nodded. He understood how things were, finally, after weeks of trying to inveigle his way back into Carl's company. Or recruit him to the cause, as Carl suspected. 'I'll catch you later then.'

'Sure. I'll be along at some point.'

As Terry walked back down the track, Carl felt relief, and a surge of guilt. A line had been drawn, and it was obvious now on which side each belonged. Unless he apologised for not inviting Terry in, and quickly, the insult would harden into a barrier, a permanent separation. Perhaps that's as it should be. Best leave Terry to his sordid little arrangement with Hendrik and Maganda, and his new religion that involved Gemma and a few other kids, and peyote, although Carl didn't know for sure what was going on. He didn't want to. Bizarre what some people would believe when there was nothing left to believe in. Carl ruffled Jess's ear, then closed the door. He turned the key in the lock.

'Do I hear a sigh of relief?'

Jess padded through to the kitchen and flopped into her basket.

'Not impressed with my hospitality, huh?'

The dog gave a deep, shuddering sigh, and curled up, cosy by the warm stove. Carl poured a glass of water and took it upstairs to his private Odeon. Sophia was still looking worried, eyes and mouth wide. Marrying Omar Sharif's wily provincial potentate, rather than Stephen Boyd's dashing but irrelevant Roman noble, was clearly giving her trouble. Film might be a world of illusion, but good ones had a grain of truth, emotional or otherwise. It was great to lose yourself in films. To forget. That's what good ones did: they flowed over you like flashing water and made you forget who you were and the fact you were watching a film. Is there anything wrong with that? Is there any harm in forgetting, for a while, your space and place in time, even now?

Carl stuffed a few more leaves into his pipe and lit up. There was only a splash of fuel in the lighter he'd found in the shed. Chuckling, he thought of the folk in the village who were trying to invent matches by taking the phosphorus out of old lifeboat flares. If they couldn't perfect their technique soon, maybe they'd all have to wait for lightning to strike a tree. Thank you, great Sky God, for sending us the power to cook and stay warm. Prometheus, or whoever, could then set off with a flaming torch, running from house to house.

'Play,' said Carl.

Sophia Loren took up where she left off. King Omar Sharif was given the girl. No contest, when there's an empire at stake. After a while he shouted, 'Pause.' He sat there, listening to the sound of the house, another man's house, settling around him. He chose some Led Zep from Alec John's old CD collection and thrashed about on the drumkit for a spell.

With the thick end of the drumstick, he crashed down, hard, on the cymbal. It bucked and gonged and quivered into silence. He sat there, the drumsticks in his hands, another man's house around him and around that, another world that wasn't his world. No matter how long he stayed here he would always feel that he belonged somewhere else, that he was an outsider. He had tried hard, and had learned new set of rules; he had focused on his daughter, on Isaac. Kids are so impressionable, they absorb habits and opinion, distill it all into their own poison, their own love. It was all transmitted, from one mind to another. It was all in the implanting.

Carl got up and went downstairs to the living room. In a black bin bag, taken from Terry's uncle's house, he found what he was looking for. He smoothed the old newspaper – yellow and brittle round the edges – flat on the drop-leaf table. His first big story. His first front-pager. Just short of nineteen years ago.

'And over the top he went, fighting the good fight,' he muttered to himself. Jess came shuffling through from the kitchen; he reached down and scratched behind her ear, the way she liked. From the drawer of the dark sideboard he took a pair of scissors.

'Just in case you take me for granted,' he said to the dog, cutting round the article. 'At any point I could resume my flourishing career – so watch out.'

The dog breathed heavily at his feet, unconcerned.

Out in the shed, he found a box of Alec John's stuff and, in it, an empty frame. Two years ago the photo of the long-dead Mrs Stoddart had been placed tenderly between her husband's folded hands. They were together, not far from Howard. In place of the photo he positioned the newspaper article, clicked the glass back into the frame, and hung it on the same hook in the porch. Through the window he saw two kids, a boy and a girl, running up the track from the main road. Carl went outside to wait for them and noticed Isaac ambling some way behind his friends, whacking bramble bushes with a stick, trying to look cool.

'If there's a party at mine,' said Carl, 'then nobody invited me.'

'It's Gary,' said the girl, out of breath. 'He's run into the redzone and hasn't come back.'

'What?' Carl started off down the path then stopped, turned and ran back into the house. 'What did he do that for?'

Isaac ran after him. 'Is it Pulse Day today?'

'Um, no, I don't know,' said Carl, rummaging through the side pockets of his rucksack. 'What was that stupid fu—' He shook his head. In truth, he had no idea when the next pulse in the delta signal was due. He used to know, used to have it marked out months ahead on the calendar. He found what he was looking for.

Car key. Deltameter.

Bolting from the house, he ran down the track to the stone byre. Both doors were flung apart and he whipped the dustsheet from Howard's car. Every so often he turned the engine over, checked the tyres. If the thing started now, when he actually needed it, he could be at the roadblock in seconds.

'Get in.'

Isaac and the other two got in. As she climbed into the back seat, Carl saw a fresh scar on the girl's pale upper arm.

'You kids still playing your stupid games, cutting yourselves open?'

The girl, Katy, pulled down her sleeve and glared at him. Carl jumped in. The car started first time.

'We don't need the safety chips any more. Gary said adults had put them in to keep us prisoners,' she said. 'Gary said we should cut them out.' Then she shouted, 'You made the world the way it is, fucking adults, so don't start giving me advice and telling me what to do.'

Carl said nothing. The car swung out of the old byre and bounced down the rough stony track. They sped off up the main road the mile or so to the roadblock.

'Maybe Gary won't be giving any more orders,' he muttered, eyeing the sullen girl in the rear-view mirror. He wondered if Isaac had asked for his own chip to be cut out. The idea made him queasy.

At the line of red boulders Carl stopped the car and they all got out. There was no sign of Gary, or the rest of the kids. Carl took out the deltameter.

Nothing.

He searched through the log, worked out when the last pulse should have been. Two days from now. Not today.

Not today.

'There they are,' shouted Katy, pointing down towards the sand dunes. 'Gary's with the rest.'

With the older boy in tow, she climbed the roadside fence and ran off down the field of thistles and reeds to join their friends, past the quarry. Oblivious to Gary and his pals, Carl looked along the stretch of road to where it curved round a long sloping outcrop of rock and grass, before vanishing inland among the hills. Gary and the other kids, jumping and running in the sand dunes, were at least 500 metres inside the redzone.

Carl stood, motionless and quiet, and looked down the road.

'What's wrong?'

It took him a few moments to register that Isaac was still beside him. 'In you get,' he said quietly.

There was not a flicker on the deltameter, right through the sinusoidal spectrum. If it had been Pulse Day, the signal would be back to full strength by now. But there was no sign of it. He licked his trembling lips.

'What's wrong?'

Carl put the car in gear and drove, taking it slow, doing 20mph, checking the deltameter as he went. At 30mph he reached the curve in the road; he checked the mileometer. A mile. Around the curve and on and down through a long dip and across a short bridge by more pine trees and then uphill again.

He stopped the car.

Two miles. Nothing. They were a lot closer to the Russian capsule now. The thick silver torpedo had not moved from its spot on the hillside for over two years, though the parachute had long been shredded by the wind. But that was a good half-mile away from the road. The capsule would keep. There was another village, he remembered, a few miles away.

Carl smiled, though tears were welling in his eyes. He coughed, blinked, his voice hoarse and uncertain. Solid plates were shifting again, as they always must, grinding towards a new alignment. Change was here. The wall of silence had opened, by how much it was hard to say.

With his left hand he reached over and grabbed the passenger seat belt, swept it around Isaac, and clicked it into place.

'What's that for?'

'So you don't get hurt.'

'Where are we going?'

'I don't know,' whispered Carl. He put the car into gear again and drove on, his hands shaking. 'We'll find something useful, and bring it back.'